P9-DNZ-144

CAUGHT UP
in a
COWBOY

JENNIE
MARTS

sourcebooks
casablanca

Published by Sourcebooks Casablanca, an imprint of Sourcebooks, Inc.
P.O. Box 4410, Naperville, Illinois 60567-4410
(630) 961-3900
Fax: (630) 961-2168
sourcebooks.com

Printed and bound in the United States of America.
OPM 10 9 8 7 6 5 4 3 2 1

This book is dedicated to
Todd
My real-life hero
The one who has shown me what
true romance really means
—Always—

Chapter 1

BITS OF GRAVEL FLEW BEHIND THE TIRES OF THE CONVERTIBLE, and Rockford James swore as he turned onto the dirt road leading to the Triple J Ranch. Normally, he enjoyed coming home for a visit, especially in the late spring when everything was turning green and the wildflowers were in bloom, but not this spring—not when he was coming home with both his pride and his body badly injured.

His spirits lifted and the corners of his mouth tugged up in a grin as he drew even with what appeared to be a pirate riding a child's bicycle along the shoulder of the road. A gorgeous female pirate—one with long blond hair and great legs.

Legs he recognized.

Legs that belonged to the only woman who had ever stolen his heart.

Nine years ago, Quinn Rivers had given him her heart as well. Too bad he'd broken it. Not exactly broken— more like smashed, crushed, and shattered it into a million tiny pieces. According to her anyway.

He slowed the car, calling out as he drew alongside her. Her outfit consisted of a flimsy little top that bared her shoulders under a snug corset vest and a short, frilly striped skirt. She wore some kind of sheer white knee socks, and one of them had fallen and pooled loosely around her ankle. "Ahoy there, matey. You lose your ship?"

Keeping her eyes focused on the road, she stuck out

her hand and offered him a gesture unbecoming of a lady—pirate or otherwise. Then her feet stilled on the pedals as she must have registered his voice. "Ho-ly crap. You have got to be freaking kidding me."

Bracing her feet on the ground, she turned her head, brown eyes flashing with anger. "And here I thought my day couldn't get any worse. What the hell are you doing here, Rock?"

He stopped the car next to her, then draped his arm over the steering wheel, trying to appear cool. Even though his heart pounded against his chest from the fact that he was seeing her again. She had this way of getting under his skin; she was just so damn beautiful. Even wearing a pirate outfit. "Hey, now. Is that any way to speak to an old friend?"

"I don't know. I'll let you know when I run into one."

Ouch. He'd hoped she wasn't still that bitter about their breakup. They'd been kids, barely out of high school. But they'd been together since they were fourteen, his conscience reminded him, and they'd made plans to spend their future together.

But that was before he got the full-ride scholarship and the NHL started scouting him.

And he had tried.

Yeah, keep telling yourself that, buddy.

Okay, he probably hadn't tried hard enough. But he'd been young and dumb and swept up in the fever and glory of finally having his dreams of pursuing a professional hockey career coming true.

With that glory came attention and fame and lots of travel with the team where cute puck bunnies were ready and willing to show their favorite players a good time.

He hadn't cheated on Quinn, but he came home less often and didn't make the time for texts and calls. He'd gone to college first while she finished her senior year, and by the time he did come home the next summer, he'd felt like he'd outgrown their relationship, and her, and had suggested they take a mini break.

Which turned into an *actual* break, of both their relationship and Quinn's heart.

But it had been almost nine years since he'd left; they'd been kids, and that kind of stuff happened all the time. Since then, he hadn't made it home a lot and had run into her only a handful of times. In fact, he probably hadn't seen her in over a year.

But he'd thought of her. Often. And repeatedly wondered if he'd made the right choice by picking the fame and celebrity of his career and letting go of her.

Sometimes, those summer days spent with Quinn seemed like yesterday, but really, so much had happened—in both of their lives—that it felt like a lifetime ago.

Surely she'd softened a little toward him in all that time. "Let me offer you a lift." The dirt road they were on led to both of their families' neighboring ranches.

"No thanks. I'd rather pedal this bike until the moon comes up than take a ride from you."

Yep. Still mad, all right.

Nothing he could do if she wanted to keep the grudge fest going. Except he was tired of the grudge. Tired of them being enemies. She'd been the best friend he'd ever had. And right now, he felt like he could use a friend.

His pride had already been wounded; what was one more hit? At least he could say he tried.

Although he didn't want it to seem like he was trying too hard. He did still have a *little* pride left, damn it.

"Okay. Suit yourself. It's not *that* hot out here." He squinted up at the bright Colorado sun, then eased off the brake, letting the car coast forward.

"Wait." She shifted from one booted foot to the other, the plastic pirate sword bouncing against her curvy hip. "Fine. I'll take a ride. But only because I'm desperate."

"You? Desperate? I doubt it," he said with a chuckle. Putting the car in Park, he left the engine running and made his way around the back of the car. He reached for the bike, but she was already fitting it into the back seat of the convertible.

"I've got it." Her gaze traveled along the length of his body, coming to rest on his face, and her expression softened for the first time. "I heard about the fight and your injury."

He froze, heat rushing to his cheeks and anger building in his gut. Of course she'd heard about the fight. It had made the nightly news, for Pete's sake. He was sure the whole town of Creedence had heard about it.

Nothing flowed faster than a good piece of gossip in a small town. Especially when it's bad news—or news about the fall of the hometown hero. Or the guy who thought he was better than everyone else and bigger than his small-town roots, depending on who you talked to and which camp they fell into. Or what day of the week it was.

You could always count on a small town to be loyal. Until you let them down.

"I'm fine," he said, probably a little too sternly, as he opened the car door, giving her room to pass him and slide into the passenger seat. He sucked in a breath as the scent of her perfume swept over him.

She smelled the same—a mix of vanilla, honeysuckle, and home.

He didn't let himself wonder if she felt the same. No, he'd blown his chances of that ever happening again a long time ago. Still, he couldn't help but drop his gaze to her long, tanned legs or notice the way her breasts spilled over the snug, corseted vest of the pirate costume.

"So, what's with the outfit?" he asked as he slid into the driver's seat and put the car in gear.

She blew out her breath in an exaggerated sigh. A loose tendril of hair clung to her damp forehead, and he was tempted to reach across the seat to brush it back.

"It's Max's birthday today," she said, as if that explained everything.

He didn't say anything—didn't know what to say.

The subject of Max always was a bit of an awkward one between them. After he'd left, he'd heard the rumors of how Quinn had hooked up with a hick loser named Monty Hill who'd lived one town over. She'd met him at a party and it had been a rebound one-night stand, designed to make him pay for breaking things off with her, if the gossip was true.

But she'd been the one to pay. Her impulse retaliation had ended in an unplanned pregnancy with another jerk who couldn't be counted on to stick around for her. Hill had taken off, and Quinn had ended up staying at her family's ranch.

"He's eight now." Her voice held the steely tone of anger, but he heard the hint of pride that also crept in.

"I know," he mumbled, more to himself than to her. "So, you decided to dress up like a pirate for his birthday?"

She snorted. "No. Of course not. One of Max's favorite books is *Treasure Island*, and he wanted a pirate-themed party, so I *hired* a party company to send out a couple of actors to dress up like pirates. The outfits showed up this morning, but the actors didn't. Evidently, there was a mix-up in the office, and the couple had been double-booked and were already en route to Denver when I called."

"So you decided to fill in." He tried to hold back his grin.

She shrugged. "What else was I going to do?"

"That doesn't explain the bike."

"The bike is his main gift. I ordered it from the hardware store in town, but it was late and we weren't expecting it to come in today. They called about an hour ago and said it had shown up, but they didn't have anyone to deliver it. I was already in the pirate getup, so I ran into town to get it."

"And decided to ride it home?"

"Yes, smart-ass. I thought it would be fun to squeeze onto a tiny bike dressed in a cheap Halloween costume and enjoy the bright, sunny day by riding home." She blew out another exasperated breath. "My stupid car broke down on the main road."

"Why didn't you call Ham or Logan to come pick you up?" he asked, referring to her dad and her older brother.

"Because in my flustered state of panic about having to fill in as the pirate princess and the fear that the party would be ruined, I left my phone on the dresser when I ran out of the house. I was carrying the dang bike, but it got so heavy, then I tried pushing it, and that was killing my back, so I thought it would be easier and faster if I just tried to ride it the last mile back to the ranch."

"Makes sense to me." He slowed the car, turning into the long driveway of Rivers Gulch. White fences lined the drive, and several head of cattle grazed on the fresh green grass of the pastures along either side of the road.

The scent of recently mown hay skimmed the air, mixed with the familiar smells of plowed earth and cattle.

Seeing the sprawling ranch house and the long, white barn settled something inside of him, and he let out a slow breath, helping to ease the tension in his neck. He'd practically grown up here, running around this place with Quinn and her brother, Logan.

Their families' ranches were within spitting distance of each other; in fact, he could see the farmhouse of the Triple J across the pasture to his left. They were separated only by prime grazing land and the pond that he'd learned to swim in during the summer and skate on in the winter.

The two families had an ongoing feud—although he wasn't sure any of them really knew what they were fighting about anymore, and the kids had never cared much about it anyway.

The adults liked to bring it up, but they were the only kids around for miles, and they'd become fast friends—he and his brothers sneaking over to Rivers Gulch as often as they could.

This place felt just as much like home as his own did.

He'd missed it. In the years since he'd left, he'd been back only a handful of times.

His life had become so busy, his hockey career taking up most of his time. And after what happened with Quinn, neither Ham nor Logan was ever too excited to see him. Her mom had died when she was in grade school, and both men had always been overprotective of her.

He snuck a glance at her as he drove past the barn. Her wavy hair was pulled back in a ponytail, but wisps of it had come loose and fell across her neck in little curls. She looked good—really good. A thick chunk of regret settled in his gut, and he knew letting her go had been the biggest mistake of his life.

It wasn't the first time he'd thought it. Images of Quinn haunted his dreams, and he often wondered what it would be like now if only he'd brought her with him instead of leaving her behind. If he had her to wave to in the stands at his games or to come home to at night instead of an empty house. But he'd screwed that up, and he felt the remorse every time he returned to Rivers Gulch.

He'd been young and arrogant—thought he had the world by the tail. Scouts had come sniffing around when he was in high school, inflating his head and his own self-importance. And once he started playing in the big leagues, everything about this small town—including Quinn—had just seemed…well…small. Too small for a big shot like him.

He was just a kid—and an idiot. But by the time he'd realized his mistake and come back for her, it was too late.

Hindsight was a mother.

And so was Quinn.

Easing the car in front of the house, he took in the festive balloons and streamers tied to the railings along the porch. So much of the house looked the same—the long porch that ran the length of the house, the wooden rocking chairs, and the swing hanging from the end.

They'd spent a lot of time on that swing, talking and laughing, his arm around her as his foot slowly pushed them back and forth.

She opened the car door, but he put a hand on her arm and offered her one of his most charming smiles. "It's good to see you, Quinn. You look great. Even in a pirate outfit."

Her eyes widened, and she blinked at him, for once not having a sarcastic reply. He watched her throat shift as she swallowed, and he yearned to reach out to run his fingers along her slender neck.

"Well, thanks for the lift." She turned away and stepped out of the car.

Pushing open his door, he got out and reached for the bicycle, lifting it out of the back seat before she had a chance. He carried it around and set it on the ground in front of her. "I'd like to meet him. You know, Max. If that's okay."

"You would?" Her voice was soft, almost hopeful, but still held a note of suspicion. "Why?"

He ran a hand through his hair and let out a sigh. He'd been rehearsing what he was going to say as they drove up to the ranch, but now his mouth had gone dry. The collar of his cotton T-shirt clung to his neck, and he didn't know what to do with his hands.

Dang. He hadn't had sweaty palms since he was in

high school. He wiped them on his jeans. He was known for his charm and usually had a way with women, but not this woman. This one had him tongue-tied and nervous as a teenager.

He shoved his hands in his pockets. "Listen, Quinn. I know I screwed up. I was young and stupid and a damn fool. And I'm sorrier than I could ever say. But I can't go back and fix it. All I can do is move forward. I miss this place. I miss having you in my life. I'd like to at least be your friend."

She opened her mouth, and he steeled himself for her to tell him to go jump in the lake. Or worse. But she didn't. She looked up at him, her eyes searching his face, as if trying to decide if he was serious. "Why now? After all these years?"

He shrugged, his gaze drifting as he stared off at the distant green pastures. He'd let this go on too long, let the hurt fester. It was time to make amends—to at least try. He looked back at her, trying to express his sincerity. "Why not? Isn't it about time?"

She swallowed again and gave a small nod of her head.

A tiny flicker of hope lit in his gut as he waited for her response. He could practically *see* her thinking—watch the emotions cross her face in the furrow of her brow and the way she chewed on her bottom lip. Oh man, he loved it when she did that; the way she sucked her bottom lip under her front teeth always did crazy things to his insides.

"Okay. We can *try* being friends." She gave him a sidelong glance, the hint of a smile tugging at the corner of her mouth. "On one condition."

Uh-oh. Conditions are never good. Although he would do just about anything to prove to her that he was serious about being in her life again.

"What's that?"

"I need someone to be the other pirate for the party. I already asked Logan if he would wear the other costume, and he refused. I was planning to ask Dad, but I have a feeling I'll get the same response."

He tried to imagine Hamilton Rivers in a pirate outfit and couldn't. Ham was old-school cowboy, tough as nails and loyal to the land. He wore his boots from sunup to sundown and had more grit than a sheet of sandpaper. The only soft spot he had was for his daughter. And Rock had broken her heart.

If there hadn't been enough animosity between the two families over their land before, Rock had sealed the feud by walking away from Quinn.

And now he had a chance to try to make it up to her. And to keep an eight-year-old kid from being disappointed. Even if it meant making a fool of himself.

He squinted one eye closed and tilted his head. If he was going to do it, might as well do it right.

Go big or go home.

"Aye, lass," he said in his best gruff pirate impression. "I'll be a pirate for ye, but don't cross me, or I'll make ye walk the plank."

Her eyes widened, and she laughed before she could stop herself. An actual laugh. Well, more like a small chuckle, but it was worth it. He'd talk in a pirate accent all afternoon if it meant he could hear her laugh again.

She took a step forward, reached out her hand as if to touch his arm, then let it drop to her side. "All right,

Captain Jack, you don't have to go that far." She might not have touched him, but she offered him a grin—a true grin.

Yeah, he could be a pirate. He could be whatever she needed. Or he could dang well try.

The front door slammed open with a bang, and Quinn jumped. As if on cue, her brother stepped out on the front porch.

Anger sparked in Logan's eyes as he glared at Rock. "What the hell are you doing here?"

Chapter 2

Q̲ᴜɪɴɴ ᴡᴀꜱ ᴛʜɪɴᴋɪɴɢ ᴛʜᴇ ꜱᴀᴍᴇ ᴛʜɪɴɢ.

What the hell was Rockford James doing standing in front of her? And offering to fill in as the pirate at her son's birthday party, no less.

But the righteous indignation was hers to carry, and she held up a hand to her brother. "Rock gave me a ride home. That stupid car broke down again, and I would have had to walk the whole way if he hadn't stopped to give me a lift."

"Why didn't you call me?"

"I forgot my phone."

He gave a grudging nod to Rock. "Well, we've got it from here. Thanks." He pulled the screen door open, then turned back and mumbled, "Sorry to hear about your head. That guy was an asshole."

She felt Rock stiffen beside her. He obviously didn't like to talk about it. But she was glad to see her brother being civil—maybe this could be the start of a truce between the Rivers and James families. She tried to keep a light tone in her voice. "Rock is coming to the party. He's going to help out by filling in as the other pirate."

Her brother raised an eyebrow, then shook his head, any remnants of a truce disappearing behind his scowl. "Like hell he is. We don't need another pirate. And we dang sure don't need *his* help."

Leaving the bike on the porch, she automatically

reached for Rock's hand and pulled him up the stairs. "Too bad. He's staying. Max wants a pirate, and I'm giving him a pirate." The nerve of her brother, telling her what to do. She fought to hold back the eye roll. He was only two years older than she was, but she'd always be his baby sister. Annoying.

It wasn't until they had stepped onto the porch that she realized she was holding Rock's hand. The shock of touching his skin and having her hand in his after all these years took her breath away. His fingers curled around hers, making her hyperaware of the wall of male standing next to her.

"You heard the lady," Rock said with a smirk.

She led him through the house and into her bedroom, where the other costume was. It was strange having him in her room again.

He looked around with interest. "Wow, you're still in your old bedroom. You've changed it up though. Got rid of the pom-poms and the boy band posters."

Pushing the door shut with her foot, she dropped his hand as if it were on fire. "That's because I'm an adult now. And a mom. I have my own boy, and he's the one I cheer for."

Memories of Rock being in this room with her flooded her mind, and her heart ached at flashes of recollection. Lying on the floor as they listened to music or worked on homework, curled on her bed kissing and touching in the frantic way that teenagers discover each other. The pictures in her head were as clear as if they had happened yesterday.

But they hadn't. She pushed the memories away—back into the spaces where she kept them, sealed off so they couldn't hurt her. That was the past. She needed to focus on the present, on Max and the birthday party that was going to start any minute now.

She pointed to the pirate costume laid out across her bed. The outfit consisted of a thin muslin shirt, a faux leather vest, and a pair of brown, striped pants. A long scarf served as a belt, with a black hat and a sword completing the costume.

"You can put that on. The guests will be here anytime, so we've got to be ready. If the pants don't fit, just wear your jeans." She glanced at his thighs, thick and muscular from years of ice skating. "Yeah, you should probably just wear your jeans."

He chuckled as he reached for the hem of his T-shirt and tugged it over his head.

She sucked in her breath.

Holy hot cowboy. The guy's chest was a solid mass of muscle.

The last time she'd seen him without a shirt, they'd been teenagers. He wasn't a teenager now. He was a man with a man's body.

The muscles in his arms flexed as he tossed the shirt onto the bed, and she almost choked at the size of them. He had the body of an athlete, toned and firm. A tattoo of his team's logo covered the top part of his right arm. She hadn't known he'd gotten a tattoo.

She didn't really know anything about him anymore. Just the bits of gossip around town and the occasional stories she heard about him from his family or on one of the sports channels on TV. She wouldn't admit it to anyone else, but she'd seen several of his games, watching him when he was on the ice and searching the player's box for glimpses of him when he wasn't.

She tried to look away but was mesmerized by his body, so foreign yet so familiar. Her gaze traveled over him, discovering new scars and marks that hadn't been there before, that he must have earned in his years on the ice.

His hair was still a little too long, curling along his neck, but it had darkened to a dirty-blond color, and his eyes were still the same greenish blue. She'd always thought they were the same color as the pond they learned to swim in, a mixture of the shades, depending on his mood or what color clothes he was wearing.

There were so many new things about him, yet he still felt like the same guy that she'd grown up with—the one who'd shown her how to ride a horse, who'd tutored her in chemistry, and who had taught her how to French kiss. And he'd been quite a teacher.

He reached for the shirt on the bed, turning slightly, and she gasped at the mass of ugly purple bruising down the side of his rib cage. She reached out as if to touch him, heard his sharp intake of breath as her fingers barely skimmed his side, and quickly dropped her hand.

"Is that from the—" She didn't want to bring up the fight again. Apparently, she didn't have to.

A scowl settled on his face, and he swiped at the discoloration as if to wipe it away. "Yeah, I guess. It's no big deal though—just a few bruises. We're always getting banged up. These are already starting to fade."

They didn't look like they were starting to fade. But the subject obviously made him uncomfortable, so she let it go and concentrated on a problem that had just surfaced in her mind. "They didn't send along any boots or shoes."

He pulled the shirt over his head. It was snug, hugging his muscled chest and stretching over his thick upper arms. "My boots will do fine."

She glanced down at his leather, square-toed cowboy boots. "A pirate wearing cowboy boots?" Oh geez—that sounded kind of hot, especially when the cowboy/pirate was Rock.

Stop it. This was the man who'd broken her heart—who'd left her behind. She wasn't about to fall victim to his charming grin and a few well-toned muscles.

He tugged on the vest and picked up the long, red scarf, a baffled look on his face. "What do I do with this?"

"You tie it around your waist. Like a belt." She sighed at his blank look and took the scarf. Sliding her arms around him, she wrapped the scarf around his waist and tied it in a knot at his hip. Her hands shook a little as they brushed over his hard abs, their solidness visible through the thin shirt.

Taking a step back, she picked up the sword from the bed and passed it to him. They needed to get out of her bedroom. She could try to push the memories away, but the ghosts of them as a couple—as young lovers—were thick. As if their souls were floating in the air, taking up all the space and making it hard for her to breathe.

The sound of a truck coming up the driveway pulled Quinn from her thoughts. Thank goodness. The guests were starting to arrive.

The door of her room burst open, and Max rushed in. "Mom! Mom! They're here! Come on! The party is starting!" He grabbed her arm and pulled, then stopped when he caught sight of Rock.

He pushed his small glasses up his nose and grinned at her. Her heart did that gushy mom thing it did every time her son smiled because she'd gotten something exactly right. "You found a pirate."

That smile on her son's face made every awkward moment with Rock worth it. "Yep, this is Captain…um… James." That was original. She gave Rock a small shrug of her shoulders, hoping he would play along. "He sailed the seven seas to be here for your birthday party today."

Max's eyes widened as he looked at Rock. "You're a pretty big pirate," he whispered.

Rock puffed out his chest and lowered his voice, affecting a deep, pirate accent. "Aye. That's from spending so much time working aboard me ship, matey. I heard some scallywag named Max was having a party, and I thought I'd stop by for some rum." He glanced up at Quinn. "Er, I mean some grog. You got any grog, boy, or am I going to have to make you swab the poop deck?"

"You said 'poop.'" Max dissolved into giggles as Rock wielded his plastic sword in the air. "You're funny."

He *was* funny. Was he seriously *still* doing a pirate voice?

She tried to keep from laughing, but the sound of Max's giggles was too much. Shaking her head, she looked down at her son. "Why don't you go say hello to your guests, and I'll try to find the Captain here some *grog*."

"Okay, Mom." Max offered Rock a wave, then raced from the room. "See ya later, Captain James."

"Nice work, matey," she said, trying to mimic his

accent as she held the door for him. "You think you can keep it up long enough to entertain a dozen hyper eight-year-olds?"

"Aye. I love a challenge." He crossed the room, stopping behind her and lowering his voice as he leaned closer to her ear. "And might I add, ye've got the finest pirate booty I've ever laid me eyes on."

She raised an eyebrow, trying to hold in a laugh. "Are you seriously flirting with me using pirate lingo?"

He winked and gave her a sharp nod of his head. "Aye, me beauty. Would you like to shiver me timbers?"

Her eyes widened, but even he couldn't hold a straight face for that one, and they busted out laughing.

It had been a long time since they'd laughed like that together.

It felt good. Right.

He held up his hands in surrender. "Sorry. That one went too far. It sounded better in my head."

"Keep that up, and you're gonna be the one walking the plank." She tried to sound gruff but couldn't quite pull it off. With a slow smile, she turned and headed for the kitchen, ignoring the butterflies careening around in her stomach at the fact that not only was Rock in her bedroom again, but he was flirting with her—and she kind of liked it.

Three hours, seventeen cupcakes, and three water-balloon fights that Rock instigated later, she sank onto the bench seat of the picnic table.

He dropped down next to her and pulled off his pirate hat. The scent of his aftershave wafted around her, and his thigh came dangerously close to touching hers. His hair was tousled from the hat and the warm day, and she had the strongest urge to reach out and smooth it down.

Her dad and Max had left to take the last of the kids home, and the scent of grilled hot dogs and sunscreen lingered in the air.

She'd thought her dad would have a coronary when he saw Rock at the party, but she told him he was doing it for Max and to chill out. Ham had grunted, and the two men had mainly stayed out of each other's way.

"Wow. You were right. Eight-year-olds are tough." He puffed out a breath, sounding more like he'd gone into triple overtime instead of wrangling up a group of rowdy children.

"You were pretty great with them." Surprisingly great. She'd had no idea he could work a crowd like that. He was funny and charming, and he'd had the kids and half of the parents eating out of his hand. Especially the moms.

One of the kid's moms fell all over herself trying to help Rock pass out the cupcakes.

And speaking of falling, if Carolyn Parker had displayed any more of her cleavage, her boobs would have popped right out of her top. Not very becoming of the PTA president and self-professed "room mom."

The moms were bad enough, preening around Rock, but the dads were just as ridiculous, trying to act cool and buddy up with him. So what if he was a famous hockey player and on television? He was still the same guy that half of them had gone to school with. Why were they treating him like such a celebrity?

Because he was. He wasn't just *some* hockey player. He was Rockford James, the star, the hockey-playing cowboy and a major player on the Colorado team. A team he was going back to, she reminded herself.

"They were fun." Rock's deep voice rumbled through her and dragged her out of her musings. "And I do have *some* skills." He nudged her leg and cocked an eyebrow. "But I do my best work when I'm not in front of a crowd."

She shook her head, the start of a smile tugging at her lip. "You're awful."

"Awful handsome for a pirate, you mean?" He flashed her one of his charming grins, teasing her as he bumped her leg with his again, then leaving his knee lightly against hers.

She could feel the heat of his skin, even through his jeans. The cotton texture of the denim rubbed against her bare leg, causing her earlier butterflies to return, swooping and swirling wildly in her belly.

Was he flirting with her? Or just laying on the charm like he'd been doing all afternoon with the other guests? Ugh. The very thought of him flirting with Carolyn Parker made her stomach go sour.

What was that about?

Actually, she knew what it was about.

The green-eyed monster was rearing its ugly head, and she didn't like it. Not one bit. She wasn't usually jealous. But who would she have to be jealous of? So much of her life was spent focused on her role as a mom: laundry, bath time, making lunches, tucking Max in at night, and reading books with him. So many books. That kid loved to read and loved being read to.

She didn't have time to think about men or flirting. Not until now, when she had Rock James sitting in front of her, the ridiculously cute guy she'd loved for half of her life, the one whose leg now pressed snugly against hers as he'd somehow moved even closer.

And the one who had torn her heart to shreds when he'd broken up with her.

No matter how cute and charming he was, there was still that.

She sighed. "What are you doing here, Rock?"

His playful grin fell, but before he had a chance to answer, her brother walked up holding a chocolate cupcake and leaned his hip against the edge of the picnic table next to her.

"Looks like you two were the hit of the party," Logan said. "Your picture will probably make tomorrow's news as the pirate couple of the year."

"What are you talking about?" she asked.

"Didn't you see Carolyn Parker taking pictures of you guys? I'm sure you'll be in tomorrow's edition of the *Creedence Chronicle*. She just got hired on there and is trying to start some new section like the society pages. I'll wager that you'll be her feature story." He peeled back the wrapper of the cupcake and took a bite. "Unless she sells the pictures to that reporter who was lurking out front earlier," he said around a mouthful of cake.

Rock's head snapped up. "What reporter?"

Chapter 3

SO THAT'S WHAT THIS IS ALL ABOUT.

It didn't have anything to do with her. Or with him wanting them to be friends again. She should have known.

Pushing his leg away, Quinn stood up and turned on him. She could feel the fury building in her chest, like bile filling her throat.

No. She would *not* cry, damn it. It was easier to be mad than to let him know he had gotten to her.

Her hands landed on her hips, and her heart slammed against her chest. "You brought a reporter to my son's birthday party? To our house? So this was all just a publicity stunt?"

His face registered shock as he sputtered, "No, of course not. Quinn, I—"

She held up her hand. "Save it. Save your excuses. This didn't have anything to do with you wanting to be my friend or trying to help make an eight-year-old's dream come true. It all has to do with your almighty career. Just like everything else in your life, hockey comes first."

"Quinn, come on. I had nothing to do with this. I hate the press. Please—" he tried again, but she cut him off.

How could he say he hated the press when he showed up in the news all the time? She didn't know what to believe.

"Just leave, Rock. Go home."

Turning on her heel, she hurried into the house, determined not to let him see the emotions she knew were evident on her face. She'd never been able to hide her feelings from him.

And she damn sure didn't want him to know he'd gotten to her. Again.

Just like he always did.

Rock slammed the front door and stomped into the living room of the two-story farmhouse he'd grown up in.

"What in the Sam Hill are you wearing?" his mother, Vivienne, asked. She stood at the kitchen island, elbows deep in a sink full of sudsy water.

"Ahoy there," one of his younger brothers, Mason, called from the recliner in front of the television. "Nice pirate duds. I hope you brought some rum and a couple of wenches home with you." He glanced over at Vivienne. "Sorry, Mom."

Rock had wanted to follow Quinn into the house, to explain and to get his shirt back, but her brother had stopped him. Not that Logan could really have stopped him if he'd wanted to get past him. He'd checked bigger guys than Logan Rivers into the boards without even a blink.

But he'd kept his cool long enough to realize that getting into a fight with her brother wouldn't help anything. The last thing Rock needed was to fuel the feud between their two families; that would only piss Quinn off more. Instead, he'd chosen to take his pirate sword and leave.

"Shut up," he growled at his brother as he sank onto the sofa.

"Geez, nice to see you too, Bro."

"Rockford James, you get your butt up off that couch and come give your mother a proper hug." Vivi was already drying her hands on a towel, and he was struck as he often was by how young and beautiful she still looked.

The combination of her being tall and constantly working in the house and on the ranch allowed her to eat cookies and macaroni and cheese and still stay slim, but it was more than that. More than the fact that her hair was still blond and worn long around her shoulders.

Vivienne James had a big heart and an easy laugh and a zest for life that drew people to her. Today, she wore jeans and a yellow cotton top, but her feet were bare, and as she padded across the kitchen toward him, he noticed her toenails were painted bright pink.

He stood and offered her a sheepish grin. Stepping forward, he wrapped his arms around her and tipped his head to her shoulder. "Sorry, Mom. I don't know what I was thinking. Bad day."

Everything felt off-kilter. Normally, he would go straight to his mom and wrap her in a hug. But nothing had been normal about the day he'd had.

She must have realized in her spidey mom-sense that something was off, because she squeezed him tightly, then pulled back, searching his eyes, her brow furrowed in concern. "How are you? How's your head?"

"I'm fine, Ma."

"You're *not* fine. You suffered a concussion serious enough that your coach sent you home to recuperate. I'm still not happy that you drove yourself up here." She slapped his arm with the damp dish towel. "But Lord knows the last time you listened to me."

He chuckled. As if.

Both he and his brothers knew that when Vivi James had something to say, they dang well better listen. Their dad had died when Rock was about Max's age, and Vivi had raised him and his two younger brothers on her own, with steady discipline and a fierce love.

She moved to the sofa and patted the seat next to her. "The rest of the dishes can wait. Tell me what's got you so worked up."

He glanced in the kitchen, then back at her. "I don't know why you're washing the dishes anyway. Why don't you use the dishwasher I bought you?"

He'd paid to remodel the old house the year before, updating it with modern appliances and tearing down the center wall to turn the kitchen and the living room into a great room. His mom had complained that she didn't want to be in the kitchen and miss one of his games, so he'd bought a flat-screen television that she could see from the big center island.

She'd accepted the new floor plan, the hardwood flooring, and most of the new furniture, but she still had some of her antiques scattered throughout, giving the house a more country look and keeping the homey feeling.

"I do use it. But sometimes I still like to wash up the supper dishes by hand. Helps me to think."

A worried expression crossed her face—just for a second, then it was gone, replaced by her normal, open smile.

What did she have to worry about? Was something going on with the farm? Mason hadn't told him of any problems. Not that he would.

Mason was the stable one, the one who always

made sure things were taken care of. He had a head for business and the steady work habits of an ox. He and their youngest brother, Colt, had both stayed to help their mom run the ranch. But it seemed to suit both of them.

Mason had made some changes, put in some upgrades, and things seemed to be going smoothly. Although you wouldn't know it, listening to Mason talk, his little brother never gave himself enough credit for a job well done.

He glanced at his brother as he passed him a bottle of beer. Tiny bubbles fizzed against his lips as he tipped the bottle up and took a long swig. The cold beer felt good on his throat, and he slumped back against the sofa.

"Thanks, Brother. Sorry for being a jerk. It's been a weird day."

"Says the guy in the pirate shirt." Mason crowed with laughter as he sank back into the recliner.

Rock grabbed a throw pillow from the couch and flung it at him.

It felt good to be home.

The morning sun shone through the curtains of his old bedroom the next day as Rock cracked open one eye and squinted at the digital clock on his bedside table.

Eight thirty. He had a moment of panic, thinking he had overslept and should have been on the ice by now.

Then he remembered. The game. The fight. The feel of his opponent's stick across his back and the sickening thud of his head cracking against the boards.

He tried to close his eyes again but felt the insistent

poking of his shoulder that had woken him up in the first place.

Rolling over, he came face-to-face with Quinn's son, Max.

He reared back against his pillow. "What are you doing here?"

"Trying to wake you up. You snore really loud." He scrunched his small nose and pushed his glasses back. He was a cute kid, his white-blond hair sticking up in messy spikes, and his glasses giving him a bookish look.

"No. I mean what are you doing *here*? In my bedroom?" A glimmer of hope sparked in his chest, and he craned his neck around Max to see out the door, but the hallway was empty. "Is your mom with you?"

"No. She dropped me off 'cause she had to work at the coffee shop this morning," he said, as if this explained everything.

"So she dropped you off here? Why?"

Max gave him a funny look like he didn't think that was a very smart question. "Because I'm only eight. And she thinks that's too young to stay home by myself. I told her I'd be fine. It's only for a few hours, but she doesn't listen to me."

"Welcome to the world of women, pal." Rock sat up in bed and ran a hand through his hair. "And I do *not* snore."

Max raised an eyebrow at him, the same look of skepticism he'd seen Quinn give him many times. "Yeah, dude. You do."

With the number of times he'd had his nose broken, there was a slight possibility that the kid might be right, but he wasn't giving in. Better to change the subject. "Does your mom drop you off here often?"

Max shrugged. "Couple days a week, if my grandpa or my uncle are busy. It's not so bad. I like Miss Vivi."

Hmm. Maybe the family feud didn't affect the women of the family. He smiled. "I like her too."

"We're makin' blueberry pancakes. She said they're your favorite and to come wake you up and tell you to get your behind downstairs if you want any." His blue eyes sparkled, and he laughed at the word *behind*.

"Blueberry pancakes, huh? Those *are* my favorite. Tell Miss Vivi that I'm jumping in the shower and will be down in five minutes."

Ten minutes later, he was sitting at the table, mopping syrup off his plate with the last of his pancakes. He stuffed the bite in his mouth just as the front door opened, and Quinn walked in, a happy smile on her face.

He tried to swallow, but the pancakes stuck in his throat.

She stole his breath, she was so beautiful. He'd seen her only yesterday, but she looked different today. Maybe it was the smile, maybe it was the fact that she wasn't in pirate garb and instead wore a pink cotton T-shirt, brown leather cowboy boots, and snug-fitting jeans that hugged her generous curves. Maybe it was the temporary truce they'd eased into the day before.

Well, they'd called it a truce. Right up until she'd pegged him for a liar and stormed into the house. So maybe not a truce anymore.

It didn't matter.

Whatever it was, she looked good.

Her smile fell as she caught sight of Rock. It obviously

hadn't been meant for him. "Oh, sorry. I thought you'd still be asleep."

"Nope. Mom made pancakes. Well, Mom and Max, I guess. Want some?"

She shook her head, and he hated the look of hurt he saw in her eyes. "No. Thanks. I'm good."

"Listen, Quinn, I didn't have anything to do with that reporter showing up there yesterday. I *hate* the press. I would never willingly bring them anywhere, least of all back to Creedence. I swear."

She slumped into the seat across from him and picked at the remaining pancake on the platter. "Okay. I believe you, I guess."

His mother came out of the laundry room off the kitchen and smiled at Quinn. "Oh good, you're here. I need you and Rock to help me with something."

He cocked his head. He knew that tone. His mother was up to something.

Quinn followed Rock out to the barn, trying not to look at his butt in his well-fitting Levi's. There was something about the way a guy's butt looked when he wore boots.

But this guy also wore skates. And his time spent in his skates obviously meant more to him than his time in his boots.

His mom had said she needed them to fix the gate on one of the stalls in the barn, that Mason hadn't had a chance to get to it, but she had a sneaking suspicion that Vivi was using the task to put her and Rock in closer proximity.

She wasn't sure yet if she minded or not.

She was still mad from yesterday—hell, she was still mad from nine years ago when he'd left the first time. But something about him still drew her, made her want to spend time with him, just be in his presence.

Why she was subjecting herself to this twisted kind of torture, she had no idea. He'd already told her that he was home only for a short time, just while he recuperated from the concussion, and then he'd go back— would leave again. So why bother spending time with him now? Why risk getting her heart hurt again?

One of the farm dogs raced up to Rock, who knelt down, laughing as he rubbed the collie's black-and-white neck, and the dog covered his face with licks.

That was why.

Listening to Rock laugh, seeing that smile on his stupid, handsome face, that was why she would subject herself to hanging out with him. Just for a little bit.

"I miss having a dog around." He held open the door leading into the barn.

She stepped through the door, her eyes adjusting to the dim interior. The scent of hay, grain, and horses filled the air, and she heard the stomp of feet followed by a soft whinny from the horse in the far stall. She hadn't been in here in years and took a step back as the memories flooded over her, almost like a physical punch to her stomach.

They'd spent so much time here, riding horses, putting up hay, laughing and talking as she watched him do his chores. Her gaze drifted to the back corner of the barn, the spot where they'd piled hay and covered it with an old quilt and lost their virginity to each other.

She tore her gaze away, hoping Rock hadn't noticed.

Too late. He'd caught her looking, and his eyes shone with amusement as a smile tugged at the corner of his lip. Maybe he wasn't thinking about the same thing she was. "Lots of memories in here." His gaze drifted to the back corner.

Crud. Warmth crept up her neck.

Yeah, he knew exactly what she was thinking about. It was just the single most pivotal part of a girl's life. It was only natural that she was thinking about it. But they sure as heck didn't have to *talk* about it. Time to change the subject. Quick.

"So why don't you get one? A dog, I mean."

He gave her a knowing smirk, then turned to the workbench and rummaged for tools. "I've thought about it, but I'm on the road too much. Wouldn't be fair to the dog."

"Don't you have someone you could leave it with during the day? Like a girlfriend?"

Seriously? Where did that come from? Thank goodness his back was to her and he couldn't see the heat flaming in her cheeks.

His hands stilled on the hammer he'd just grasped. His tone was light, but she felt the weight of it, like their conversation was hanging in the air. "Nope, no girlfriend. How about you? Got a man in your life?"

"Yeah, I've got three."

He dropped the hammer and turned around, his eyes wide. "Three?"

She laughed. That was too easy. "Yeah, but they're all related to me. My son, my brother, and my dad. I don't have the time or the inclination for anything else."

Arching an eyebrow, he parted his lips as if to comment—why was she looking at his lips?—but he let the subject drop. Instead, he pointed at the broken stall door. "Let's take a look at the damage."

She followed him across the barn and stood back as he leaned down and assessed the gate.

"It looks like the screws are stripped on this hinge. It shouldn't take but a few minutes to fix it. You can..."

She had been busy checking out his butt again as he'd leaned down and didn't notice when his words drifted off midsentence. Not until he made a grab for the fence post and swayed on his feet did she catch on that something was wrong.

Reaching out, she grabbed his shoulder for support. "Whoa there, you okay?"

He brushed her arm away, his voice gruff. "I'm fine." But his pale coloring told her otherwise.

"Why don't you sit down?"

"I don't need to sit down."

She narrowed her eyes, glaring at him with her best Mom stare.

"Fine. I'll sit down." He sank to the ground, resting his back against the fence post.

She sat next to him, her shoulder barely grazing his. "How bad is it?"

"I don't know. Pretty bad, I guess. Bad enough to have the coach send me back to the ranch to recuperate."

"Why to the ranch?"

"Just so I'll have somebody around if the symptoms get worse."

Panic filled her chest, and she pushed to her feet. "Was this worse? Should I call someone? Should I call 911?"

He chuckled and grabbed her hand, stopping her and

pulling her back down next to him. "Hell no, you don't need to call 911. I just stood up too fast. Got a little dizzy. Could have happened to anyone."

She settled in next to him again, satisfied with his answer. For now.

Glancing up at his head, she noted the cut above his left eyebrow and wondered if it had resulted from the same fight. "It was a pretty good hit. And a total cheap shot. That guy's such an asshat. I'm glad he got suspended. They're not gonna let him play for the rest of the finals, even if they get a run at the Cup."

His body was turned slightly to hers, and he cocked his head to the side, his eyes wide with disbelief.

"What? Didn't you know he got suspended? He's out for the rest of the season."

A cocky grin pulled at one corner of his mouth, then slowly turned into a full-fledged smile. "If you saw the hit, that means you were watching the game. You were watching me play."

He said the words like an accusation, and she felt like a naughty kid who'd just been caught with her hand in the cookie jar.

"I didn't say that," she sputtered. "I never said that I watch you play. I don't even like hockey."

"Then how do you know about the Cup?"

"Everybody knows about the Stanley Cup. It's a thing. Like the Super Bowl. That doesn't mean I watch *you*, specifically."

"Then how'd you see the hit? Or know the guy is an asshat? Which he is, by the way."

Her mind raced, searching for a plausible explanation. She could say that she saw it on the news. They showed the replay often enough. But then she'd just have to spin another lie to keep that one going.

She let out a sigh. "Okay, yeah. I was watching you play. I catch a game sometimes. And it *was* the playoffs."

"Which we are now out of," he said with a grimace. "Thanks to my not paying attention."

"What? Are you kidding me? That wasn't your fault. You couldn't have anticipated that. It was a cheap shot, and boarding is bullshit," she said, referring to the term used when one player rams into the back of another and shoves them into the sideboards. The move was illegal and often resulted in the player getting kicked from the game.

But this time, it resulted in Rock's head hitting the boards and knocking him out. She'd never forget the sight of his head cracking into the sideboard and the feeling of panic in her chest as she'd watched him sink to the ice.

Even now, just thinking about it, it still made her mad as hell. "I don't care if the guy was a rookie. He should have known better."

She glanced up at Rock. His grin was back.

"Yeah, it sounds like you just catch an occasional game."

Heat crept up her neck, and she shoved against his shoulder. "Oh, shut up. Quit giving me a hard time."

"What kind of a time would you like me to give you?" He lifted his arm and dropped it easily around her shoulders, his expression going from playful to sinfully sexy in a matter of seconds.

All the air felt like it had been sucked from her chest. She hadn't been this close to him in years, yet the pressure of his arm across her shoulders felt exactly right.

The scent of him surrounded her—soap and aftershave and a hint of maple syrup.

She couldn't move, couldn't breathe. Her body felt frozen as she watched his gaze travel down from her eyes and land on her lips.

He leaned down, just an inch, then stopped, searching her face for—what?—permission? She couldn't give it but couldn't deny it either. She couldn't do anything. Except wait.

And try to breathe.

All she could do was hold perfectly still as he leaned even closer, his lips just a fraction of an inch from hers.

She closed her hands, tightened them into fists at her sides as the sensation of butterflies plunged and careened into the walls of her stomach.

He was still looking at her lips, regarding them as if he were a starving man and they represented his last meal.

Reaching his hand up, he skimmed his fingers across her neck before they came to rest on the side of her face. His thumb brushed across her bottom lip.

She sucked in her breath, a quick gasp, as a shiver tingled down her spine.

Every nerve in her body was on hyperalert, anticipating, craving, waiting, dying—for the touch of his lips.

With the softest touch, he leaned closer, his palm still holding her cheek, and with just a passing graze, the lightest glance, his lips brushed hers.

Chapter 4

IT WAS BARELY A KISS, JUST THE SLIGHTEST TOUCH OF THEIR
lips, but it was Rock's lips—lips that even after all of
these years, felt as familiar as her own.

Her breath caught in her throat, but she didn't pull
away, couldn't pull away.

His mouth slanted across hers, deepening the kiss as
she melted into him. Literally melted against his body
as if all of her bones had vanished, replaced with molten
heat that surged through her veins, warming her from
the inside out.

He tasted like maple syrup and blueberries and Rock—
and the smallest of sighs escaped her lips. His hands
cupped her cheeks, holding her face in a tender embrace.

She gripped his shoulders, holding on, forgetting
everything as she kissed him back. Sinking in to the
feeling—to the sensation of being thoroughly kissed—it
felt so damn good. Oh God, he felt so good.

The scent of him, his soap, his aftershave—something
musky and expensive—swirled around her, both familiar and mysterious. She wanted to climb into his lap,
to wrap her legs around him, to slide her hands under
his shirt and explore the new contours of his muscles,
to kiss and touch every scar, every inch of his body. A
body that she knew, yet didn't.

Memories swirled through her, memories of kissing
him, touching him. He was her first love, her first kiss,

her first everything, and she had loved him with everything she had to give.

They had loved each other. And he had walked away, left her behind.

Holy shit.

What the heck was she doing?

She pulled back, her palms flattening against his shoulders as she straightened her arms. "I can't." Gasping, she ignored the sting of gravel that bit into her hands as she scrambled backward. "I can't do this."

"*Quinn.*"

"No. No. No." She shook her head, trying to clear her muddled thoughts. It was as if she'd been swimming in a beautiful perfect lake, the water warm and fluid around her, then something had brushed past her leg, and she remembered that the lake held a monster that swam just below the surface, and suddenly she couldn't get out of the water fast enough.

She backpedaled, then pushed to her feet, determined not to get pulled down into the water again, not to get sucked in to the whirlpool that was Rockford James.

"I gotta go." She took two steps forward, then stopped and stomped her foot, a small cloud of dust kicking up around her boot heel. "Damn it. I can't just leave you here."

A grin tugged at the corner of his beautiful mouth.

"Not because of that," she sneered. Her shoulders fell as she let out a sigh. "Because you're hurt."

His cocky grin fell, replaced by a scowl. "Let me get this straight—you're pissed but you're not gonna walk away because you feel *sorry* for me? Well, screw that. You can keep on walking, lady."

"I can't. That's not who I am. I don't walk away when someone needs me."

He winced. "Who says I need you?"

A flash of pain pierced her heart. No one. No one had said that. And Rock *didn't* need her. Apparently, he didn't need anyone except himself. "It doesn't matter. I'm a mom; it's what I do. You're hurt, and I'm not walking away."

"You guys need a hand? Somebody hurt?" A younger version of Rock walked around the barn, a copper-colored golden retriever on his heels.

"Nobody's hurt," Rock growled. "I'm fine."

"Hey, Colt. I'm glad you're here," Quinn said to Rock's baby brother. He looked so much like Rock, the same sandy-blond hair, the same broad shoulders, sometimes it was hard for Quinn to be around him, just the sight of him bringing up too many painful memories. "I've got to go. Can you watch him?"

"Nobody needs to watch me. I'm not a child."

The golden ran over to Rock and set to licking his face in greeting.

No, he wasn't a child. And he wasn't the teenage boy who'd left her behind, the boy who still lingered in her mind and haunted her dreams. No, he was a man. A man who with one kiss, had just turned her inside out and shaken her to her core.

Shoving her hands in her pockets, she tried to control their trembling, then turned on her heels, and walked back to the house.

—◇◇◇—

Rock held out his hand and let Colt pull him up. "How you doing, little brother?"

The younger man pulled him into a bear hug. "A lot better than you, by the looks of things. What's going on with Quinn? I don't think I've ever seen her so rattled."

"Yeah, me neither." He wasn't sure if he wanted to share that it was his fault, or that it might have something to do with the fact that he'd just kissed her. Okay—it had everything to do with the fact that he'd just kissed her.

But he needed to mull that over a little on his own first—because he also wasn't sure if he was ready to face how rattled he felt either.

"Sorry I missed you last night," Colt said.

"It's cool. Mom said you were working a late shift at The Creed," Rock told him, referring to The Creedence Tavern, the local pub and restaurant in town. "Since when did you start working there?"

"I don't work there. I was just filling in for Dale last night because his wife went into labor."

"No way. I didn't even know she was pregnant."

He shrugged. "It's only been for about the last nine months now."

Rock elbowed him in the side. "I was gonna come down and see you, but Ma wouldn't let me out of her sight last night."

His brother chuckled. "Yeah, I bet. So, how's your head? For real."

"For real?"

Colt nodded, his gaze solemn.

"For real, it hurts like a bitch sometimes and other times not at all. I'm sore and pissed and embarrassed that I let that punk get the drop on me, and I feel like I let the whole damn team down and we're out of the finals because of me."

"Whoa. That's a lot. I know you've got some pretty broad shoulders, but I didn't realize you carried the whole team."

He sighed. "Shut up. You know what I mean. I just feel like I let 'em down. And I hate that the coach sent me home to 'recuperate.'" He lifted his fingers to make air quotes.

"It must have been pretty bad then."

"It's a few dizzy spells and some bruises. But I'm not a freaking invalid, and regardless of what Quinn Rivers has to say about it, I do *not* need a babysitter."

Colt held up his hands. "All right, dude. Although you'd be hard-pressed to find a prettier babysitter than Quinn. She used to babysit me, and I never seemed to mind."

Rock let out a chuckle. "Point taken. I just don't want her, or anybody, making a fuss over me. That includes Mom."

"Good luck with that one." He gestured toward the pasture. "I'm headed out to check on the calves. Want to keep me company? Stretch your legs a little?"

"Sure." He picked up a stick and threw it for the dog as he fell into step behind his brother. It *would* be good to stretch his legs and to focus on something besides the blond cowgirl who smelled like vanilla and whose kiss still sent him reeling, making him dizzy in ways that had nothing to do with the concussion.

Two hours later, Rock took a biscuit from the plate and inhaled the sweet, buttery aroma before taking a bite.

Okay, he could admit, there were a few good things

about being home, like sitting around the table with his mother and his brothers, and the taste of his mom's homemade biscuits.

"Pass the roast beast," Mason said, indicating the platter brimming with roasted beef, potatoes, and carrots.

Rock and Colt took after their mother, inheriting her blond hair and Norwegian stock. But Mason was the one who looked just like their father, with his shock of black hair and the five-o'clock shadow of dark whiskers that seemed to show up by noon.

They'd lost their dad in a farming accident when they were little, and Rock sometimes wondered if it was hard on his mom to have a son who shared such a likeness with the man she lost. The man they'd all lost.

Rock had been nine years old, barely older than Quinn's son now, when he took on the role of the man of the house, stepping into his father's boots to take care of his mother and younger brothers.

Maybe that's why he felt so responsible for what happened with the team, and why he felt like he'd let them down. He was used to taking responsibility, for shouldering the burdens of those around him.

He passed the platter to his brother. "I took a walk with Colt this morning. The calves look good."

"Yeah, we're branding them and putting 'em out to pasture over the next few weeks. We're scheduled to start at Rivers Gulch day after tomorrow. Probably take us a couple days to get theirs done, then they'll come over here in a week or two and help us with ours."

"Wait. You're going over to Rivers Gulch to help them with their branding?"

"We all are. Including you. We can use the extra

hand. We've both got close to three hundred head this year."

"But what about the 'feud'?" He lifted his fingers in air quotes. "Since when do we go over and help Hamilton Rivers do anything."

"Oh Lord, son, you've been gone too long," his mother said. "We only worry about the dang feud when it's convenient. But we're neighbors, and we share grazing land, and when there's work to be done, we come together and get it done."

Colt nodded. "We've been branding together the last several years, and it helps both of us. Plus, it's kinda fun. We eat first, and Quinn always puts out a great spread. So does Ma."

They were referring to the annual tradition of branding and castrating their calves. Every spring, they roped and branded their own, then let them out to pasture together to spend the summer grazing on their shared land. In the fall, they culled the herd, separating out their cattle by their brands and bringing them back to their respective ranches.

Both the branding and the roundup were big events on the farm.

"I'm glad to help," Rock said, speaking around a mouthful of biscuit. "But I don't think either Ham or Logan would want me around."

"They'd be happy to have the extra hand. Like Mom said, it's easy to put aside our differences when there's work to be done. And Logan's not such a bad guy."

Rock arched an eyebrow at his baby brother. "You sound like you're friends with him."

Colt shrugged. "He helps out down at The Creed

sometimes too, and I've known him my entire life, so yeah, I'd say we are friends."

"You're friends with the guy that used to tease you and always make you be the goalie when we played hockey on the pond?"

"Dude, you used to make me do that too. And that was a long time ago. We were kids."

"Well, I was over there yesterday, and he's still pissed at me."

"Can you blame him?"

"Point taken."

"Look, you've been gone a long time. We're neighbors. It's easier to get along. And just because the guy thinks you're a douche, which by the way, sometimes you are, doesn't mean the rest of us have to be part of your drama."

Vivienne held up her hands. "All right, that's enough. We're going to Rivers Gulch to help with the branding, they're coming over to help us—that's just the way it is. Rockford, we'd be glad to have your help, if you're feeling up to it. Now I would like to get back to the meal, and I prefer if you not call each other feminine cleansing products while we eat."

All three men grimaced.

"Ew."

"Gross, Mom."

Rock let out a groan.

Vivi chuckled. "Pass the gravy."

Two days later, Rock sat in the passenger seat while Mason pulled his pickup into the driveway of Rivers

Gulch. Vivi sat between them, and Colt rode in the back with the two dogs.

The bed of the truck was full of gear to help with the branding, and they made quick work of unloading while the dogs ran around and greeted everyone.

Logan was already at the grill and called the crew in to eat.

Rock followed his family into the front yard, where two long picnic tables were covered in red vinyl table-cloths and set with plates and silverware. Three large pitchers of iced tea and several baskets of rolls were already on the tables.

Besides the James and the Rivers families, they both had their hired men come along to help, making a total of ten people to feed. The group gathered together, grab-bing rolls and filling their cups with tea as they settled around the table.

The scent of grilled meat filled the air, and someone had set up a wireless speaker so an old country song was playing softly in the background. With the sound of quick guitar-picking and banjo strums, the day had a festive feel to it, and Rock's spirit lifted for the first time in the last few days.

Not that he'd been moping around the house the last day and a half. Okay, yeah, he'd been sort of moping. More like brooding—that had a more manly feel to it.

Whatever it was, it felt like crap. It was bad enough that his body hurt, but he also felt like crap for the way things had ended with Quinn.

And his bad mood was apparently evident enough that the rest of his family noticed. Although they all handled it differently. His mom had made his favorite blueberry cobbler the night before, Colt had challenged him to a game of foosball, and Mason had asked him if he was on his period.

Even though he appreciated the cobbler, it was good to snap out of it.

Why he was wasting energy on something that had ended years ago was a mystery to him. He needed to redirect his focus to something he could control, like working out and getting healthy, blueberry cobbler withstanding.

He needed to look to his future, not focus on things in the past that he couldn't change.

Quinn was just a girl—er, woman—whom he used to know. It's true, she was his first love, but so what? That didn't mean he had to moon over her forever. And it didn't mean that she still had any kind of hold over his heart.

Yeah, right. You keep telling yourself that, buddy.

The screen door slammed, and he looked up to see Quinn walking down the porch steps, a bowl of potato salad in her hands.

Her hair was in a braid and pulled through the hole in the back of a pink ball cap. She wore a black tank top, low-heeled boots, and snug jeans that hugged her curvy hips. A pouch holding a multi-use tool hung from the brown leather belt encircling her waist.

Quinn Rivers was a country girl through and through. Tough enough to run a stallion at top speed through a barrel-racing course and serve a bunch of hungry cowboys a meal complete with yeast rolls and homemade potato salad, yet still feminine enough to have Rock's hands sweating and his mouth starting to water.

And it wasn't from the rolls.

It was from the tall, gorgeous woman who stopped in the middle of the steps, her back held straight, as she waited for Max to follow her, his small arms laden with a big jar of pickles.

Her laughter rang through the air at something Max said, and she set the bowl on the table and reached for the jar in her son's hands.

"I got it," Rock said, hastening from his seat to grab the jar and set it on the table. "How you doing, Max?"

Quinn's easy smile faltered, just for a moment, then she forced it back in place. Her smile didn't quite meet her eyes as she avoided Rock's gaze. "Max, you remember Rock from the other day."

Max grinned up at him, his eyes bright behind his round glasses. "Hiya, Rock. Are you gonna be a pirate today?"

Rock chuckled. "Nope. Gonna be a cowboy."

"Too bad. You made a pretty good pirate."

He liked this kid. Squinting one eye closed, he did his best pirate imitation. "Thanks, matey. But I'm afraid I'm in trouble with the captain, and she's gonna make me walk the plank."

Max giggled and climbed over the bench seat of the picnic table. "You're weird. But funny."

"Yeah, he's funny all right," Quinn muttered as she took a seat next to her son.

Rock slid in next to her, lowering his voice and resting a hand on the small of her back. "You think maybe we can have a parley?" he asked, referencing the pirate term for *truce*. "If I tell you I'm real sorry and promise to swab the decks?"

"Fine, but you have to stop talking like a pirate." Their legs were pressed next to each other, and Quinn discreetly slid an inch away, just enough that their thighs were no longer touching. She also removed his hand from her back. "And don't even think about touching my *booty*."

He chuckled, okay with the directive, for now. As long as she was talking to him again. Although he'd had plenty of thoughts the last few days about touching her booty, and all the rest of her.

Before he could come up with a clever response, Ham stood up at the head of the table and held out his hands, signaling the group to quiet down for the blessing.

Rock held out his hand to Quinn, who grimaced as if it had cooties, but took it anyway.

He tried to focus on Hamilton's prayer, but all he could think about was the fact that he was holding her hand, the weight of it comfortable and familiar in his. He rubbed his thumb over her knuckle.

"Amen."

"Amen," she said, pulling her hand away and avoiding his gaze as she focused on helping Max with his plate.

Rock picked up the potato salad and dropped a spoonful on his plate. That was okay. At least he'd made progress, and it felt like they were back on good terms again. Tentative good terms, but good terms nonetheless.

He'd earned a smile, and that was enough for him.

—⁂—

Quinn let the lasso fly, and the loop sailed through the air and landed perfectly around the calf's neck.

Her heart raced as she tightened her grip, pulling the

rope taut as she sprinted toward the calf and wrestled him to the ground.

There was a certain rush to roping a calf, from the skilled precision of the lassoing to the physical contest of wrangling it off its feet. Her dad had taught her and her brother to rope when they were little, and they were both proficient.

Her skills were a little rusty, since she didn't find a lot of use for roping anymore, but it was fun to participate in the annual branding ceremony.

And it was a ceremony, complete with the time-honored traditions of having a big meal together first, then setting up the branding pot and having a round of cigars while the branding irons heated.

A lot of ranches were using chutes to brand, but Hamilton Rivers wasn't big on change and liked the traditional ways of doing things. "If it ain't broke, don't fix it" was a common quote heard from his mouth.

Unless the new way saved him money, then he was much more amenable to a change.

Quinn sometimes liked the old ways too. There was something comforting about keeping to tradition, to teaching her son methods of doing things that her dad had taught her, and his dad had taught him as well.

She'd be fine if they let go of the cigar part of the tradition—although she might miss the sweet tobacco scent mingled with the propane and smoke that was all part of branding day.

And the scent of tobacco was preferable to the stench that the brand gave off when it hit the calf's skin.

They had a system, and everyone had different jobs. She and Colt roped while Logan and Mason did most of the wrestling and holding the calf down while it was vaccinated, branded, and sometimes castrated. Ham and a couple of the hired men did most of that, and Vivi ran the branding station, keeping the irons hot and refilling syringes with vaccine.

They'd all done this together for the past few years and knew the system. Except for Rock. He was usually still playing this time of year and hadn't been home for a branding in years. And not since the two ranches had started working together.

Vivienne had assigned him to do the vaccinations, a job that still required some strength and skill, but wouldn't put as much of a physical strain on his already bruised and beaten body.

But she'd never known Rock to do things the easy way, and he was right in the thick of things—working next to his brothers and hers, doing the vaccinations, *plus* slinging rope and wrestling calves.

As much as she tried to ignore him, Quinn seemed to be aware of him everywhere he went—whether he was across the corral helping Mason or kneeling next to her, vaccinating the calf she'd just roped. His presence alone added another layer to the day, and detracted from the concentration she needed to do the job.

It was enough to keep an eye on Max, who was either running around with the dogs, reading a book, or advising Vivienne about how to fill the syringes with the exact amount of medicine.

He approached her now, running toward her, a rock held out in his hand. "Mom, check this out."

"Max, get back!" she yelled just a second too late.

Chapter 5

QUINN'S WARNING CAME TOO LATE AS MAX CHARGED toward her.

He knew better, but the excitement of whatever he'd discovered obviously outweighed his caution. He plowed forward, not paying attention to the calf on the ground in front of her, or maybe he saw it and subconsciously thought it was already tied and secure.

Regardless of what he was thinking, the calf's feet were still loose, and one of them shot out, connecting squarely with Max's thigh and knocking the boy to the ground.

His eyes went round, filling with tears as he cried out.

Quinn let the calf go, racing the loose length of rope as she ran to where Max had fallen.

Rock had been closer, and he was already picking the boy up and setting him on his feet. "You all right there, buddy?"

Max nodded, swallowing back the tears and rubbing at his leg.

"You gotta watch out for these damn little boogers. You get too close, they'll git ya," Rock said, patting the boy on the shoulder.

"You sure you're okay?" Quinn asked, falling to her knees in front of Max and throwing her arms around his small shoulders.

Only the slightest tremble indicated his fright as he gave her a tight squeeze, then let her go. "I'm okay,

Mom. I got too close, and the damn little booger got me."

She raised an eyebrow at Rock, who was stifling a laugh.

"I see. Well, I'd prefer that you not swear, but in this instance, I'll allow it. Don't make it a habit." She held back a grin, but it faded when she saw the bloody scrapes on his palms. "Let's go in the house and get you cleaned up."

"Quinn, we need you over here," her dad called.

He must not have seen Max get kicked. Or maybe he had and didn't think it was that bad. Hamilton Rivers was the kind of dad who thought skinned knees and bruises were part of the learning process and frequently told his kids to "buck up" and "shake it off."

"I can take him in," Rock offered.

Quinn lifted her head, searching Rock's face to see if he was serious.

"What? I have two younger brothers. I can handle some antiseptic spray and a Band-Aid," he assured her.

"Okay, but I'll come in with you for a second. Just to take a look at his leg."

Rock leaned down, offering the boy a ride on his back, and Max climbed up, clinging to his shoulders.

The main bathroom in the house didn't seem that small until she was crowded into it with her son and the muscled bulk of Rockford James.

He set Max down on the counter and turned on the water. "Run your hands under there to wash the dirt off them," he instructed the boy while Quinn rummaged through the medicine cabinet and pulled out a tube of antibiotic ointment and a box of Band-Aids.

She pulled off Max's cowboy boots and stood him on the toilet seat.

"Mo-om," he said, pushing her hands away as she reached for his jeans.

She pulled back, surprised by her son's sudden modesty. "Sorry. I just want to check your leg."

Max glanced up at Rock, who gave him a nod and turned his back, giving the boy some privacy.

Quinn gasped at the red bruise that had already formed. He was small for his age, and his thigh looked pale and thin against the fist-sized bruise.

Rock turned around and peered down at it. "Oh yeah." He offered Max a manly grunt and held up his hand for a high-five. "That's a good 'un."

Max responded with a brave grin and smacked Rock's outstretched hand.

"I'm going to get you a pair of shorts. And an ice pack," she said, fleeing into the hall so Max wouldn't see her cry. She closed her eyes and pressed her hands to her lips, swallowing the emotion of seeing the ugly bruise on her little boy's skin.

"Just a sec," she heard Rock say, then felt him step out of the bathroom and pull her against him in a hug.

His voice was soft as he whispered close to her ear. "He's okay. I looked at it. It's just a bruise. It's a good one, but the skin's not torn or scratched. He'll be all right."

She clung to him, letting herself take comfort in his strong embrace for just a moment before she pushed back and swiped the tears off her cheeks with the back of her hand. Taking a deep breath, she pulled herself together. "Thank you. I'm fine. Just give me a minute."

"You sure?"

"Yeah, just keep him company a second while I grab him some other clothes."

"No problem."

He turned and stepped back into the bathroom, and she hurried to Max's room.

Returning a few minutes later with a first aid gel pack from the freezer and a pair of soft, cotton shorts, she sucked in her breath at the sight of Rock standing in the bathroom with his shirt pulled up as he showed Max the colorful array of bruises that covered his back.

Dang, but that guy did have some serious muscles. And rock-hard abs.

The bruises on his back tore at her heart, not in quite the same way Max's had, but she hated to think of Rock being hurt.

She handed Max the shorts, and he pulled them on. "Why don't you stay inside for a bit?"

"Ahh. But Grandpa needs us."

Ham had spent the last week talking about how important today was, and Max had obviously taken his grandfather's words to heart.

"He can get along without us for a little while."

"Why don't you go?" Rock offered. "Ham's gonna be expecting you to come back, but he doesn't care one way or the other if I'm there. I can stay inside with Max."

She gazed up at him and noticed for the first time the weariness around his eyes. It was hard to imagine Rock as anything but the strong, capable man she'd always known him to be, but he had taken a major hit a few days ago and had a severe enough concussion that his coach had sent him home.

Maybe this would make Rock take it easy without making him admit that he might be tired.

"Maybe you could read him a few books and keep the ice pack on his leg," she suggested, then lowered her voice. "Get him to lie down for a bit without using the word 'nap.'"

"Sure. I can do that." He lifted Max and carried him out of the bathroom. The boy looked small against Rock's well-built frame. "Don't worry about us. We'll be fine."

She hesitated for a moment, weighing her decision to leave Max after he just got hurt with facing her dad's annoyance and condescension about her babying her son too much. "I'll be back to check on you in a bit."

But Max didn't seem concerned. Rock had set him down, and Max was already pulling him by the hand toward his room and telling him he knew exactly which books he wanted him to read.

------ w ------

Rock grinned as Max gave him a tour of his room, pointing out practically every toy he owned and every odd piece of junk he had collected and the significance behind it.

"And this is the rock that I found when we were on a hike a few weeks ago. I think it has a fossil in it." Max handed it to Rock, who peered down at it and declared that it was indeed a fossil.

"Isn't that cool?" Max said, putting the rock back and moving on to the next thing. "And this is my bank. See, it has three sections, one for saving, one for spending, and one for givin' to the church. When I get my allowance or birthday money, I split it up and put some in each section." The piggy bank was clear and shaped like three little buildings, a home, a bank, and a steepled church. Coins and bills partially filled all three sections.

Rock admired his dedication. "What are you saving for?"

The boy scratched his head and pushed his glasses back up his nose. "I'm not a hundred percent sure. I was saving for a bike, but I got a really neat one for my birthday, so now I'm either saving for this new *Star Wars* LEGO set or a Disgusting Science Kit."

This kid cracked him up. "What's a Disgusting Science Kit?"

"It's like this kit that you can use to do experiments, like grow your own germs, or you can make stuff too, like fake snot."

He chuckled. "That does sound disgusting."

"I know." Max grinned and finished the circuit of his room, then grabbed three books from his bookshelf. "Wanna read these? They're my favorites."

"Sure."

Max's twin bed sat in the corner of the room, and Rock sat down, taking a second to prop up the pillow, then leaned back against the headboard. Max climbed in next to him and snuggled against his arm.

Dang if he wasn't a cute little bugger.

Rock positioned the gel pack across Max's small leg, then peered down at the books. "Dinosaurs, a wizard kid, or time travelers. Which one should we read?"

Max arranged the books in a pile, then pointed to the one on top. "This one first, then the others."

This one *first*? How long was this kid planning on him staying? All night?

"So, is this one of the books your dad reads to you?"

Ah, crap. Where the heck had that come from? He had no idea why he had just asked that and felt like a total shit as he witnessed the instant change in Max.

The boy stilled, his whole body transforming. His shoulders shrunk inward, and his spine went slack. His voice was soft as he answered, "No. My dad doesn't read books to me. He doesn't do anything with me."

"Do you ever get to see him?" He said the words before he could stop himself. He wished he could take it back, but now that the door was open, there was no closing it.

"No. I don't ever see him. I've never even met him." His gaze stayed focused on his lap, and he picked at a seam on his shorts. "Sometimes I like to imagine that he's a soldier in the army or maybe a spy. So then, the reason he is gone and doesn't come around is 'cause he's fighting for our country or saving us from terrorists. Like 'cause he's a hero, ya know?"

Physical pain tore at his heart, and Rock wanted to scoop Max into his arms and protect him from the assholes of the world. Like assholes who got teenage girls pregnant then walked out on them, and like the deadbeats who walked away from their kids, from their responsibilities as men.

But he couldn't say that—couldn't take away from the hope this sweet kid was holding on to. "Maybe he is."

"Did you know my dad?"

Rock shook his head. "No, not really. I knew who he was. I played a little football for my high school, just to stay in shape for hockey, and our schools played ball against each other, so I knew who he was, but I didn't really know him."

What he did know of the guy was that he had a reputation as a bully and a troublemaker. He knew he'd been in some trouble with the law, even as a teenager, and that he liked to pick on guys smaller than him.

And he definitely *wasn't* a hero.

He wished he could get Monty Hill on the field against him now—or better yet, across the ice. He'd give whole new meaning to dropping the gloves and taking that guy out.

But he couldn't. He couldn't do a damn thing.

Except wonder what the heck Quinn could have been thinking when she hooked up with a guy like him.

The familiar anger churned through his gut. It happened every time he thought about Quinn with someone else, especially a loser like Hill. And knowing that Hill had hurt her, and he couldn't do a thing about it, made the fury ten times worse.

If he were being honest, he knew that some of that anger was aimed at himself.

He'd hurt Quinn first—when he'd left her behind. Hell, he'd practically driven her into the loser's arms.

He couldn't blame her. She'd been young, and the guy she'd thought she trusted had just let her down. No wonder she'd fallen victim to a chump like Hill.

There was nothing he could do about it now. Hill was gone, but Quinn and Max were still here.

All he could do was try to prove to Quinn that he was here now, that he wanted to be her friend again. Maybe wanted to be more than friends again.

A niggling thought whispered inside of his brain that he wasn't here for her. He was here *now*, but he was leaving again, as soon as his coach called him back to the team.

That thought caused his head to pound, so he pushed it away and focused instead on the little boy who curled against his arm, waiting for him to read a story.

"So, you say this book has some time travelers in it? That sounds cool."

Max tipped his head up and grinned at Rock. "Yeah, it is. They go to different places in every book, and they're funny."

Good. They could use some funny after that bleak conversation.

Rock smiled down at Max, then opened the book and started to read.

———

Quinn had spent longer than she'd anticipated outside, and she stretched out her sore muscles as she walked down the hall toward Max's room.

She didn't hear anything coming from his room, and she peered around the doorjamb and had to stifle a laugh.

Rock was laid out on the twin bed, sound asleep, and Max was sitting next to him, leaning against his shoulder and quietly reading a book.

The boy looked up as Quinn stepped into the room. "He fell asleep halfway through the book, and I didn't want to wake him up," he whispered. "I heard Uncle Logan talking about him, and he said that he got hurt pretty bad, so I figured he needed his rest."

Her heart melted, as it often did, at the pure sweetness

of her son's personality. "That was really nice of you. How's your leg?"

He shrugged. "It's okay. I feel bad about not helping Grandpa. Is he mad?"

She shook her head. "No. He's fine. We're almost finished. They're just cleaning up. How about if I stay and watch Rock for a little bit, and you can go outside and see if you can help?"

He nodded, setting his book down and carefully easing off the side of the bed.

Quinn gave him a quick hug, glancing down to check on the bruise and trying not to wince at the deep-purple color.

She helped him with his sneakers, then listened as his footsteps raced down the hall, followed by the faint slam of the screen door as he headed outside.

Taking his place, she gently sat on the edge of the bed, trying not to disturb Rock. She let out a breath as she peered down at his handsome face, his chin so defined that it could have been chiseled from stone.

His hair fell across his broad forehead, and she wanted to brush it back, then run her fingers through it—the way she used to do when they were teenagers.

They had known each other their whole lives, had spent so much time together. They'd been in the same class at school, had ridden the bus together, and Rock had been the one who insisted they all get skates and learn to play hockey on the pond that separated their two ranches.

He'd been a part of every milestone in her life: her sweet sixteen, her first rodeo, losing her mom. And she'd been there for his: for every hockey game he'd played, for his graduation, for the day he got his first truck.

They'd always been comfortable around each other, cared for each other, and each could practically read the other one's mind. Even now, even with all the years that had passed, she doubted anyone knew her the way Rockford James did.

Although she couldn't say the same about him, because she never would have believed he could have left her the way he had when he got offered the scholarship and the chance to play college hockey. Evidently, she hadn't known him as well as she thought she had.

"You've got a pretty great kid," he said, his voice still husky with sleep.

She peered down at him, watching the crystal-blue eyes that were as familiar as her own, blink open and gaze up at her. His lips curved into an impish grin, and she smiled back.

Dang it. She couldn't help it. She'd always been a sucker for his grin.

"I know," she said. "I came in, and he was reading a book and watching over you while you slept."

"I didn't fall asleep. I was just resting my eyes."

"And snoring."

His forehead creased. "Why does everyone keep saying I snore?"

She chuckled, trying to keep it casual, even though she'd just realized that she was in a bed alone with Rock. "We made it through most of our calves. I think we have fifty or sixty left. We're taking a break to eat, then we'll finish them off tonight. You planning to stay for supper?"

"What are we having?"

"Chili and corn bread. It's been cooking in the Crock-Pot all day."

"Is it Ham's recipe?"

"No. It's mine. So don't worry, it doesn't have any onions."

He grinned, and her stomach went all topsy-turvy. "You always could read my mind." His grin turned flirty, and he ran the back of his fingers over the curve of his hip. "Do you know what I'm thinking about right now?"

"You're probably thinking that if you don't move your hand, you might get slapped. I don't care how big you are, cowboy, I can still take you out."

He laughed, a loud belly laugh. "You are probably right." He pushed himself up on his elbows and winced.

"You okay?" Those bruises covering his back had to hurt.

"I'm fine." He brushed off her concern. "You don't need to coddle me."

She swallowed. That hadn't been one of the assorted things that had come to mind that she had imagined doing to him. Best to focus on something else. She stood up from the bed. "Good. Then you can help me serve the chili."

Five long hours later, Rock fell into bed. His body ached. He was in good shape, but working on the ranch and wrestling calves used different muscles than he was used to exercising.

He couldn't believe he'd fallen asleep in Max's room earlier that afternoon.

But waking up to Quinn next to him had made the unexpected nap worth it.

Even all these years later, she still looked great, like the same girl he'd known—and loved—most of his life. And she still made his heart race and his palms sweat, just like when he was a teenager.

Memories of time spent with her filled his head—and his dreams—as he drifted off.

—∿∿—

The morning came too quickly—its arrival announced by the bright strip of sunlight coming through the windows.

Rock let out a groan, squinting against the sun as he checked the time. His eyes widened. He was surprised to see that it was past eight already and he'd slept in again.

He crawled out of bed and scratched his stomach as he stumbled down the stairs and into the kitchen. His mom handed him a cup of coffee. He leaned down and kissed the top of her head, and she wrapped her arms around him in a hug.

"How's your head?"

"Good. Better every day."

"Well, don't get better too quickly. I kind of like having you around," she teased. "You want some waffles?"

"Yes, ma'am," he answered, swiping a piece of bacon off the platter by the stove. "Anything I can do to help?"

"Nope. Just sit down and keep me company is enough. Tell me what's new."

He didn't have much to tell her. They'd always been close and usually talked on the phone a couple of times a week. She stayed pretty current on the happenings in his life. But now, after his brother's comments the day before, he wondered if he hadn't been paying enough attention to what was happening with her and the ranch.

Had he missed something that was going on?

"I'm good, Mom. You know everything. Why don't you tell me what's new with you. Everything good? Things with the ranch okay?"

She tilted her head. "Are you worried about me, Son?"

"Do I have reason to be?"

"No. Lest you forget, I'm the parent here. I'm the one who does the worrying." She turned her back to pour batter into the waffle iron, but he thought he'd caught a flicker of something in her eyes.

The front door slammed open, and his brothers walked in, followed by their two dogs. Mason's border collie stuck to his side, but Watson, the golden retriever, raced directly for Rock, wagging his tail and his body in delight, whining as he begged to be petted.

"Nice of you to join us, princess," Mason joked from the sink where he was washing his hands. He dried them on a towel as he sat down at the table. "We've been up and working for hours while you've been in here getting your beauty rest."

"From the look of your ugly mug, you should have stayed in and slept a little longer yourself." Rock picked up a piece of bacon and tossed it at his brother.

Mason caught it and crammed it into his mouth.

"That's enough of that talk," Vivienne said, setting a platter stacked with waffles on the table. "None of you have a clue about needing beauty rest. All of you boys are too handsome for your own good."

Mason grinned at her. "Thanks, Mom. I'm going to add that to my dating résumé—my mom thinks I'm handsome."

Colt chuckled and sat down at the table. "That'll win you some favor for sure."

Rock reached for a waffle, but his mom slapped at his hand. "Sorry, Ma." Duly chastised, he bent his head as his mother blessed the meal.

They put their joking aside to focus on passing the food and filling their plates.

"So, are you going to the game with us tonight?" Mason asked before shoving a forkful of waffles into his mouth.

"What game?"

"Colt's softball game. He plays on a league with The Creed. Tonight's the game against Franklin, so half the town will likely show up."

Franklin was the neighboring town to Creedence, and their biggest rival. It didn't matter if it was football, baseball, or 4-H animals—if Franklin was involved, the whole town was rooting against them.

A sour feeling filled Rock's gut as he thought about the rival town, and he knew it had more to do with than just softball. Franklin was the also the town Monty Hill was from.

"Tonight's a playoff game, so it should be a good one," Colt said. "And we've got a good team this year."

Rock was glad to see that Colt was still involved in sports of some kind. He'd always been a natural athlete, and it was a cryin' shame what had happened with his hockey career.

He'd had a promising future, was a rising star in the

minor leagues, and could easily have moved up into the pros, if one bad injury hadn't taken it all away.

It was a crushing blow. Colt's entire future changed in the span of less than a minute.

And the kid had been good, could have been better than Rock, with a few more years under him. Not that Rock would ever tell him that. Although Colt already knew. Everyone knew.

That's what made the whole thing even worse.

Stupid injuries.

"You pitchin'?" Rock asked. Colt had always been good at whatever sport he tried, but he had a great arm and could throw a ball with the speed and accuracy of a pro.

"Yeah. It's coed, and we've got some great girls on our team. I think we could take the championship this year."

Rock tried to push down the disappointment about his own team being out of the running for the Stanley Cup this year. Better to focus on his brother's success than his own failings. "Sounds good. I'll be there."

"We can all go into town and grab a burger together at the diner before the game." Mason reached for another waffle and turned to Rock. "I'm working on fixing that far stable in the barn this morning. One of the mares kicked out a section. Wanna give me a hand after breakfast?"

"Sure." He nodded, and the conversation turned to the endless list of chores that needed to be accomplished on the ranch.

He spent the day working with his brothers, lending a hand and pitching in where he could. It felt good to be working with his hands, to be helping his family. Even though he didn't come home as often as he wanted to, he easily fell back into the comfortable companionship of his brothers. They might joke around a lot, but it was obvious they loved each other and were fiercely loyal to each other.

Rock wasn't sure how long he wanted to stay out, so he took his truck when they left the ranch later that night. He had two he kept at the ranch. A new Ford with all of the trimmings, and his old blue truck that he'd driven as a teenager. He'd paid a local guy to refurbish the old truck, adding a new engine and a fresh coat of paint. The pickup held a lot of memories, and he typically drove it when he was at home.

But there were already enough old memories swirling in his head, so he drove the new truck into town tonight.

The diner's cheeseburgers were just as good as he remembered, and his stomach was full as he parked behind Mason's rig and followed his mom and brother toward the baseball fields.

Creedence might be a small town, but they took their sports seriously and, several years ago, had installed a nice sports complex, complete with four baseball diamonds and two soccer fields. Having the substantial donation from Rock might have helped as well.

The four diamonds were color-coded and spread out from a center area that had a snack bar, two locker rooms, and public restrooms.

The scent of grilled hot dogs and popcorn filled the air. Even though he was stuffed from supper, he couldn't resist the smell of popcorn and bought a round of tubs and sodas for him, his mom, and Mason.

"Thanks, honey," Vivi said, taking the offered cup.

She nodded toward one of the diamonds. "Colt's team is playing on the blue field tonight. I think I see him over there warming up."

It took them ten minutes to cross to the field and climb up the bleachers. Not that the walk was that far, but between the three of them, they found that one of them had to stop and chat with almost every person they ran into.

Rock fielded questions about the team and the fight and his injuries. He smiled and joked, happy to visit, but found his gaze continually searching for one particular tall blond. He hadn't seen her yet and didn't want to admit that hopes of running into Quinn may have influenced his decision to come out to the game tonight.

Not that he didn't want to support his brother, but the off chance that he might run into his neighbor was also a strong factor.

He heard her familiar laugh as they climbed the bleachers behind the field, and he looked up to see her and Max sitting a few rows ahead. Her hair was loose, falling in golden waves around her shoulders, and the white tank top she wore accentuated her slim, tanned arms.

She had on a pair of khaki shorts and tennis shoes, and even in such a simple outfit, she was breathtakingly beautiful.

A rush of heat coursed through him, both from the sight of her long, tan legs and from the wave of anger inspired by the too-smooth-looking cowboy standing next to her who was making her laugh.

Chapter 6

DESPITE HIS ANNOYANCE AT THE CHUMP WHO WAS CHATTING up Quinn, Rock smiled at Max, who was waving and calling out for them to come sit with him.

"I didn't know they'd be here," he said quietly to his mom.

She turned back to him, an innocent smile on her face. "Oh, didn't I mention it? Logan plays on the team with Colt."

"No. It must have slipped your mind."

Yeah right. Nothing slips that woman's mind. He'd wager a hundred dollars that she knew Quinn and Max would be here, and double down that their presence was the main reason she'd encouraged him to come along.

Mason climbed the two rows in front of them and spread out the blanket their mom had him carry in from the truck. Vivi sat down, conveniently leaving plenty of room for Rock to sit next to Quinn, and Max clamored across the bleachers to sit next to Mason and Vivi.

"I'll see ya later," the cowboy was saying as Rock dropped onto the bleachers next to Quinn.

He didn't know if his angry glare had anything to do with the guy leaving or not, and he didn't really care. "Who was that guy?" he asked, the question coming out a little harsher than he'd intended.

Quinn raised an eyebrow. "Well, hello, Rock. Nice to

see you too. Yes, the weather is lovely tonight, and oh yeah, it's none of your business."

Yeah, definitely came out too harsh. He held his hands up in surrender. "Sorry. You're right. What I meant to say was 'Hey, Quinn, how you doing? Isn't it a great night for some softball?' Is that better?"

"Barely."

He shifted in his seat, setting his drink on the bleachers in front of him and trying not to stare at her amazingly long legs. "So really, who was that guy?"

She let out a laugh and shook her head. "You are terrible. He's just a customer from the coffee shop where I work."

He huffed. "A customer that seems interested in more than just your coffee-making skills. So, did he ask you out?"

"Why, Rockford James, if I didn't know any better, I'd think you were jealous."

He shrugged. "What if I am? Or what if I just felt like punching that guy in his fat, stupid nose?"

Her eyes widened. "Wow. That is so mature. I can tell that you've really grown up."

He ignored the jab, used to their verbal sparring. "You didn't answer the question."

This time, it was her turn to shrug. "No. He didn't ask me out. But he asked for my number."

His blood boiled, and he tried to rein in the sparks of jealousy that were firing through his veins. "I hope you told him to shove it."

"No, I didn't. Because I'm a civilized person who doesn't go around telling perfectly nice people to shove it."

He cocked an eyebrow.

"But I also didn't give him my number."

A smug smile tugged at the corners of his lips, and the fire in his veins cooled.

He was working on a witty comeback, when another person walked up the bleachers to talk to Quinn.

This time it was a girl, probably in her midtwenties. Her hair was mousy brown and unkempt, her bangs too long and hanging in her eyes. She wore faded jeans and a black tank top with a marijuana leaf embossed on the front. Real classy.

Rock felt Quinn stiffen next to him as the girl warily approached. She looked familiar but he couldn't quite place her, more like he'd known her as a kid instead of as an adult. He shoved a handful of popcorn in his mouth and watched their exchange.

"Hi, Quinn. How you doing? How's Max?" She was too thin, her bare arms skinny, and she picked at a scab on her wrist, her gaze bouncing from Quinn to Rock to Max and back to Quinn.

"Hi, Megan. We're doing fine. Is one of your brothers playing in the game tonight?"

Her tone was purposefully light, but Rock knew her well enough to hear the tension in her voice.

The girl squinted toward the field. "Yeah. Merle is playing third base."

He looked out and spotted the third basemen. Another rush of anger hit him as he saw the last name Hill emblazoned on the back of the guy's T-shirt, and he scanned the field to see if Monty was also playing. He almost hoped he was. His fantasy of punching the guy in the throat might come true sooner rather than later.

The girl shifted to her other foot. "Well, um, I haven't

seen you in a long time, and I just wanted to come over and say hi." Her gaze darted to Max again, who was giggling over some joke that Mason was telling him. "He's getting big. He's cute too. If you ever need a babysitter, you could call me, or whatever." She tried for a timid smile, revealing a row of small, crooked teeth, their enamel dull, the product of either poor hygiene or the inability to afford proper dental care.

"Thank you. I'll keep that in mind. It was nice of you to say hello," Quinn answered, although she didn't sound like she really thought it was that nice at all. Her tone stayed cordial though.

"Okay, well, I guess I'll be seeing you around." Megan offered her a small, awkward wave, then turned and walked away, leaving the stale scent of smoke behind.

Rock leaned in toward Quinn and lowered his voice. "Was that…?"

She let out a shaky breath, but her body stayed stiff. "Yep."

"So she's his…?"

"Yep."

"And is she part of Max's…?"

"Nope."

"That's what I thought." He handed her his half-empty tub of popcorn. "Here."

"What's this for?"

"I figured since you were finishing all of my sentences, you might want to finish my popcorn as well."

"Smart." She offered him an impish grin and popped a piece into her mouth.

He kept his shoulder pressed against hers just in case she needed the support. "You okay?"

She nodded and finally relaxed her shoulders. "Yeah. I knew since we were playing Franklin, that there was a chance some of his family would be here. I don't have reason to run into them very often, and the majority of them don't acknowledge us. Megan's the only one who ever even speaks to us or acts like she wants to be part of his life."

"Why? It's not the kid's fault."

"Apparently, it's easier to act like we don't exist. Especially since that's what Monty does. Since his father refuses to claim him, none of the rest of the family does either."

Rock's hands clenched into fists, and he glanced back at Max to make sure he wasn't listening. "What the hell is wrong with that guy? How could he not want to be part of his own son's life? Max is a great kid. Why would he not claim him as his own?"

"Because if he doesn't claim him, he doesn't have to pay child support."

"But you could have a paternity test, take him to court."

"Why would I? If he doesn't want to be part of Max's life, then it's his loss. And I sure as heck don't need his money or his interference in how I raise my son."

He scanned the crowd of people in the opposing bleachers. "Do you think he's here now?"

She shook her head. "No. Last I heard, he moved to Texas. I think he's doing the rodeo circuit down there. I haven't talked to him in years, and even if he were here, he wouldn't want to talk to me, and I dang sure don't have anything to say to him."

Rock's heart ached for the little boy whose father didn't want to even acknowledge his existence. He knew what it was like to grow up without a dad, but there was a big difference in having a dad who was taken by an untimely death and a dad who left on purpose.

A loud crack sounded as the first batter whacked the ball out of the field, and the people in the bleachers rose to their feet to cheer.

Quinn's attention shifted as she looked onto the field and saw who the batter was. "That's Logan!" She pushed to her feet, cheering along with the crowd as her brother took off at a sprint, rounding first, then second, then third, then sliding into home.

"Yes," she cried, throwing her arms around Rock's shoulders in a hug.

He hugged her back, but knew the exact moment she realized she was hugging *him*, could feel her body stiffen and then pull away.

She pushed her hair back and sat down on the bleachers, ignoring Rock and acting as if she hadn't just hugged him in celebration as she yelled, "Attaboy, Logan."

A smile crept across his face.

Hey, it was progress.

In his book, anytime she wasn't mad at him or lashing out at him with a snarky barb was improvement.

As he sat back down, Max squeezed in between him and Vivi and leaned against Rock's leg. "Hey, did you see that? My uncle got a home run."

"He sure did." Rock held up his hand to give the boy a high-five. "You a big fan of baseball, Max?"

He nodded, his small glasses bobbling on his nose.

"You play on a team?"

"No, I don't like to *play* baseball so much. But I like to watch it, and to read about it."

Rock chuckled. This kid. "What's your favorite base-ball book?" He didn't want to cause Quinn any more discomfort, so he let the topic of her ex drop and talked to Max about books and the game. The kid was smart and funny and easy to listen to.

Heck, he was a better conversationalist than some of the guys on his team.

He settled in, watching the game, cheering for his brother, and talking with his family and Quinn and Max.

Even though he seemed relaxed, he was still acutely aware of every instance that Quinn's arm brushed his, or her leg pressed against his thigh. The scent of her hair almost drove him nuts each time she leaned across him to chat with Vivi about something.

Colt's team won by seven runs, and the atmosphere was excited and happy as the townsfolk of Creedence left the stadium, exchanging high-fives and congratulatory handshakes.

Max giggled every time he slapped someone's held-out hand. He grinned up at his mom. "Everybody's so happy, we should celebrate and go out for ice cream."

Way to go for it while Quinn was in a good mood. The kid was cute *and* smart.

"We'll have to ask Uncle Logan when he comes out if he wants to stop on our way home."

Rock gestured toward the parking lot. "I can give you a lift if you don't want to wait. I'm heading that way anyway." He winked at Max. "And I was thinking about stopping for a chocolate-dipped cone on my way home."

Quinn arched an eyebrow at him. "Really?"

He shrugged, offering her his best innocent smile.

"Can we, Mom? Please? Uncle Logan takes forever to come out."

"Fine. It seems like I'm outnumbered." She pulled her phone from her pocket. "I'll just text Logan and let him know we got another ride home."

—◦◦◦—

Quinn groaned at the mass of cars filling the parking lot of the Tastee Freez. Apparently, they weren't the only ones who'd had the idea of stopping for ice cream.

Rock parked and got out, then held the door for Max to scramble out behind him. But Quinn hesitated, her hand on the handle of the door.

It had been bad enough that Rock had sat next to her at the softball game, but now all of these people were going to see them taking Max out for ice cream.

Small towns were notorious for having everyone involved in everyone else's business, and Creedence was no different. They loved their gossip and could spend hours speculating on what other people were doing.

And her showing up at the hotbed of Creedence's activity with the hometown hero—and her old boyfriend—Rockford James, could practically guarantee that the town's tongues would soon be wagging.

Maybe we won't run into anyone we know.

Ha. Like that was going to happen. Everyone knew Rock. Even if they had never met him, everyone in town claimed that they *knew* the local celebrity.

This was a bad idea. They should have waited for Logan. Going out for ice cream with her brother wouldn't cause gossip to flood the community.

Rock didn't live here anymore. He didn't know how

interfering these people could be. He just got to come home, soak up the glory of a few stops at the grocery store or The Creed, then head back to Denver.

Thinking about that reminded her Rock's current visit was also temporary. He might be here now, but he was eventually going back.

Usually, she knew when he was back home and could stay out of his way. What the heck had happened this visit, and why was he suddenly so interested in renewing their "friendship"?

And really, that kiss a few days ago had felt like a lot more than "friendly."

This whole thing, the kiss, the going out for ice cream, the way he'd touched her hand, had her feeling like her tenuous hold on her feelings for Rock were spinning out of control.

And she didn't like it. Control was the one thing she craved, and she worked to keep her and Max's life in a steady routine that both of them could count on. Being a single mom left all of their life decisions up to her, and she did her best to make good choices and keep their world on an even keel.

And Rock James was *not* a good choice. Nothing about him or how she felt when he was around her was anywhere close to an even keel. In fact, most of the time, she felt like she was sliding off her axis and clinging to normalcy by the ends of her fingernails.

Just watching him walk up to the ice cream parlor caused her anxiety to ramp up. He was so dang good-looking. He was funny and easygoing, and everybody loved him. Everyone wanted to give him a high-five, to talk to him, to touch him.

Even her. Lord help her, she wanted to touch him too.

Thoughts of touching him, and of his big hands touching her, had kept her awake, tossing and turning for the better part of the last two nights. And being tired was not helping. If anything, it was weakening her resolve to stay away from him, or at least drawing clear boundary lines.

She couldn't sit in the truck all night. Opening the door, she stepped out, and he turned and offered her a grin. A grin that had her resolve melting and those boundary lines blurring like watercolor paints.

"You still like mint chocolate chip?" he asked as she joined him in line.

"I'm surprised you remember," she answered drily.

"No you're not. For cripes' sake, Quinn, we've known each other most of our lives and grew up together. We've been here hundreds of times, and you always get the same thing. I know what your favorite ice cream flavor is, what your favorite color is, I know how much salt you like on your fries, and that you don't like mustard on your hot dogs. I know your favorite book, your favorite band, and that you don't like your food to touch or the color orange."

Her body had stilled as he rattled off the list of things he knew about her, surprise and pleasure filling her at what he recalled.

He leaned closer, lowering his voice, and his warm breath tickled her neck. "I *know* you, Quinn Rivers."

She bristled a little at his arrogance. "You don't know everything. For your information, I *do* eat mustard now."

His lips curled in an impish grin. "But I nailed everything else, didn't I, darlin'?"

She shrugged.

His expression turned serious, and he kept his voice low and close to her ear. It felt intimate, him whispering private things to her while they stood in such a public place. "I remember, because we used to be inseparable; you were like my other half. You weren't just my girl; you were my best friend. And I remember *everything*."

She swallowed at the sudden emotion clogging her throat.

Because she remembered everything too. Remembered what it felt like to ride around beside him in his truck, to be the first person he looked for in the stands after he'd scored a goal, to have his warm, naked body wrapped around hers. But she also remembered the indescribable pain of her broken heart when he'd left her behind.

When he went off to be a hotshot star and left his country-bumpkin girlfriend in the dust of the dirt road heading out of their small town.

"I remember everything too," she whispered, not trusting her voice to betray the intensity of the feelings he'd just brought to the surface.

"Quinn—" he started to say, but Max jumped up, pulling on his arm and telling him it was their turn at the window.

What would he have said? she wondered as she listened to him place their order. How would he have possibly explained away his actions? Would he have apologized? More to the point, would she, *could* she forgive him?

Did she even want to? Would it make any difference?

Really, it had been nine years ago, a lifetime. Max's lifetime, at least. Did it even matter? Who was it helping to hold on to this grudge?

They said that forgiveness could set you free. Whoever the elusive *they* were. But had *they* had their hearts broken by the guy they thought they were going to spend the rest of their lives with?

It sounded so easy—just let it go. Like the song said. But could she just let it go? Let go of her outrage, her righteous indignation, her bitterness at the decisions of a teenage boy who'd been seduced by the bright lights of his hockey dreams coming true?

Rock handed her a cone, interrupting her thoughts. A drop of the minty green ice cream had dripped on his knuckle, and she had the sudden urge to pull his hand toward her and lick it off.

She grinned. Now *that* would get the local gossips talking.

"What's that grin about?"

Shoot—she'd been caught fantasizing about slurping ice cream off him. But she sure as heck wasn't going to admit that to him.

He didn't really know *everything* about her—it's not like he could read her dang mind. "I was just thinking that us being here together was going to give the locals something to talk about tomorrow."

"Tomorrow? Heck, they're probably already burning up the phone lines right now." He leaned down, his face close enough to hers that she could smell the chocolate on his breath. "We could really give 'em something to talk about."

Her body stilled, mesmerized by the nearness of his lips to hers.

Holy cow—snap out of it, girl.

She reared back, thwarting his attempt at stealing

another kiss. "Don't even try it, mister. Just because we're not on the ice doesn't mean you can't still earn a punch in the nose."

Rock threw his head back and laughed. "That would get them talking too."

The sound of his laughter eased some of the tension building in her chest, and she let out a breath and licked the melting ice cream from around her cone.

He led them to a bench away from the center of the crowd, and they sat down with Max between them. Rock threw an arm easily around the back of the bench and stretched out his long legs in front of him.

Quinn had to turn away, the sight of him relaxed and licking an ice cream cone was causing a different kind of tension to build, and sparks of heat to swirl in her belly.

She needed to get ahold of herself and focus on Max. He'd ordered a chocolate-dipped cone, and the ice cream was already melting and dripping down the front of his shirt.

He didn't often get dirty, and she loved this adorable, messy side of her little boy. She sometimes wondered if he picked up on her need for control and order, and that's why he kept his room tidy and his toys organized.

Ruffling his hair, she dropped a kiss on his forehead, then handed him a napkin.

They talked easily about the softball game and spent time catching up on the news of the town and people from their school. Their school had been small, and they knew everyone in their classes and most everyone in the classes around them.

Finished with their treats, they got back in the truck, and Max fell asleep within a few minutes. His body slumped against her side, held up by the strap of the seat belt as she stroked his hair.

"You're a good mom," Rock told her, a wistful smile on his face.

"How do you know? You've only been around us a few days." He might have been sweet-talking her, but the praise warmed her just the same.

"I just know. It doesn't take long to be able to tell."

"Maybe you can tell because you have such a great mom as an example."

"True. But it's also obvious how much you love Max, and he seems like a bright, well-adjusted kid."

"He is. He's the best. I love him so much sometimes the magnitude of it hurts my chest. He's the best thing that's ever happened to me."

"See, it's saying stuff like that." He took his eyes off the road for a second to give her a meaningful glance. "I'm proud of you."

She turned her head away, looking out the window so he wouldn't see the sudden tears that had sprung to her eyes. *Sheesh*. She must be tired; she wasn't usually this emotional, but Rock's words and the fact that he noticed meant something to her. "Thank you," she said quietly.

"I mean it. I think you're amazing. And I have the utmost respect for what you do. Sometimes I feel like my whole life is about hockey, that everything I do surrounds the team, the schedule, the next game. Someone tells me where to go, when to be there, what to wear. I don't make any of the decisions, I just show up and play the best I can."

"That's not entirely true. And a lot of people depend on you to play well. You also have people watching you, judging you, scrutinizing your every action. If I screw up and feed Max a peanut butter and jelly sandwich for breakfast, or don't get three fruit servings in him during the day, nobody knows but me."

"I have a feeling you don't screw up very often. It sure seems to me like you've got this whole 'mom' thing pretty well figured out."

"That's nice of you to say. But I think you've got this whole 'millionaire superstar hockey player' life pretty well figured out too. You drive a fancy car, and I imagine that you live in a gorgeous house. I've seen what you've done for your family's ranch and for the town. It doesn't seem like life is too rough for you."

He shrugged. "I'm not saying my life isn't good. You know I dreamed of playing professional hockey since I put on my first pair of skates, and I'm lucky I get to do what I love every day and get paid well to do it. But this life isn't going to last forever. And sometimes I think about what I gave up in order to follow my dreams. *Who* I gave up."

They pulled into the driveway of Rivers Gulch. He stopped the truck in front of the house but didn't get out.

Instead, he turned to face her and stretched his arm out along the back of the seat. "I was an idiot. A stupid teenage kid who was only thinking about himself. I got caught up in being a big shot hero, but I didn't act heroic. I acted selfish, and I'm sorry. I should have tried harder to make us work, should have given you a chance to be part of my new life. That one decision has always haunted me, and I've often wondered how things could have been if I hadn't broken things off with you that summer. If I'd only had you come with me and tried to make a place for you in my world."

Instead of choosing your career over me and break-ing my heart.

The words were there, on the tip of her tongue, ready to be spewed with the bitterness and anger that usually hit her when she thought about it. But tonight she didn't want to feel angry and sour. All night she'd been think-ing about forgiveness and letting that resentment go.

Her dad liked to tell her that things happen for a reason. She didn't always have to know the reason, and a lot of times the reason may never be clear, but it's there just the same.

And her reason was lying on the seat next to her. She looked down at her son, who was still sound asleep, his body curled against her, his breathing even.

She let out a small sigh. "I was a stupid teenager too. And I made a few dumb decisions myself, but they resulted in the best thing that's ever happened to me. If all of that old stuff hadn't happened the way it did, I wouldn't have Max."

He smiled down at the boy. Not a phony smile like some of the guys who'd tried to ask her out gave her son, but a real smile that told her Rock really did care about Max. "I know. I think about that sometimes too. And I don't want to bring up all the old hurts of the past, beyond the point of telling you that I'm sorry. I can't take back what I did or change what happened back then. But I can change what I do today and tomorrow. I'm tired of fighting with you, of being enemies, I want to be your friend, if nothing else."

He picked up a loose strand of her hair and twisted it between his fingers. "You were the best part of my life, and for the past eight years, I feel like a piece of me has been missing. And that piece is you. I want you back in my life, Q."

"I don't know what to say." She didn't know how to even process what he was saying or why her body had responded with warmth at hearing him use the old nickname.

"I know I hurt you, but damn it, I'm tired of us being enemies. I don't want to push, but I want you back. And I know that I'm gonna catch hell from Ham and your brother, but I'm willing to risk it." He offered her a grin and a quick wink. "How about we start with something easy, like you let me take you out to dinner? Tomorrow night?"

Her heart lifted at his offer, but she shook her head. "No, I'm sorry. I can't."

Chapter 7

ROCK REARED BACK, HIS GRIN FALLING AND HURT FILLING HIS eyes. "I understand."

Quinn reached out her hand and rested it on his outstretched arm, surprised at the surge of heat that shot through her veins at simply touching him. "I want to. I'm tired of us being enemies too. When I said I can't, I didn't mean that I can't *ever*. I just meant that I can't tomorrow night. I have a thing at Max's school."

His smile returned. "Oh. Yeah. No problem. What I meant to say was I'd like to take you to dinner. What night would be good for you?"

"I can't do tomorrow, but I can do the night after. Will that be okay?"

He nodded. "That would be perfect."

"It's a da—" She'd started to say *it's a date*, but it wasn't really a date. It was just dinner. Between two old friends. "It's a plan," she said instead.

"Do I get to come to dinner?" a sleepy voice asked as Max blinked his eyes awake.

Quinn laughed. "I thought you were asleep."

"I was. I just woke up and heard you talking about going out to dinner." His eyes were fluttering closed again, and he let out a yawn.

"Well, you don't get to come along to this one. Maybe next time." She smiled, thinking how he likely wouldn't remember this conversation in the morning. "You want me to carry you in?"

He shook his head. "No. Rock."

Her eyes widened. That was interesting. Max didn't usually warm up to people so quickly. Maybe he was comfortable around Rock because he was around his brothers so often. She glanced up at Rock, offering him a small shrug.

"Sure. I'll carry you in. And I'd love to do something with your mom and you later this week. Maybe I could take you guys ice skating? Would you like that?"

"Mmm-hmm," Max muttered as Rock picked him up and carried him toward the house.

Quinn followed, her stomach twisting in confusion. Something about this scenario felt so achingly right. Like this was how it was supposed to be all along.

Yet she knew this wasn't how it was and wasn't how it was going to be.

The three of them weren't going to be a family.

Rock hadn't asked her to marry him. He hadn't even said he wanted to be romantically involved. He'd said he wanted to start fresh and be *friends* — that he'd missed her friendship.

But still, what about that kiss?

And did she even want to be more than friends?

He was home, and everything seemed so great, but he was going back to Denver as soon as his coach cleared him to play again.

That thought sent spirals of misery plummeting through her already dizzy stomach, and she stumbled up the stairs, her feet tripping on the last porch step. She reached out instinctively, and Rock shifted Max's weight to one side and grabbed her arm, holding her steady as she regained her balance.

"Whoa. You okay there?" he asked.

"I'm fine. Just missed the step in the dark." The porch lights were plenty bright, but it was easier to blame the night than admit she was thinking about him. She reached for the front door and held it open for him.

"Was that mint chocolate chip spiked with Bailey's? Is that why it's your favorite?" he teased as he passed in front of her and headed down the hall toward Max's room.

Ha. Her ice cream had been alcohol-free but dang if she didn't feel like she could use a stiff drink right about now.

They didn't bother to turn any house lights on. There was enough illumination coming through the windows of the house to navigate their way to Max's room, where she pulled back the covers, then turned and slipped off his sneakers and socks while Rock held him. She normally wouldn't let him go to bed without brushing his teeth, but it didn't seem worth waking him up to do it tonight. She'd just make him brush twice as long in the morning.

Rock laid him down, and she pulled the covers over him as he snuggled into the pillow.

She brushed his hair back and pressed a quick kiss to his forehead, then followed Rock out of the room, turning to pull the door most of the way closed behind her.

Turning back, she ran into the solid mass of Rock, who had stopped in the hallway.

He reached out to steady her again, but this time he slipped an arm around her waist as she raised a hand to his chest. She heard his soft chuckle, and it sent a little shiver racing down her spine.

A silvery patch of moonlight fell onto the floor behind him, but his face was shadowed as he leaned toward her. "That's the second time you've stumbled tonight. I don't remember you being this klutzy before." His voice was low, a husky whisper.

"I'm not usually klutzy at all. It's just when I'm around you."

"I make you stumble?"

She gazed up at him, knowing how close she was, her hand flat on his chest, knowing she should step back but not wanting to pull out of the circle of his arms. "You make me dizzy. Like my head is spinning."

"Do you need me to hold you up?"

Did she? Did she need him at all?

She wasn't sure. But she knew that she wanted him. Wanted him like a starving animal wanted food.

"I'm not sure what I need," she said, her words coming out breathier than she'd meant them to.

He dipped his head, his lips next to her ear, his low voice its own seduction. "I don't think I knew what I needed until now. I've missed you, Quinn."

She let out the softest sigh, her eyelids fluttering closed. The scruff of his whiskers grazed her cheek, the barest touch heating her skin.

His breath caressed her neck, causing her to soften. Like a golden pat of butter on a hot biscuit, she melted against him, her resolve thawing as the molten heat of his body drew closer to hers.

"Have you missed me?" he whispered. "Do you ever think about me? About us?"

She swallowed at the emotion suddenly burning her throat. "I used to. All of the time. But it hurt too much.

I had to stop—had to put you out of my mind." She wanted to pull away, to stop this torture, but she couldn't.

It was like she was suspended in time, locked in his arms, paralyzed by the delicious torment of having him near, of his lips so close to her skin, whispering the words she'd waited so long to hear.

"I'm sorry. I'm so sorry that I hurt you. I would take it back if I could. I swear I would."

She believed him. Something about the dimly lit hallway, the way his hands gripped her waist, the break in his voice that took her back to the moments spent with the teenage version of this man. The break that told her he had been stripped bare, that he was speaking the truth, giving her the most honest version of himself.

But they weren't teenagers anymore, weren't kids who could ignore everything except their own reckless impulses.

And, God help her, she was feeling reckless, like nothing else mattered in the world except the feel of Rock's hands on her body and the brush of his lips on her skin.

Need and desire coursed through her, and all she wanted, craved, yearned for, was his touch.

She swiveled her head, nuzzling her cheek into his soft hair. Her fingers curled around the fabric of his shirt, gripping the folds in tight fists. Her mind swirled with words she wanted to say, actions she wanted to take, and she opened her mouth to speak.

But in the back of her mind, she registered the familiar sound of the low creak that signaled her father's bedroom door opening, and reality crashed back in.

She opened her hands, releasing Rock's shirt, and

clasped her fingers together against her chest. She took a quick step back, fighting to catch her breath—and her grip on the situation.

"Everything all right out here?" Ham asked. "I thought I heard something. That you, Rockford?"

"Yes, sir."

"We're fine, Dad." She swallowed, hearing the tremble in her voice and hoping her dad hadn't picked up on it. "We were just putting Max to bed."

He grunted. "Seems pretty late for visitors. Some of us have to get up for work in the morning."

Oh brother. She let out a frustrated breath. "It's not that late, Dad. It's not even ten o'clock." He probably hadn't even been asleep. He usually stayed up through the evening news. It was more likely he'd heard Rock's pickup pull in and was checking to see why he was still there.

"I was just leaving," Rock said, tipping his chin toward her and offering her a grin. "Good night, sir."

She followed him to the front door, where he stopped in the doorway and turned back to her, shaking his head. "Man, being here brings back so many memories. That felt just like when we were teenagers, and your dad caught me trying to kiss you and ran me out of the house."

"*Were* you trying to kiss me?" She tilted her head, amazed at her own boldness.

He offered her a flirty grin. "Then or now?"

"Now."

"Yeah, I guess. I was hoping to get around to it anyway."

A smile tugged at the corners of her lips. How could this guy always charm a grin out of her?

"But you already agreed to go out to dinner with me, so I don't want to push my luck."

Her grin faltered for a second, and the realization that she was disappointed he wasn't going to kiss her now surprised her.

He must have noticed, because his smile widened, and he leaned down and dropped a quick kiss on her lips, just the softest of touches, but enough to send a battalion of butterflies swirling through her stomach.

"I'll call you tomorrow," he said, then let the screen door shut softly behind him.

The next day dragged by for Rock. All he could think of was Quinn and taking her out to dinner the following night.

He was up early and had gone for a run, then spent a few hours lifting and going through dry drills. The concussion protocol allowed him to continue to work out, and his body had been itching to get back in the gym.

But since the closest gym was miles away, the old weight bench and barbells they'd used growing up would have to do. That, and helping his brothers out with chores around the farm. He'd hauled bales and mucked out stalls and spent hours running fence.

Vivi cajoled him into spending a few hours inside after lunch, bribing him with homemade cookies if he would watch a movie with her.

He was canny enough to know what she was doing, but he was also smart enough to know that his body, and his head, needed the rest. As an athlete, he was pretty in tune to his body and what it took to keep him in top physical health. Not that he didn't occasionally indulge in something decadent, but for the most part, he watched his diet and tried to eat healthy.

He could feel himself getting better, feel the muscles healing and getting stronger.

The run this morning had felt good—good to be using his body. But it didn't matter how strong he got, his mom would never stop worrying about him. He was pretty sure that's why she'd talked him into hanging out with her.

He wasn't sure how she'd talked him into watching the romantic comedy.

He knew he needed to take care of himself, to let his body rest, and to heal. But he hated this feeling. He was the Rock—the one who was strong, the big brother, the eldest son, the dependable teammate. He was the one who got things done, who moved the puck, who scored the goals, and who was there for his mom and his brothers. He wasn't the one who needed to be taken care of. That was his job—to take care of everyone else.

His eyes blinked open, and he stretched his arms over his head and let out a yawn.

How long had he been asleep? He wasn't sure, but he looked over and saw his mother staring at him intently. "Hey, Mom."

Her eyes softened around the edges, and a small smile curved the corners of her lips. "I love you, Son."

"I love you too." He raised an eyebrow. "What's up?"

Vivienne James was a tough-as-nails woman who had impeccable aim with a flyswatter or a wooden spoon when her boys stepped out of line, but also had the deepest capacity for love and had always been generous with praise and words of encouragement for all of her sons.

Sometimes he wondered if his mom was trying to give them double the love, to somehow make up for the loss of their dad. If so, she was succeeding.

Vivi's heart was bigger than the whole state of Colorado, and when she hugged a person, they felt it to their very soul. Neither he, nor his brothers, ever doubted the depth to which they were loved.

Even though Vivi often told him that she loved him, this felt different. Like there was a little more emotion behind it. Like something was going on.

Uh-oh. What if she were sick? Or there was something wrong with one of his brothers.

"Nothing's going on," she said, but the concerned look in her eyes betrayed her. She patted his leg. "I'm just worried about you."

Oh. Someone *was* sick. But it wasn't her or his brothers. She was worried about *him*.

He huffed out his breath. "I'm fine, Ma. Quit fussing over me."

She held up her hands. "Okay. It's just that I can't remember the last time I saw you fall asleep during a movie."

"Yeah. It was such a riveting plot."

She nudged his leg and let out an easy chuckle. "Hey now. That's one of my favorites. The ending gets me every time." Her voice took on a more serious tone. "A concussion is nothing to mess around with. I just want you to take care of yourself."

"I am."

"Speaking of messing around—what's going on with you and Quinn?"

Smooth. Real smooth.

"Nothing. What do you mean?" He tried for wide-eyed innocence, but his mom wasn't buying it—not that she ever did.

"I heard you're taking her out to dinner tomorrow night."

"Dang. Colt has a big mouth." He knew he shouldn't have spilled the details to his little brother.

"It wasn't Colt who told me. It was Quinn."

"Yeah? Quinn told you? Did she sound excited?"

His mom arched an eyebrow. "You certainly do."

He shrugged. "I just want to put the past behind us and quit fighting."

She studied his face. "I'd like that too. But she's not as tough as she looks. Be careful with her. I love that girl like she's my own kin. I don't want to see you hurt her again."

He cringed at the word *again*. "I know, Mom. I don't want to hurt her either. That's why I'm trying to make amends. I hate all the anger and bitterness between us. I just want to be her friend."

His mom didn't say anything, but one of her eyebrows shot up.

"I do," he insisted. "She was a big part of my life. I miss having her in it." Even still, he found himself wanting to call her when something funny happened or when he had news to share.

"I understand. And I hope you all can work it out. She's been through enough. Small towns might take care of their own, and they do love Quinn, but I still heard them talk about her and how that weasel Hill has never done right by her, and the talk wasn't always flattering. She holds her head high, but she's not as strong as she acts. So like I said, just be careful with that girl. You hear me?"

"I hear you."

He'd been accused of being selfish before. Hell, he *was* *s*elfish, thinking only of himself when he'd left Quinn all those years before.

And that wasn't all. He hadn't really faced it yet, but he knew that his selfishness was in part to blame for why he'd been hurt.

In hockey, their mantra, handed down by the great man, Gretsky himself, was that good players score, great players pass. He should have passed the puck during the play that he got slammed on. But he knew he could score, knew he could get the game-winning goal.

He'd seen his teammate open in front of the net, had heard the slap of his stick against the ice as he called for the puck, but Rock had held on, had skated up the boards, dominating the puck as he readied to cross to the crease. That's when he'd been hit.

If he'd only passed the puck, the hit might never have happened.

If he'd only let go of his pride and selfishness.

But he had the chance to do that now—to make up for some of the hurt that he'd caused.

To make things up to the one he'd hurt the most.

—◦◦◦—

Quinn couldn't seem to focus as she absently twirled a few strands of spaghetti around her fork.

She and Max were having dinner that night, but all she could think about was the impending dinner that she'd be eating the next night with Rock.

Where would he take her? What should she wear?

What the heck would they talk about?

And what if he tried to kiss her good night?

Stop. She couldn't go there.

He'd said he wanted to patch things up, to be friends again.

He was confusing the heck out of her, and thinking through all of the possibilities was making her head hurt.

She looked across the table at Max, a grin curving her lips as she watched him chase a meatball around his plate, trying to spear it with his fork. He made another stab at it, and the meatball shot off the side of his dish and rolled across the table toward her.

He looked up, his eyes wide, as he waited for her response.

It was only the two of them at dinner. Her father and brother had taken off earlier to run errands in town and had phoned that they were grabbing a burger at The Creed.

Which was fine with Quinn. She treasured time she got to spend alone with Max. Even if he was lobbing spaghetti sauce–covered meatballs across the table at her.

She peered down at the meatball as it rolled to a stop by her plate. Glancing up at Max, she held her arms up in the air in a U shape and yelled, "Score."

His eyes grew even rounder, then he burst into giggles, and her heart melted like chocolate in the warm sun. There was nothing in the world as sweet as the sound of her son's spontaneous laughter.

She considered picking up the meatball and chucking

it back at him. He would really dissolve into laughter, but she stopped herself before starting that mess. Instead, she scooped the meatball into her napkin and smiled over at her son. "How about you try to get the meatballs in your mouth instead of on the table?"

"I was trying. It just got away from me," he said.

She knew what that was like. Things got away from her on a daily basis, including her reaction to a certain hunky, hockey-playing cowboy.

Leaning forward, she cut the remaining meatballs on Max's plate into bite-size pieces.

He gave her an appreciative grin. "Thanks, Mom."

"You're welcome. Now finish up so you can get in the shower. I think you've got spaghetti sauce in your hair."

He giggled, then popped a bite into his mouth.

She picked up her tea and took a sip, her mind wandering again.

"Do you think my dad likes to read books?"

Quinn almost choked on her drink.

Where the heck did that come from?

She swallowed as she tried to formulate an answer. "I'm not sure. Why do you ask?"

"I was just thinking about him the other day when Rock was reading me those books. I was thinkin' that maybe if I could figure out what kind of books he liked, I could send him one, and maybe then, you know, he might want to come and see me so we could read it together."

Pain seared her chest, and she struggled to breathe against the feeling of a giant fist squeezing her heart. And that fist was the only thing that was keeping her heart from breaking in two.

She wanted to pick Max up, to gather his small body

in her arms, and cuddle him against her. All of her mama-bear instincts were kicking in, and she wanted to protect him from anything—or anyone—that could hurt him.

Anyone like Monty Hill. Like the son of a bitch who refused to even claim him as his own. She looked down at Max's sweet face, his eyes wide and innocent behind his glasses, and a surge of love flowed through her. A surge stronger than anything she'd ever felt for another human being.

A tiny human being that she wanted to protect from the ugliness of the world and from his stupid, deadbeat dad. But she couldn't say that. She had always tried to keep her feelings for Monty in check when she was around Max, not wanting the boy to feel any of her animosity and worry that it somehow had to do with him.

She could take it, could take anything, bear any burden, if it meant shielding the sweet, precious heart of her son.

"Your dad is a pretty busy guy. I'm sure he would want to read books with you if he could. I think he travels a lot."

"Do you think he ever travels to Colorado? Maybe he could come for a visit," Max suggested with a shrug of his thin shoulders.

"I don't think he gets out this way very often."

The boy's shoulders sagged as he let out a sigh.

She hated to set up a false expectation, but she also wasn't ready to break her child's beautiful, forgiving heart.

"Hey, how about if we make some root beer floats and sit out on the front porch?"

Max's eyes lit with excitement, and he stuffed the last few bites of meatball in his mouth.

It was probably a cheap trick to distract him with an offer of sugar and soda. But it was better than the alternative, which was to tell him that it didn't matter how many books they sent him, his dad wasn't ever coming for a visit.

Heck, she wasn't even sure if the Neanderthal knew how to read.

Chapter 8

ROCK SUCKED IN A BREATH, HIS GAZE FIXED ON THE BEAUTI-ful woman who flashed him a smile as he stepped out of the car.

She strode down the steps toward him, dressed simply in a pair of jeans, a fitted, teal-colored T-shirt, and a pair of sandals. Her hair was loose and fell in wavy curls around her shoulders. A silver necklace draped around her slender neck, and some kind of blue, sparkly hoops dangled from her ears.

She was stunning. But she could have been wearing a paper bag, and she'd look amazing in his book.

"Hey, Rock," she said, her voice almost sounding shy as she ducked her head.

This was new. Quinn Rivers hadn't been shy a day in her life.

And especially not with him.

They'd always been comfortable, easy with each other.

So why were his palms sweating and he was standing awkwardly by the car, wondering what to do? Should he hug her? Kiss her on the cheek?

She stopped a few feet away from him and focused on the car, saving him from deciding. "You brought the Porsche tonight instead of the truck."

"Yeah, I thought it would be more fun to drive the convertible." He'd considered bringing the truck, but it held a lot of memories for both of them, and he figured tonight would be tense enough without adding in the nostalgia of the old truck. "Is that okay?"

"That depends." Her lips curved up in an impish grin. "Can I drive?"

He chuckled and felt the knot loosen in his gut. "Sure." He held open the door.

She passed in front of him, the heady scent of her shampoo and perfume swirling around him, almost making him dizzy, as she slid into the driver's seat.

He climbed into the passenger side, his gaze captivated by the way her hand caressed the supple leather seats. It didn't take much to imagine her hand gliding seductively along his skin in the same manner.

Just friends, he reminded himself, tearing his eyes away from her slender fingers and focusing on buckling his seat belt.

"How fast does it go from zero to sixty?" she asked, glancing at the long driveway leading out of the ranch.

"Fast enough."

"Let's see." She put the car in gear and punched the accelerator.

He let out a laugh and grabbed the dash, grinning at the look of reckless joy and freedom on her face as she flew down the driveway.

All he could do was hold on—to the car, and to his heart.

"Where are we going?" she yelled over the noise of the wind.

"I thought we'd go to the Wagon Wheel," he hollered back, referring to the steak house just outside of Creedence. The food was good, it had patio seating next to a mountain stream, and he remembered it had always been a favorite of Quinn's. "But we need to stop for gas first."

She nodded, her attention fixed on the road.

Ten minutes later, she turned into the Quik Stop, pulling up to the gas pump and turning off the engine.

An old red pickup was on the other side of the pump, and Rock recognized the guy standing next to it.

Lennie Larson had been a classmate of theirs from high school. He'd played football with Rock and his brothers, and his stocky frame had made him a good defenseman. But it seemed his stockiness had turned soft, and a round roll of beer belly hung over the top of his belt.

He wore a red shirt that was almost as faded as his truck, a dark stain dribbled down the front as if he'd recently dropped a bite of his lunch on it, and his once light-brown hair had darkened and thinned.

Rock waved as he got out of the car and approached the gas pump. "Hey, Lennie."

"Hey, Rock," he answered, his bottom lip protruding out from the round bubble of chew packed inside. He raised his chin and smiled as he glanced toward the car. "Hey there, Quinn."

She grinned back, running her hand along the side of the door. "Hi, Len. What do you think of my new car?"

He let loose a thick stream of tobacco juice. "Pretty nice." He pulled the back of his hand across his chin, swiping away the stray drip of juice.

"I just got it." She flashed a flirty grin at Rock, who just chuckled as he filled the tank with gas.

"You had a pretty good season," Lennie said, speaking

to Rock, but his eyes were still taking in the trappings of the sports car. "Tough break about the Cup."

A hard rock settled in his gut at the mention of the team and their missed opportunity at the championship. He pulled the pump handle free and shoved it back into the holder, then twisted the cap back on and snapped the compartment door closed. "Yeah, tough break."

He didn't know what else to say. There wasn't anything else to say. They were out. They'd blown it this year. *He'd* blown it this year.

He slid back into the passenger side of the car, grumbling, "Let's go."

"See ya, Lennie," Quinn called before starting the engine and pulling out of the gas station. She patted his leg. "Don't let it get to you. It wasn't your fault."

She still had a way of always knowing what he was thinking. He rested his hand on hers, clasping her fingers in his as he let out a sigh. "Thanks."

He'd felt the slightest jolt in her arm when he'd closed his fingers around her hand, and she let it rest there for just a moment, then pulled her hand free and grasped the steering wheel.

Did she really want to get a firmer grip on the wheel, or was she just trying to pull away from him?

He didn't know.

But he did know that he didn't want the black cloud of his injury to cast a shadow on their date. Not that it was a date. But on their dinner plans. He blew out his breath, trying to let the negative energy go with the expelled air.

The car sped down the road. She handled it well and was obviously enjoying herself, which made him happy.

"Just so you know," he told her as they pulled into the parking lot of the restaurant, "I haven't ever let anyone else drive this car."

She angled into a parking spot and cut the engine, then turned in her seat to face him. "That's what you used to say about your truck too."

He clapped a hand to his forehead. "I'm glad you brought that up *after* I let you drive. Otherwise I might not have given you the keys."

"What? Why? I'm a good driver."

"Remember when I let you drive my truck home from the lake and you hit that tree?"

Her eyes widened, then she let out a laugh. "Oh my gosh, I forgot about that. And I barely tapped it. Besides, you could hardly call that a tree. It was more like a bush."

"Sure, okay." He liked teasing her as he got out and opened the door for her. He automatically raised his arm to rest it around her shoulders, then pulled it back at the last second. Quinn was laughing and teasing with him again, the most she'd spoken to him in years. Best not to push his luck.

The hostess sat them at a creek-side table on the patio and took their drink orders. Quinn ordered a glass of wine, but he stuck with water.

"You don't want a beer?"

"Nah. Not when I'm driving. And I really don't drink a lot during the season." Although that was true, he was also worried the alcohol would contribute to the headaches he'd been having, but he didn't need to share that with her.

The waitress brought their drinks, and they both ordered steaks.

Quinn studied him over her glass of wine as she took

a sip. "You are different. I can't totally pinpoint all of the differences, but it's there. It's like you're...more responsible. More grown up, I guess."

"Gosh, I hope so. Especially if you're comparing me to the asshole teenager that I used to be."

She cocked an eyebrow at him.

"Don't get me wrong. I'm sure I can still be an asshole, but I try not to be an asshole *and* an idiot at the same time."

A small smile tugged at the corner of her lips. "I'll give you that one."

"Seriously, I have grown up. I have a job, a house, bills, responsibilities. I'm not the same kid who left here nine years ago."

I'm not the selfish kid who left you behind.

He didn't say it. But he didn't have to. He knew she was thinking the same thing. He could tell by the way her smile faltered and she absently picked at the seam of her napkin.

"You're different too, you know," he said, lifting his glass and tilting it toward her. "You're the epitome of responsible. You're a mom." He shook his head as he took a sip of water. "It's hard to believe you have an eight-year-old son."

"It's hard for me to believe too." Her eyes took on a faraway gleam. "But you know, sometimes the brightest consequences come out of the darkest times."

"Max is a pretty great kid," he said, not wanting to rehash the same hurts again. Reaching out, he touched her hand—didn't hold it, just rested the tips of his fingers on her knuckles as he offered her a smile. "He must have your genes."

"Lord, let's hope so."

She didn't have to say the rest of it. He knew what she was thinking, just from the worried expression around her eyes and the tight set of her mouth.

"Don't worry. Hill's not even around. And I can already tell that he takes after you in so many ways. And Ham and Logan are good men. They set fine examples for him."

"Thank you. That's what I'm hoping."

He shook his head, a question on the tip of his tongue, a question that he'd wanted to ask for years. "How'd you get mixed up with Hill anyway?"

She shrugged. "I don't know. I didn't even know him. He was just a cute guy at a party. I'd been drinking, way too much, more than I'd ever done before, or since, and he seemed nice—a little rough around the edges maybe, and a little bit of a bad boy. And the exact opposite of you. He was just the kind of guy that I know you would have told me to stay away from. Which is probably what made me go off with him. I wanted you to hear about it. To hear that I was already with someone new—someone you would hate. I wanted to punish you. To make you come running back for me."

She glanced up at him, old hurts shining in her eyes. "It didn't really work out the way I'd planned though."

"Yeah, it did. Except I'd already come back for you. I was just too late."

"What are you talking about? You never came back."

"Yes, I did. I knew I'd made a mistake, but I was too pigheaded and stubborn to admit it. And the first chance I had to come home, I did. I was planning to show up at your house and grovel until you took me back. It wasn't until I got back to town that I heard about you and Hill. And that I was too late. That I'd screwed up and missed my chance."

"Why didn't you ever tell me?"

"Why would I? As far as I was concerned, you'd made your decision, and you'd moved on. Without me. I went back to Denver and threw myself into school and my career and tried to forget about you."

"Did you?" Her voice softened, almost to a whisper. "Forget about me?"

"Never." He rubbed his fingertips across the side of her hand. "Not for a single day."

She pulled her hand away. "Then why didn't you ever come tell me? What the hell took you so long to apologize?"

He winced at the anger and resentment in her tone, but a grin slowly crept across his face. "I do love it when you get fired up," he answered in a slow, sexy drawl.

She narrowed her eyes, trying to keep a straight face, but the corners of her mouth tipped up, and she let out an exasperated chuckle. "You're still the only person who can tease me out of a good mad."

"That's because I don't want you to be mad anymore." The teasing tone was gone, replaced with a more serious one. "I meant it when I said I was looking to put the past behind us. I've missed you."

She stared at him, her eyes searching his face. "I can't tell if you're being for real."

Funny enough, it was the realest he'd been with a woman—hell, with himself—in a long time. After he'd lost Quinn, he'd set himself on a course of self-ishness, taking what he wanted, when he wanted, and not thinking about who he hurt or how his actions were affecting others.

The only people he cared about were his brothers, his mother, and his teammates. With them, he gave his all. With everyone else, he could care less.

Until now.

Until the last few days, when he'd run into Quinn and the past had smacked him in the face. He'd thought he might have a chance to win back some of himself and win back the friendship of the only girl he'd ever truly loved.

"Ya know, it's funny we're talking about Monty tonight," she said, smoothing her napkin across her lap. "Max brought him up last night, and he doesn't usually talk about him. Like hardly ever."

"What did he say?"

"He asked me what kind of books he liked to read. It was totally random and out of the blue."

Uh-oh. Maybe not totally random.

"The only thing I can think is that maybe reading books with you the other day might have brought up some feelings about wanting to read books with his own dad."

He had a feeling that was exactly what happened. Damn it, he should have kept his stupid mouth shut. "So what did you say?"

"I didn't know what to say. I try not to say anything bad about his dad. Heck, I try not to say anything about him at all. I try to act like the man doesn't even exist. And I think that's how he acts about us too."

"Idiot. Him, not you."

"I know what you meant. And he is an idiot. He's a jerk and an asshole that's missing out on having a relationship with one of the best kids ever."

"It's his loss."

"I know that. And I don't really care about him or what he's feeling. But I care about Max. I worry sometimes. I worry about him not having a normal family."

"What the heck is a *normal* family?"

"You know what I mean. I hate that he doesn't have that steady, whole family unit."

"Well, you didn't have that steady, whole family unit."

"My point exactly."

"Stop beating yourself up. He's got you, and Ham, and Logan. And you're doing a dang fine job with him. He's smart and funny and seems like a perfectly well-adjusted kid. Kids are resilient. They take stuff in stride."

"I hope that's true. I want to believe that's true."

"Believe it," he assured her.

Although what the heck did he know about it? He didn't have kids, didn't really even know that many kids. For all he knew, Max could turn out to be a serial killer. But he didn't think so. Not in his gut.

In his gut and in his heart, he knew Max was a sweet boy. A good kid.

The kind of kid he'd like to have some day. He and Quinn were just the kind of family Rock had always imagined he would have.

A wave of guilt washed through him. What was he doing getting mixed up in their lives? He wasn't their family, and he wasn't going to be. He had a life, in a different city, in a different world. A world of professional hockey, where he traveled and spent the majority of his time in ice rinks and locker rooms and gyms.

He was only in town for a short time. It wasn't fair to give her or Max the impression that he was sticking around. Did he think he could just drop in, play the hero for a little bit, then take off again?

Was he doing that with Quinn? Was he leading her on — setting her up to think he was back when he knew he'd be going to Denver as soon as his coach gave him the all clear?

After all that stuff he'd just told her — about how he'd changed, was more responsible — was he still just being selfish? Was he still thinking only of his own needs and not of the needs of a little boy? Or of the little boy's mother, who had been through enough, as his own mother had recently reminded him.

He opened his mouth to say something, he didn't know what, but he was saved from having to speak by the arrival of the waitress, who set steaming-hot plates covered in thick slabs of steak onto the table. A plump baked potato sat next to each steak, a rounded scoop of butter melting down the outside of the crispy skin.

"Anything else I can get you folks?" the waitress asked.

Rock cleared his throat. "We're good," he said, finally finding his voice. "Thanks."

Quinn looked down at her plate. "This looks delicious."

"What are you waiting for? Dig in," he told her, thankful for the distraction. This he could handle. Talking about food was easy. Talking about the past, not so much.

He just needed to keep the conversation light. They'd dredged up enough history for the night. Time to focus on something else.

He watched her cut a piece from the steak and stick the bite into her mouth.

Her lips sealed around the tines of the fork, and she closed her eyes and let out a moan as she chewed.

Holy crap. It wasn't enough that her laugh had funny, tingling sensations running down his spine, or that the way her thick hair curled against her slender neck made his hands itch to run his fingers through it, now she was going to destroy him with the way she ate. Everything about Quinn was beautiful to him, but now this woman even made eating steak look sexy.

Rock's mouth had suddenly gone dry at the sound of her soft moan of pleasure, and he took a sip of water and focused on his own steak. Taking a bite, he realized why she'd made that incredibly sexy sound. "Dang. This is good."

"So good," she said, sticking another bite in her mouth.

He liked to watch her eat. Liked to watch the way she dug into and enjoyed her food, gaining pleasure from each bite.

They spent the next few minutes in comfortable silence, prepping their food and eating.

"So, tell me about your job," he said, setting his fork down.

"Oh gosh, I don't think we have enough time. There's so much to say. So much excitement happening in the ever-changing world of preparing fancy, overpriced coffee drinks."

He chuckled. "Do you enjoy it?"

"It's a job. And some days it's fun. I like getting out of the house and talking to people. I only work part-time, and Sarah tries to schedule me when Max is in school, so that's good. Plus it gives me some money of my own and makes me feel like I'm not so dependent on my dad."

"I was surprised to hear that my mom babysits him sometimes."

"Yeah, your mom is amazing. I don't know what I'd do without her. Especially when Max was little. She's the closest thing he will ever get to having a grandma."

He must really have been out of touch. "I had no idea that my mom helped you so much. Even back then."

Quinn's shoulders went up in an off-hand shrug. "You weren't around. You were gone all the time, either at school or traveling with the team. I used to hope that I would run into you, when I was at your house. Then I stopped, and hoped that I wouldn't. Because you hardly ever came home. And once you went pro, it seemed like you never came home at all."

Was that true? He thought back over the last few years. It wasn't like he didn't see his family. They came to Denver often enough, and he'd bought season tickets for them to attend games whenever they could make it down.

He saw them, but it was usually in between the things he had going on. And they made the trip to the city more often than he made it back to the ranch. He tried to get home, at Christmastime and always for a few weeks in the summer, during the off-season. But something was always going on, something that demanded his attention, which kept him away from the ranch. Something that was always more important.

His shoulders sagged as shame filled him. Vivi never complained, never hassled him or made him feel guilty for not making it home more. She'd only ever acted proud of him.

He didn't feel very proud of himself right now. Had he neglected her and his family?

"You're right. I haven't made it back home much. The team keeps me pretty busy."

"It's a big commitment. And maybe if I were all famous, like you, I wouldn't come home as much either."

But she would. Not that he was "all famous," but he knew Quinn would always make time for her family.

The waitress approached with the check. "You want dessert? We make a pretty mean peach cobbler."

"Oh, that's Max's favorite," Quinn said.

Rock handed over his debit card. "We'll take three peach cobblers, to go."

Quinn raised an eyebrow as the waitress walked away. "Three?"

"Yeah. Didn't you say it's Max's favorite?"

"You do surprise me, Rockford James."

"Good." He offered her a wink and a smile, trying not to think about all of the ways he would like to surprise her. Like with flowers, or diamonds, or by taking her mouth in a passionate kiss.

He looked out over the rushing water of the stream. A path wound along the side of the creek. "You want to take a walk? We can put the dessert in the car and then see if we can work off a little of those baked potatoes?" And get his mind on something besides thoughts of kissing her.

Although from the way his mind had been working all night, it was going to take more than a stream-side stroll to accomplish that.

―⁓―

Quinn paused at the edge of the stream and stooped to

pick up a flat, smooth stone. She held it up to Rock. "Remember how we used to have stone-skipping competitions down at the pond?"

"Of course."

"Everything was a challenge to you. You were always so competitive."

"I still am," he said with a chuckle as he searched the ground for a rock to skip.

They had spent hours at the pond that sat between their two ranches, she and Logan, and Rock and his brothers. It was where they'd learned to swim in the summer and where they'd all learned to ice skate in the winter. Rock had been smitten with hockey from the first time he'd donned skates, and he'd convinced them all to learn so he'd always have someone to practice with.

Being the oldest, he could talk them all into doing just about anything. But his love for the game of hockey was a singular and passionate desire. Enough that he talked his mom into signing him up for a league in the closest town that offered one, and they spent hours driving to weekly practices and games.

Both of his brothers played, and even Logan played for a season or two, but none of them had wanted it, had needed it, the way Rock did. Even as a kid, hockey was in his blood. She could see it in every game he played, in the hours he spent practicing skating on the pond in the winter, and shooting pucks in the barn all year round.

She always knew that he would try for a career in hockey, and she'd always supported him in that dream. Always believed in him, and had assumed she would join him in following that dream. That was until he left her behind to follow it on his own.

Remnants of that heartbreak snuck into her thoughts, and her chest tightened as emotion filled her throat.

What was she doing out on a date—or out to dinner or whatever the heck this was—with him? Why was she letting his stupid, crooked smile and his stupid, gorgeous blue eyes get to her?

This was the guy who'd taken her heart and smashed it into a million pieces, who'd left her broken and ruined, who'd walked away and never looked back.

Except, apparently, he had looked back—he'd come back to get her. But it had been too late.

It was too late then, and it was too late now.

It didn't matter how many sparkles of heat shot through her or how ridiculously muscled his arms were or how his offer of peace between them filled her heart with a secret longing of hope, the cold, hard truth was that he wasn't back. Not really. He was back only for now.

She knew that as soon as he recovered, he would be hightailing it back to Denver as fast as his speedy little convertible could take him. So why was she letting herself fall under his spell?

Why was she laughing and—for cripes' sakes—blushing every time he'd teased her or offered her a compliment tonight?

She sucked in a deep breath. She couldn't let herself fall victim to him again, couldn't let him back into her heart—couldn't let him hurt her again.

He'd broken her heart and ruined her for any other man, but he hadn't broken her spirit.

Old wounds fought their way to the surface, and she tried to push them back down, tried with the only weapon she had against them. Flickers of anger seeped through her, like a den of snakes waking up, uncoiling and slithering outward, like a starburst of poison radiating from her heart and out through her chest.

Gripping the stone tightly in her hand, she turned away from him and flung it at the water. The stone skipped across the stream, bouncing across the water several times before disappearing.

"Wow. You've gotten better," Rock teased.

Yes, she had. She *had* gotten better. Not just with skipping stones, but in life. She'd gotten over him and put the past behind her.

Yeah, right. Keep telling yourself that, sister.

She whipped around, anger fueling her, ready to tell him what she thought of him, of what he'd done to her.

But her footing slipped on the slick rocks of the bank, twisting her ankle and throwing off her balance. She cartwheeled her arms, letting out a sharp cry and stumbling as she fell toward the stream.

Chapter 9

STRONG HANDS GRABBED HER ARMS, PULLING HER BACK AND saving Quinn from falling into the creek.

"I've got you," Rock said as he pulled her against his hard, muscled chest.

She gripped his shirt, clutching the fabric between her fingers as she struggled to catch her breath.

"You're okay," he assured her, but still held her tightly against him.

She let herself melt into him, just for a moment, letting her defenses down to relish in his embrace, to savor the feel of his sturdy arms around her as her soft body molded into his hard one.

As if it had a power of its own, her cheek pressed into his chest, and she inhaled his scent—a heady combination of laundry detergent and expensive musky cologne.

He held on to her, not moving, not pulling away, just standing on the bank, the sound of the creek rushing in the background, and holding her in his arms.

She didn't move either—didn't slide her arms around his waist, but also didn't break away. She just stood in the circle of his arms, letting herself take comfort in his embrace, feeling the angry snakes in her chest settle and curl back into slumber.

Maybe they *could* be friends.

Maybe she could let Rock back into her life. He had been a foundation of her childhood and her time in school. He had always been there, and she had felt the absence of him in her life, not just in the romantic aspect, but in the simplest moments of something happening and having her first thought be of wanting to tell him about it.

They had shared everything. And he had always been there for her to talk to. To confide in. To share the details of their lives.

"I've missed you," he said softly into her hair, mirroring her thoughts just as he used to. Sometimes she swore she couldn't have an original thought because Rock seemed to always be thinking the same thing or knowing just what was on her mind.

She tipped her head back, gazing up at him and swallowing back the emotions filling her throat. "I've missed you too. I was just thinking about how we used to share everything, even the smallest details of our lives, and now it's like we don't know anything about each other. I really only know what's going on with you from the media reports and the few things I've heard from your mom."

He grinned. "My mom is like a news station herself. She always knows what's going on."

"Yeah, but regardless of how big your ego is, we don't talk about you very much. Even though you're still like the six-foot-four, blond-headed elephant in the room. I think she's always worried that it would hurt me more to talk about you, so we usually avoid the subject altogether."

He blinked. "Well, that's disappointing."

Even though she tried to keep her lips set in a tight line, she could feel the corners threatening to tip up as he jostled her against him.

"We can't do anything to change the past, Q. All

we can do is try to change the present to make a better future. We can't go back, but we can go forward. I may not have been there for everything that's happened in the last nine years of your life, but you can fill me in. You can still tell me about it. And I'd like to hear. All of it."

She doubted he really wanted to hear all of the gory details of being a single mother, especially since so much of it involved poop, vomit, crying (on both her and Max's parts), and bargaining with a small human to please, please, please, for the love of all that is holy, please just *try* some broccoli.

But he did seem sincere, so she nodded, her head moving slowly up and down in hesitant agreement. "Okay. We can try." She did want to try—wanted to be his friend—wanted to have Rock back in her life.

She just wasn't sure what having him back would end up costing her.

He let her go, slowly dropping his arms with what felt like reluctance, but was maybe only wishful thinking on her part. "How about we just walk? And you can tell me all about Max."

"Okay," she said again, already missing the warmth and strength of his embrace.

She took a few steps down the path, testing her ankle. It seemed to be okay, and she put more pressure on it as she walked.

Rock fell in step next to her. Out of the corner of her eye, she saw him reach out his hand as if to take hers, but he must have changed his mind, because instead of taking her hand, he stuffed both of his into his front pockets.

They walked along the stream, and he listened to her talk, asking questions and laughing at her silly stories about Max. He seemed to be really interested, not like some of the guys she'd tried to date, whose eyes glazed over as soon as she mentioned anything to do with her son.

Not that this is a date, she reminded herself as they reached the end of the path. A bench had been set up among the trees, and a sign showed a small trail that led from the creek into town.

Without saying anything, they turned and followed the trail, coming out of the trees onto a sidewalk. They turned left and kept talking as they wandered back up the sidewalk to where they'd left Rock's car in the restaurant's parking lot.

"You want to drive back?" he asked as he held the driver's door open for her.

"Do you even have to ask?"

They'd put the top up and left the bag with the desserts on the seat before they went for a walk, and the sweet scent of cinnamon and peaches filled the interior of the car.

It was close to nine, and the night had turned cool, but Quinn put the top down again anyway. There was something freeing about driving the convertible with the light of the moon shining down on you.

But they were still in the mountains in Colorado. She turned the heat on, directing it at their feet, and pulled out of the parking lot. Within a few minutes, they left the town behind, driving through the country as they passed the town cemetery and the grain elevators.

Rock stretched out his arm, casually hanging his hand over the headrest behind her. "This car looks good on you," he said, the flirty tone back in his voice.

Must be the moonlight.

It was affecting her too. It was romantic, cruising down the highway with the top down, country music playing low on the radio, and Rock's hand resting so close to her neck she could almost feel the heat of it.

She was tempted to lean her head back, to press against his fingers, knowing he'd turn his hand over and run his fingers through her hair. Knowing, because that's what he'd done a hundred times before when they'd driven down this same stretch of road on their way home from school, from town, from a dance.

Memories of the two of them in high school flooded her mind, and she blinked at the tears that suddenly clouded her eyes.

What the heck was that about?

She cleared her throat, pushing back the emotion and the memories as they drove past the drive-in theater, the screen currently dark.

"Do they still show movies out here?" Rock said, craning his neck to read the faded marquee.

"Every weekend in the summer," she told him. "I keep thinking I'm going to take Max to a show, and every year we get too busy to go."

"Man, I loved going to the drive-in. Remember how we used to fill the back of my pickup with blankets and pillows?"

"And eat popcorn and licorice until we were sick to our stomachs?"

He chuckled. "Yeah, but that greasy butter was so good. I still remember the night we saw *Up*. You loved that movie. You bawled your eyes out."

"So did you."

"That was just my allergies acting up."

"Allergies, my ass." She laughed, but heat bloomed in her belly as she saw the way his eyes shifted to look at her rear.

Keep your eyes on the road. Never mind the fact that he'd just checked out her butt.

"Hey, why don't we go tomorrow night?" he suggested. "We can bring Max."

Another date? Tomorrow night? Her shoulders tensed. "Um, maybe."

He must have picked up on her hesitation. "We can all go. We'll make it a party. I'll get my mom and my brothers to come, and you can invite Ham and Logan."

She let out a laugh. "That'll be the day that Hamilton Rivers shows up at a drive-in movie."

"Okay, maybe not Ham. But I'll bet my mom will come along."

Hmm. It certainly didn't sound like a date. Especially if he was suggesting that his mom and her brother come with them.

The tension in her shoulders eased. "Yeah, okay. It does sound fun. And Max will love it. We'd better check out what's showing first though and make sure it's suitable for him." Although she already knew from looking into it the previous summer that they usually played a family-friendly movie as their first showing.

It meant a lot to her that Rock had thought to include Max.

The tension that had just eased out of her returned with a vengeance as she turned into the driveway leading up to her house.

What would happen when they went to say good night?

Would Rock try to kiss her? Hug her? Shake her hand?

What if he did try to kiss her?

Would she let him, or should she try to deftly turn her head? And what if he *didn't* try to kiss her? Would that be better or worse?

Just the thought of Rock pressing his lips to hers, of him taking her mouth in another kiss like the one he'd given her at the ranch a few days before, had her stomach swirling with a mixture of anticipation and dread.

She slowed the car to a crawl, delaying the arrival at her front porch by another few moments. Eventually, she had to stop. Either that or she'd have to drive Rock's beautiful convertible up the porch steps and into her living room.

Pulling up in front of the porch, she put the car in park and turned off the engine.

The night was still, incredibly quiet, especially after the chaos of the wind and noise of the convertible.

An owl hooted, and she heard the faraway whinny of a horse. The click of her seat belt was almost deafening as she released the buckle and got out of the car.

Rock was already out too, coming around to her side of the car to walk her to the door. He had the bag with their desserts in one hand. "I had fun tonight. Thanks for coming with me."

She sucked in a breath and felt the heat of his hand against the middle of her back as he guided her up the steps. "Me too. Thanks for dinner."

He handed her the bag. "Here's the dessert."

"Thanks." She took the bag, thankful to have something to hold on to. Twisting the plastic handle between her fingers, she hesitated, not sure if she should offer him a hug or just open the door, run inside, and pray he took off quickly.

Maybe she should invite him in. They could have the peach cobbler. But what if her dad, or worse, her brother, were still up. That's all she needed right now, to have one of them give Rock the third degree over their dinner out.

The plastic bag rustled with her nervous fidgeting, and he reached out and rested his hand on top of hers.

Could he feel the tremble in her fingers?

"Good night, Quinn." He leaned in, his hand still on her back, pulling her up against him as he brushed a quick kiss against her cheek, his mouth barely touching the corner of her lip.

She caught her breath, too late to turn her cheek—in either direction.

The warmth of his body sent licks of heat surging through her veins, and her stomach dropped, filled with looping, weaving swirls.

She reached for him, taking one hand away from the death grip she'd had on the to-go bag, but he'd already backed away, turning his back as he jogged down the steps of the porch.

"See you tomorrow night," he said. "I'll text you tomorrow to work out the details."

"Sounds good." She pressed open the front door and slipped inside, praying that both her father and her brother had already gone to bed.

She was in luck.

Not bothering to turn on the lights, she stuffed the desserts in the fridge, then slipped down the hallway to check on Max.

Flickering lights shone from under her father's door as she passed, and she assumed he had the nightly news on as he got ready for bed.

Poking her head into Max's room, she saw his small form curled in his bed, the covers twisted around his legs.

She carefully pulled the blankets free and covered him up, tucking his stuffed dog in next to him. He was probably getting too old for the stuffed animal, but he'd had it since he was born and there didn't seem to be any harm in him still sleeping with it once in a while.

He was growing up too fast for her. How could he already be eight? She ran her fingers tenderly through his hair and placed a soft kiss on his forehead. He'd always been a sound sleeper, and the good-night kiss didn't even faze him.

But it hit her hard, how quickly the years had already passed, how much she'd wanted to teach him, to show him already, how many things she'd messed up, and how many things she'd accidentally gotten right.

Her chest hurt, as if it wasn't big enough to hold the enormous amount of love that she had for this boy, her precious son. Sometimes she thought the magnitude of it would break her, that her heart, her body couldn't conceivably hold the unmeasurable volume of love that she felt. Was it like this for every mother? Every parent?

She couldn't imagine that anyone else could possibly love their child as much as she loved Max. She would do anything for him, anything to protect him, anything to keep him from harm.

Without a second thought, she would die for him.

And she would also kill for him.

That thought startled her. Where the heck had that come from?

Too many memories and emotions had been swirling

around her the past few days. She tried not to think about Max's dad, tried to pretend that he didn't even exist.

But all this talk of the past, combined with seeing Megan, and all of Max's questions, had her thinking about Monty.

He'd made the decision to walk away and to deny that he was even Max's father. The bastard. He had no idea what he was missing in not knowing his beautiful son.

But what was Max missing by not having a father?

Max was hopping up and down with excitement on the porch as Rock's pickup pulled into the driveway the next night.

A funny hitch skipped in Quinn's heart as she realized that he was driving the same truck that he'd had in high school.

Except now it had a flashy new paint job and the engine sounded as if it were running smoother. He must have had it restored.

Rock's grin was as wide as Max's as he got out of the truck and headed for the porch. "You guys ready to go see a movie?"

"Yes!" Max yelled and launched himself off the porch and into Rock's arms.

Rock faltered for only a second, then he swung the little boy around in a circle and carried him over to the pickup. "What do you think of my truck?"

"I think it's so cool." Max crawled across the bench seat and settled himself in the middle as Quinn grabbed their stuff. She'd packed a tote with extra drinks and snacks, figuring that the concession prices would be outrageous. And she'd tucked in jackets, knowing it could get cool once the sun went down.

Rock clamored back around the truck and held out his arms. He planted his feet and gave her an impish grin. "You wanna jump too?"

"No. Not even a little bit." She shook her head, trying to hold back a grin. "You're a goofball."

"Yes," he said, taking the tote bag from her and carrying it to the truck. He held open the door. "But I'm a goofball with blankets and pillows and even a heater."

She peered into the bed of the truck, and it was indeed stocked with comforters, pillows, and a portable heater. A couple of lawn chairs and a cooler were also stacked next to the blankets. "It looks like you're prepared for the zombie apocalypse."

"Hey, I like to be prepared." He shut the door after she'd climbed in and circled the front of the pickup. Squeezing in next to Max, he put the truck in gear and tapped on the dashboard. "You all ready to have some fun?"

"Yes." Max giggled and squirmed with pent-up energy. He hadn't had anything to eat since supper, but he was acting like he was hopped up on sugar and caffeine. He was really excited for this movie idea.

Evidently, Rock was too. His grin matched Max's as they talked easily about which superhero was their favorite.

Rock had texted her earlier that day to say he had checked out the movie playing that night, and it was the latest superhero action flick. He'd invited Vivi and his brothers to come along, and they'd all agreed.

Quinn brought the subject up over lunch with her dad and brother, telling them the whole James family would be there and that they were invited to come as well. She could not have been more surprised when her dad nodded and said it sounded like fun. She'd bet Ham Rivers hadn't been to a movie in over a decade.

Logan said he would try to show up as well. So, apparently, it was going to be a party at the drive-in. She'd texted Rock back that her whole family was in, and he'd offered to pick her and Max up a little early so they could get a good spot.

She'd tried to get Max to take a nap this afternoon, but he'd been too excited. She could feel the ripples of excitement coming off of him now as he riddled Rock with questions.

"How high do you think the screen is? How do they get the picture on the screen? Can we get popcorn? With butter? Did you know we made butter in our class, in a jar?"

Rock took his questions in stride, answering each one in the order he'd been asked. "Pretty dang high. Some kind of projection magic. Of course we're getting popcorn with lots of butter. And Milk Duds. And that sounds cool, about the butter in the jar." He glanced over Max's head and offered Quinn a smile. He seemed to be having as much fun as her son. And didn't seem fazed at all by his constant barrage of questions.

She'd never met such an inquisitive kid as her son. He had a question for everything. His desire for knowledge and for understanding how things worked sometimes wore her out.

But Rock was keeping up, even throwing in silly responses or made-up answers if he didn't know the real ones.

Quinn listened with half an ear, lost in her own thoughts and memories of being back in this truck with Rock.

"Why do they call it a Milk Dud?" Max asked.

"'Cause they're made out of milk chocolate and they stick to your teeth, so when you eat them, it looks like a cow chewing her cud, which rhymes with 'dud.'"

Quinn raised an eyebrow at that one.

Rock shrugged, his grin contagious, as he obviously enjoyed this game.

"How many cows do you have?"

"Hundreds."

"Have you ever ridden a cow?"

"Yes, when I was a kid. But not with a saddle, because we didn't have one that big."

"Have you ever ridden a horse?"

"Yes, lots of times."

"What's a bastard?"

Chapter 10

ROCK'S SMILE FELL, AND HE FELT LIKE HE'D BEEN SLAMMED in the chest with a brick.

He blinked as he looked to Quinn for help.

She looked about as stunned as he felt.

Max must have heard the word somewhere. Probably on television. At least that's what he hoped. He figured the truth was the best way to go. Especially with this kid. "Um, so a bastard is someone whose parents aren't married to each other."

He could tell Quinn was holding her breath as Max processed this information.

"So then are you a bastard?" he asked.

Sometimes, yes.

But somehow, he didn't think that was the best answer to give to an eight-year-old kid. "No, my parents were married. My dad just died. And it's really not a very nice word to call someone."

"Oh." He wrinkled his small forehead in concentration.

"Max, where did you hear that word?" Quinn asked gently.

"I heard Grandpa and Uncle Logan talking about my dad, and they said he was a bastard for not ever wanting to come and see me. But that doesn't make sense. Because if you're not married to my dad, then that means I'm a bastard too. And they didn't make it sound like a good thing."

"No, they shouldn't have said that at all," she said through gritted teeth.

"Are my dad's parents not married either?"

"I'm not really sure, honey."

"Then maybe he is a bastard too."

"Okay, can you please stop saying that word? Like Rock said, it's not very nice. It's the kind of word that can mean more than one thing. You know, like…" She paused, as if trying to come up with an example.

"Like the word 'punch,'" he offered. "You know, it can mean like a delicious fruity drink, or it can mean to take your fist and punch someone."

"Like I might do to your grandfather and uncle," Quinn mumbled.

"So what's the other thing that it means?" Max asked.

"It can also refer to someone who is not a very nice person," Rock said.

The boy frowned, and his eyebrows squished together. "So, does that mean that they don't think my dad's a very nice person?"

"Or, in this case," Quinn said, "I think they meant it was not very nice of him not to come and see you."

"Yeah, that isn't very nice of him." He lowered his voice. "I wish he would come and see me."

Rock's heart twisted inside his chest. Poor kid. He could kill that idiot Monty Hill. He *was* a bastard.

He slowed the truck and made the turn into the drive-in. "Oh look, we're here."

Max craned his neck to see over the dash, then turned his head back toward him. "Hey, Rock?"

"Yeah, buddy." He held his breath. What was this kid going to ask him now?

"Do you think they have root beer? 'Cause that goes real good with popcorn."

He let out a soft chuckle. "Yeah, I think they have root beer."

"Do you think we can get some?"

"I think we can manage that." He snuck a glance at Quinn, who offered him a bewildered shrug as if to say she had no idea where her son came up with this stuff. "If it's okay with your mom."

Max whipped his head back toward Quinn. "Is it okay, Mom?"

"Sure."

"Yes." He did a tiny fist pump. "And don't forget you said we could go ice skating sometime in the next week. We're still going ice skating, right?"

Rock laughed again at Max's sudden switch of conversation topics. He wasn't sure the kid had even remembered his offer to take him skating. He'd been half asleep when they'd talked about it. "Yeah, we're still going. I didn't forget."

"Max, don't push," Quinn admonished. "Rock's a busy guy."

"It's okay. I always have time to go skating." He was itching to get out on the ice again and hoped the casual setting would give him a chance to test out how he felt being in skates after the concussion. He grinned at Quinn. "Plus, it will give me a chance to show off some of my mad skating skills."

She raised one eyebrow. "I've seen your skills."

He lowered his voice. "Not for a while now. And some of my skills have definitely improved."

A soft, pink blush rose on her cheeks, and he couldn't

keep the grin off his face. He'd used a flirty tone, and he liked that her mind automatically went to *those* skills.

"Why don't you focus on your driving skills so you don't run into the ticket booth," she said, shutting down any further discussion on that topic.

For now, at least.

He chuckled as he eased forward, then stopped at the ticket booth and pulled out his wallet.

The red-haired teenager in the booth looked up from the book she was reading and smiled. "Hey, Rock." She peered into the truck's cab and waved. "Hi, Max. Hi, Quinn."

"Hey, Ginger." He recognized the girl. She and her whole red-haired family attended the same church his family had always gone to. This really was a small town.

He handed her his debit card. "Seven adults and one child's ticket."

The girl peered questioningly into the back of his truck.

"My mom and brothers will be along shortly, and so will Quinn's dad and her brother. Can you hold their tickets here for them?"

"You don't have to pay for us," Quinn said, pulling a twenty from her pocket and holding it out to him.

Rock waved her money away. "I've got it. This was my idea, and I invited you. I invited everyone, so it's my treat."

"Good luck explaining that to my dad."

Ginger handed him three tickets and a cardboard placard to put in his windshield.

"Thanks. And if Ham or Logan give you any trouble about me covering their ticket, just let them pay for

CAUGHT UP IN A COWBOY 135

themselves and give their tickets to a family that looks like they could use a couple of free tickets."

The teenager grinned. "Got it."

She was probably relieved that he gave her an out so she wouldn't have to argue with Hamilton, who was known for sometimes being a cantankerous cuss.

"Thank you." Quinn shoved the bill back into her pocket, then pointed to an open section in the middle of the lot. "That looks like a good spot over there."

Several cars had already arrived and were setting up for the movie.

"Looks good to me." Rock eased the truck down the lane and backed into an open spot, thankful to have something else to focus on. He cut the engine and opened the door. "We can use the lawn chairs and the cooler to save the spots on either side of us for our families. I know Colt said he was going to bring his pickup as well."

They piled out. Rock lifted Max into the back end of the truck and instructed him to start pulling out the blankets and pillows. He dropped the tailgate and held out a hand to help Quinn.

She paused next to him. "I'm still in shock over seeing the old truck. I didn't know you still had it."

He ran a hand lovingly over the tailgate. "Yeah, I tried to sell her a couple of times and just couldn't do it." He gave her a sideways glance. "Too many memories, I guess."

She let out a sigh. "I swear we spent every day of the summer in this thing."

"And I took you to prom in it too. I still remember trying to get you into the cab in that fluffy pink dress."

And he remembered trying to get her out of that same dress later that night. And succeeding.

He could tell by the pink tinge that flared in her cheeks that she was thinking about the same thing. It wasn't often that Quinn Rivers blushed. And he'd seen it twice already in one night. Maybe he was getting to her.

"Anyway," she said, obviously flustered. "What's in the cooler?"

He grinned. He liked seeing her flustered. "I'm not sure. Mom packed it, so it's probably got a veggie tray and a fruit platter."

"You're probably right." She chuckled and pulled the lawn chairs out. "I'll get these set up so we can save their places."

They spent the next ten minutes getting the back end set up with a nest of pillows and blankets.

A horn honked, and Colt's truck backed in to the spot next to them. To Rock's surprise, Ham was riding shotgun, and Vivi and Mason were in the back seat.

"Logan changed his mind, so we picked Ham up on our way," Colt explained as they piled out of the truck.

"Grandpa," Max called, scrambling out of the truck and racing toward Ham and Vivi. He gave his grandpa a high-five, then threw his arms around Vivi's legs, and she leaned down and planted a kiss on his head.

"The popcorn's on me," Rock called to the group. "Who wants some?"

Everyone raised their hand. Like he even had to ask.

"Come on, little brother," he called to Colt. "You can help me."

"Can I come too?" Max asked.

"I wouldn't leave without you." Rock grabbed Max

and lifted him onto his shoulders, ignoring the sudden feeling of light-headedness he got from bending down. Max weighed next to nothing. It wasn't going to hurt him to have the boy resting on his shoulders.

Max bounced up and down, radiating excitement, but also causing small explosions of pain as his swinging feet struck the bruises on his side.

Maybe he'd let him walk back.

Quinn fell into step beside him, and several people waved and called out to them as they walked toward the concession shack, which was already filling with people.

Apparently, the drive-in was the place to be on Friday night in Creedence.

He nudged his brother as they got in line and lowered his voice. "Give me a hand with this guy, will you?"

Colt gave him a questioning look, then it must have dawned on him that it had something to do with Rock's injuries, because he nodded and reached out his hands for the boy.

"Come here, kid. Show me what kind of soda you want." As tall as Rock, he easily lifted the boy from his brother's shoulders and set him on his own. He pointed to the display boards behind the counter.

"Root beer," Max said. "Rock, they have root beer. You said we could get it. Can we get it?"

"Max, we brought drinks," Quinn said.

Rock laughed and turned to Quinn. "It's okay with me. I did tell him he could have it."

"Fine. It seems like I'm outnumbered."

Rock laughed as he approached the counter, counting the people in his head, although he knew his mom had most likely brought individual plastic bowls to split up the popcorn. "We'll have four buckets of popcorn with butter, three boxes of Milk Duds, and a box of M&M's." He knew both of his brothers would want their own popcorn and a box of candy, and the M&M's were for his mom. "And a root beer for Max." He cocked an eyebrow at Quinn. "Are Butterfingers still your favorite?"

Her eyes widened, then she nodded. "But you don't have to—"

"And a box of those Butterfingers," he told the cashier, passing her his card.

"Hi, Ms. Bishop," Max called, waving to the woman standing in line next to him. He leaned forward and tapped Rock on the head. "That's my teacher, Ms. Bishop."

Rock turned to the pretty brunette. She had on jeans, tennis shoes, and a T-shirt that read *I love my second graders*. She was also surrounded by four kids of varying ages, although she didn't look old enough to have a teenager.

He held out a hand. "Hi, Ms. Bishop. I'm Rock."

She offered him a friendly smile. "I know who you are. It's nice to meet you, Rock. And please, call me Chloe." She smiled and waved at Quinn.

Colt nudged him.

"And this is my brother Colt. He's the handsome one in the family."

Chloe nodded at Colt, the corners of her lips turning up in a different kind of smile—the kind of shy one apparently reserved for handsome little brothers. "Hello, Colt. It's nice to meet you too."

"Same here," Colt replied.

Wow. Way to really impress her with your conversation skills, dude.

Max tapped Colt on the head. "We gave her that shirt last year. I was one of her second graders."

She tipped her head back, grinning up at Max still sitting on Colt's shoulders. "Yes, you did. And I just found out that they're moving me to third grade, so I'll be your teacher next year too."

"Yay!" He called down to Quinn. "Mom, did you hear that? Ms. Bishop is gonna be my teacher again?"

"Yes, I heard."

"And that's Madison. She's in my class too." He waved down at the little girl standing at Chloe's leg. "Hi, Maddie."

The girl timidly peeked around Chloe's legs, then raised her hand in a small wave.

One of the older kids stared at Rock. "Do you play hockey?"

He nodded.

"I knew it. I seen you on TV."

Ms. Bishop put an arm around the little girl standing next to her. "These are the Johnson kids. They live next door to me, and I take care of them sometimes when their mom isn't feeling well."

"She means when our mom gets drunk and forgets to come home," the teenager mumbled.

"Nice to meet you guys," Rock said, ignoring the teenager's comment.

The young girl pulled on Ms. Bishop's arm. "Do you think I could get a slush instead of popcorn? I don't like popcorn all that much."

"Well, I'm not sure…" Chloe said, looking around at the other kids.

"You can all have a slush. *And* popcorn. Snacks are

on me tonight." Rock signaled to the cashier, who still had his card. "Put their stuff on my card and make sure they all get something, food and a drink."

"You don't have to do that," Chloe said.

"You didn't have to take four of your neighbor's kids out to the movies either. It's my pleasure."

"Thank you. That's very kind of you."

"It's nothing, really." He felt pressure on his hand and looked down to see that Quinn had twisted her pinkie around his. She wasn't looking at him, wasn't paying any attention to him at all. She was standing next to him, but her body was turned away from him, and she was talking to one of the Johnson kids.

No one could probably even tell that she was touching his fingers.

But he knew.

He felt the pressure on his hand.

And in his heart.

Dang. He was in trouble here. Real trouble.

The cashier passed him their food and the drink for Max. Between the three of them, they juggled the popcorn and candy, and Max held his own drink, resting it on the top of Colt's head as they made their way out of the concession shack.

As usual, their walk back was slow, because everyone they saw wanted to say hello, to ask about his mom, to comment on the season, and a few mentioned the hit. He'd rather talk about his mom's well-being and the status of the weather than have to remark on his injury.

He wanted to forget about the concussion, about the bruises covering his body, about the dull ache in his head, and just enjoy being at the movies with his date. And her kid, and his brothers, and their parents.

Hmm. Maybe *date* wasn't the best word.

They made it back to the trucks and passed out the snacks. His mom had been busy setting out drinks and napkins. Pulling out the plastic bowls, she split up one of the buckets, dishing up popcorn for herself, Max, and Ham.

Quinn's dad had made himself comfortable in the back of Colt's truck, and Max climbed off Colt's shoulders and scrambled up to sit next to his grandfather. Colt helped Vivi into the truck bed, and she settled on the other side of Max.

His brothers sprawled out in the lawn chairs, and he and Quinn took their drinks and a bucket of popcorn and crawled into the back end of his truck.

Leaning against the pillows, he reached for a handful of popcorn, acutely aware of the places Quinn's body pressed against his. She didn't exactly snuggle in next to him, but she was close enough that her shoulder brushed his and the side of her hip and thigh were nestled against him.

The rowdiness of the drive-in settled down as the lights dimmed, and the huge screen came to life. Fifteen minutes of previews later, the movie finally started.

Rock tried to concentrate on the movie. It was good. That wasn't the problem. The problem was the gorgeous blond whose hand kept brushing his as they both reached for popcorn, and whose hair kept tickling the side of his arm, and whose shampoo smelled like vanilla and something floral and utterly, sinfully feminine.

He liked the way she softly chuckled at the clever

dialogue in the movie and busted out laughing when something really funny happened. Her laughter touched something inside him, something deep and hollow that the sound seemed to fill.

He'd missed her laugh. He'd missed hanging out with her, talking to her, bouncing ideas off her.

He'd also missed holding her, missed having her soft curves sink against him. He was usually smooth with women, easily resting his arm casually around their shoulders. But nothing seemed casual or easy about this new truce between him and Quinn. He didn't want to move too fast or do anything that would scare her away.

Which was probably why his arm felt like a foreign appendage that he didn't know how to hold or where to set. He was getting ready to fall back on the old stretch-and-yawn routine to get his arm around her—that was always smooth—and no woman ever saw through that move. Yeah, right?

He wasn't used to this feeling—this awkward sense of worrying about how his movements and reactions affected the woman with him. Not that he wasn't a gentleman around women. He was. If he wasn't, Vivi would hunt him down. But he was used to being around the puck bunnies or women he met that cared only about his status and who he was and being seen on the arm of an NHL player. He didn't have to do anything to impress or sway their opinion of him.

Not that he was trying to impress Quinn, but he was trying to sway her opinion of him. Sway her into thinking that maybe he wasn't such a bad guy after all, and maybe she could still be interested in being around him.

She stretched forward to straighten the blanket

around her legs, and he saw an opportunity to casually rest his arm behind her so when she'd leaned back, his arm would already be there.

Was that too cheesy of a move?

Maybe he should just go with the yawn and stretch—it might be more obvious, but it got the job done.

He just had to go for it. Reaching out, he dropped his arm into the empty spot behind Quinn's shoulders just as she was leaning back.

She hesitated, pausing for a moment as her shoulders touched his arm, then she settled into the crook of his arm, and he let out a sigh of relief.

He looked up at the screen, realizing he'd missed the whole last scene as he'd been piddling around, trying to figure out how to get his arm around this woman, but he didn't care. Her warm body was curled against his side, and that's all that mattered.

A clattering noise at the end of the truck drew his attention. Max was crawling up over the tailgate and scrambling across their blankets to snuggle in between them.

The little boy fit perfectly, and as he looked up at Rock and offered him a toothy grin, something melted inside Rock's heart.

He might be a bad-ass tough-as-hell hockey player, but he seemed to be a marshmallow when it came to this little kid and his mom.

A smile stole across his face as he settled back against the pillows and looked up at the screen, his heart happy.

An hour later, the overhead lights of the drive-in flickered on as the credits rolled across the screen.

Rock blinked, struggling to wake up, to orient himself.

Dang. He must have fallen asleep.

His leg was tingling and numb, and his neck hurt from leaning sideways at an odd angle, but the shoulder he was leaning on was nice, the fabric of Quinn's cotton shirt soft against his cheek.

"Wake up, sunshine," she whispered into his ear, her breath tickling the skin of his neck.

He sat up, stretching as he let out a yawn. He couldn't believe he'd fallen asleep. Stupid concussion.

"Sorry. Didn't mean to fall asleep on you." Dragging the back of his hand across his mouth, he was thankful that at least he hadn't been drooling.

"It's okay. We could still hear the movie over your snoring," she teased, offering him a grin. "Barely."

He granted her a wry grin. "I missed the ending. Was it any good?"

Her teasing grin softened. "Yeah, it was. The whole night has been good. Really good."

"Especially the root beer," Max piped in.

Rock looked down to where the boy was still tucked in between them.

Yes, it was a good night, indeed.

He was still thinking that twenty minutes later when he carried a sleeping Max through the darkened Rivers home and into his bedroom.

He might have fallen asleep during the movie, but Max had conked out on the way home, so worn out from the full day that he wasn't sure if anything short of a foghorn could wake this kid up.

Quinn had led him down the dark hallway and pulled Max's comforter down so Rock could lay him in the bed.

Max snuggled into his pillow, and Quinn pulled the

blankets over him and tucked them in around his small body. She kissed his forehead and murmured that she loved him, then motioned Rock toward the door.

He stepped into the dark hallway and stopped as she pulled the door of Max's room shut behind her.

This is where they'd been a few nights before, but this time, he wasn't sure he could walk away with just a quick peck good night. He'd been watching her mouth all night—as she talked, as she laughed, as she pressed popcorn between her soft, pink lips.

Lips that he wanted to capture in a kiss.

The only problem was that once he started kissing her, he wasn't sure he could stop.

Slow down, buddy.

She hadn't given him any indication that she wanted him to kiss her. Just because she'd allowed his clumsy attempt at putting his arm around her at the movies and because she'd touched his hand in the concession stand didn't mean she wanted to make out with him.

He turned back to her and tried to lean casually against the wall. "Thanks for going to the movies with me." He kept his voice low, not just because Max was asleep, but because the moment seemed to call for it— the late hour, the intimacy of the dim hallway.

Her hair shimmered in the rays of moonlight that shone through the front windows, giving her blond hair a silvery glow. His heart pounded against his chest just looking at her.

She was so beautiful.

She dipped her chin, staring at the floor, then raised her eyes to his. "Thanks for taking us." Her voice was soft, breathy.

She stood right in front of him, only a few inches separating them. He wanted to reach out, to touch her hair, her shoulder, to settle his hand on her waist. But he couldn't. This new relationship, the one where they agreed to be friends, was so fragile, he didn't want to upset the delicate balance they'd achieved.

He wanted to kiss her, wanted to kiss her so badly he could taste it, but more than that, he wanted her in his life. And didn't want to scare her away.

Memories of the last time he'd tried to kiss her filled his head, and he'd darned near scared her away for good. He needed to take it slow, not push.

She tilted her head, looking up at him, studying his face. "I used to know every feature of your face, every story behind all of your scars. But now you have new features, scars that I don't know how you got."

He held his breath as she reached up and ran her fingers lightly across the tiny scar next to his lip. He'd gotten it when a stray puck had grazed past his face during practice. He'd just taken his helmet off.

He opened his mouth, wanting to tell her the story, but no words would come. All he could focus on was the gentle pressure of her fingertips next to his mouth. Without thinking, he moved his face, turned it just the slightest toward her hand, and kissed the ends of her fingers.

He heard her intake of breath, and the sound sent frissons of heat swirling through his belly.

She moved her hand, sliding her palm up to cup his cheek, and he pressed his face into her fingers. Raising his hand, he set it on top of hers.

"You're killin' me, Q," he whispered.

Her eyes widened, and her lips parted. "Why?" Her answer was barely above a whisper.

"Because I'm trying to take it slow and not push you, to respect our friendship." He paused and raised his eyes, gazing sincerely into hers. "But I want to kiss you so bad it hurts."

It did hurt. Every muscle in his body was tense with need; every nerve was taut with anticipation. He felt like a tightly wound spring, and he wasn't sure he could hold back from releasing the tension.

Quinn leaned closer, raising her chin so her mouth was scant inches from his. Close enough that he could feel the heat of her skin, smell the cinnamon scent of her gum.

This was too much. She was too much of a temptation. He thought he could hold back, but he was wrong.

Chapter 11

DIPPING HIS HEAD, ROCK TOOK HER MOUTH IN AN ALL-consuming kiss.

Screw soft and light. He needed to feel her, to taste her.

His hands slid around Quinn's waist, and in one movement, he twisted them both around and pressed her back against the wall.

His mouth consumed hers as he kissed her with all of the passion he'd been suppressing the past few days—passion he didn't even know was in him. He couldn't remember the last time he'd kissed a woman with this much feeling—this much desire.

Wait—yes, he could. It was the last time he'd kissed Quinn. This woman he held in his arms. Against a wall.

She gripped his shoulders, her fingers digging into his arms as she arched into him.

Her lips were supple and hungry, and her body molded perfectly to his.

A low moan escaped her, humming against his lips—and it was about the sexiest fucking thing he'd ever heard.

He wanted her, needed her, couldn't get enough of her.

His tongue found its way between her lips, and he could taste the sweet cinnamon of her gum.

He reached down and slid his hands under her butt, ready to lift her up, when a flash of light crossed the hallway, followed by the low thrum of a truck's engine.

Damn. Colt must be dropping Ham off.

Rock pulled back, his breath coming in hard gasps, his head spinning with dizziness.

Quinn blinked up at him, her hair tousled, her lips slightly swollen.

He reached up, grazing her bottom lip with his thumb. "Woman, you are about the sexiest thing I've ever seen."

She smoothed her hair as a grin tugged at the corners of her lips. "I'm a mess."

He leaned close, dropping his voice. "You look like a woman who's just been thoroughly kissed."

She let out a soft sigh, her own voice low and husky. "Not thoroughly enough."

He let out a laugh and pulled her into a quick bear hug before her dad came through the door. "Damn, I've missed you."

Quinn sat up in bed and plumped her pillow, then lay down again. She tried one side, then the other, but couldn't seem to get comfortable.

A glance at the bedside clock told her it was close to midnight, a time when she would normally be deep in sleep, exhausted from the day. Her body was tired, but her mind was restless, her thoughts tumbling and jumbled, thinking about Rock and the past few days. And always coming back to the way he'd kissed her earlier that night.

The kiss had been full of passion and promise, his mouth crushing against hers with want and need.

She couldn't help but wonder what would have

happened if they hadn't heard Colt's truck coming down the driveway to drop off her dad.

Her cell phone buzzed, and her heart leapt. Who the heck was texting her this late?

A text at midnight usually meant something was wrong. Or that Carolyn Parker, the PTA president and an insomniac workaholic, was sending out late-night reminders of what parents needed to bring to school for a bake sale or function.

But school was out for the summer.

She sat up in bed and reached for the phone, letting out a quick gasp as she saw the message was from Rock.

You still up? his message read.

She typed a response. Yep. Can't sleep.

Why not?

Thinking about stuff.

I can't sleep either. I'm thinking about you.

Her heart raced, and her fingers trembled as she held them above the keyboard. How should she respond to that? Be witty and make a sarcastic remark? Joke it off?

Be honest?

She tapped the keys and hit Send before she could think too much about it. I'm thinking about you too.

What are you thinking about me?

A grin curved her lips, and she settled back against her pillows. Just about how nice it's been to hang out with you the last week. And how much fun it's been.

I'm thinking about that kiss.

Oh my.

She didn't know what to say. She could feel the heat rushing to her cheeks, and she was glad he wasn't here to see it. Although he would love it.

And tease her relentlessly.

Before she could respond, another message popped in.

What are you wearing?

She laughed. Okay, this one she could handle. She glanced down at the thin tank top and cotton pajama shorts she had on. A long flannel nightgown and fuzzy socks.

Sounds hot. He followed his message with a winky-face emoticon.

It is. Smiley face. Seriously sexy. Winky face.

No, I mean it actually sounds hot. Too hot for summer.

She watched the blinking dots signaling he was still typing.

You should take it off.

Her breath caught. She swallowed as her mouth suddenly went dry.

She could imagine how those words would sound in Rock's deep voice, and a shimmer of heat ran down her back.

The only light in the room was from the phone's screen, and the dark made their conversation seem more intimate.

Clutching the phone, she waited as she watched the dots flashing again.

But leave the fuzzy socks on.

She let out a laugh, then covered her mouth, hoping she hadn't woken anyone up with her sharp burst of laughter.

Fuzzy socks are my downfall. I've always found them ridiculously sexy, his next message read.

Giggling, she typed back, I had no idea you had a fuzzy sock fetish. Send. I'll buy another pair.

Buy several. Winky face.

She squirmed in her bed, imagining the implications of *several* nights with Rock, with fuzzy socks or not.

They were making progress, getting more comfortable with each other. She liked it. She wanted more of it—wanted more of him. Whether it was the safety of being in her bedroom alone or the intimacy of talking to him in the dark while she lay in bed, she felt closer to him, more vulnerable, more willing to take a chance. I like playing around with you. I miss this, she typed.

I miss you.

The air suddenly felt thinner, and she sucked in her breath. I miss you too.

Feel like playing around some more?

What did you have in mind?

Just wondering if I were there, would you let me kiss you again?

Maybe. Send. Probably. Send. Yes.

Would you let me touch you?

His words sent a flurry of heat swirling in her belly, and her nipples puckered. There were no flirty winky emoticons with that message.

Her fingers hesitated over the phone before typing out a single word. Yes.

She watched the screen, holding her breath as she waited for his next response.

All I can think about is touching you. Filling my hands with you. Feeling you against me.

Oh.

Her body melted into the pillow, and she drew her legs up under her as sensations that she hadn't felt in a long, long time surged through her. She spent so much time thinking of herself as a mom, that she'd forgotten what it felt like to be a woman.

To have her body tingle and prickle with desire, with need.

It had been so long since she'd let her guard down, let herself feel that deep yearning for a man's touch, for a man's weight resting on top of her.

But she wasn't craving just any man. Her body wanted only one man. The only man she'd ever loved.

It wanted Rock.

Reading his words, *Rock's* words, on the tiny, dimly lit screen awakened yearnings in her that she'd forgotten she even knew how to feel.

But what she did remember, what she couldn't seem to forget, was how he'd hurt her. How he'd broken her heart and left her behind.

But he's trying to fix that, her inner self screamed at her. *Give him a chance*. He was trying. And what he'd been doing was working. Obviously.

But this was taking things to the next level. Wasn't it?

Or was this just harmless flirting? Just playing around with her? Like he said.

What would it hurt to play a little back? To tease him a little? She shouldn't be the only one in torment.

I'd like that, she typed and pressed Send before she could change her mind.

It couldn't hurt anything to do a tiny bit of flirting. It was all little text messages, a few words in a dark room. It's not like he was here.

She watched the little dots flicker then stop, then flicker again, as if he were writing something, then stopped, then started again.

Her hand was sweaty on the phone, she was gripping it so tightly as she waited for his response. Even though she was anticipating it, she still jumped a little when the phone buzzed in her hand, and she let out a sigh as she read his message.

Remember when I used to cut across the pasture in the middle of the night and sneak into your window?

Yes. Of course she remembered. She remembered all of it—everything about her time spent with him. She remembered opening the window and watching him crawl in. Remembered the thrill of him gently lying down on her bed beside her, and how softly he'd touched her.

Remembered spending hours curled against him, kissing him, touching him, loving him—all the while both thrilled at him being there and terrified as she worried that her dad would find out.

But it didn't matter—because she'd never been unable to resist the pull of Rock.

Evidently, she was still unable to resist the pull of him, since she was flirt-texting with him at midnight.

What if I showed up at your window tonight? Would you let me in?

Holy moley. What if she said yes and he showed up? At her bedroom window?

Would she let him in?

She smoothed her hair and glanced down at herself, a thrill coursing through her at the sight of her pebbled nipples pressing against the thin pajama top. The idea of him being here, in her bedroom, seeing her in her skimpy pajamas, both excited and terrified her. Just like when she was a teenager.

This whole thing felt like one of the crazy things she used to do when she was a teenager—a wild and reckless act that would often result in both a fun time and an eventual grounding once her dad found out.

But she wasn't a teenager anymore. She was an adult and a mom. She didn't make crazy and impulsive decisions anymore—like the one that led her to *being* a mom.

Now she was responsible and mature. And she didn't encourage boys to sneak into her bedroom at night.

But Rock wasn't a boy anymore. He was a man. A man with hard abs and big, muscled arms, and the same crystal-blue eyes that she still saw in her dreams.

A man who had her insides tingling and yearning for his touch.

Stable, responsible, grown-up—those were the words that described her now. She didn't do wild and reckless anymore.

But maybe it was time she did. Being a mom didn't mean she was dead.

And the idea of Rock in her bedroom had her thoughts going in lots of directions—and none of them fell into the category of responsible.

Why not? What the heck? Live a little, right?

And just because she said yes didn't mean he *would* come over. All he'd asked was if he *did* come over, would she let him in?

She typed the three letters, then hesitated over the Send button.

Images of her as a teenager filled her head—running through the fields, swimming in the pond, galloping across the pasture, her hair flying behind her—and always with Rock by her side. He was in every part of her childhood, her teenage years. And she'd missed him as an adult.

Not just romantically, but missed his laughter, his gentle teasing, his sound advice.

She hit Send.

She held her breath as she waited for his response.

But the screen stayed white. No blinking circles to indicate he was typing.

Her teeth were clamped tightly together, and she let out her breath and tried to relax as the screen dimmed and then went black.

Maybe he'd fallen asleep while he waited for her reply.

Her shoulders sagged as she heaved a soft sigh.

It was probably for the best.

A knock sounded at her window.

Chapter 12

QUINN JUMPED AND LET OUT A QUIET YELP AS HER GAZE SHOT to the window.

Rock was standing there.

Right outside her window. And grinning like a loon.

He waved her over.

Oh. My.

She'd done it. She'd said yes.

And now he was here.

All she had to do was open the window and let him in. Into her bedroom.

She pushed back the covers and climbed out of bed.

Where the heck was her robe? Too late.

Just open the window.

Crossing the room, her heart hammering against her chest, she couldn't take her eyes off him. He wore a burgundy team T-shirt and loose cotton shorts, and his hair was mussed around his forehead.

He looked hot as hell.

What was she doing? Was she crazy?

Opening the window was what she was doing, sliding up the frame and stepping back as he popped the screen free from the other side and crawled through.

"I think this window was bigger when I was a kid," he whispered as he squeezed his large frame through.

He was so much bigger than he used to be—his hands, his arms, his chest, even his feet seemed bigger.

She fought back a giggle as she wondered if *everything* about him was bigger.

Her nipples puckered again as she wondered—hoped?—that she was about to find out.

He left the window open and took a step toward her.

She was tall herself, but he made her feel small as he towered over her. She loved it.

"Hi," he whispered, the grin still beaming from his face.

"Hi," she replied, suddenly shy and intensely aware of the outline of her breasts and her taut nipples poking through the thin top. Maybe he wouldn't notice.

He stood still, not touching her yet, but his gaze traveled up and down her body, and she felt the heat of his once-over every bit as if he'd actually run his hands across her.

His eyes stopped at her chest, and his grin widened.

Yeah, he noticed.

Gulp.

He reached out his right hand, swept it around her waist, and settled it on her back. He raised his left to her face and tenderly touched her cheek.

His touch sent a shiver of need racing down her back, and she fought to breathe.

His grin faded, and his lips parted, just slightly, just enough for his tongue to dart out and run across them.

He didn't say anything, just looked down at her, his gaze locked on hers in an intense stare as his palm softly held her cheek.

Turning his hand over, he slowly—so achingly slowly—ran the back of his fingers down her throat, down her chest, trailing to the center of the V in the neck of her tank top, then skimming across the top of the exposed part of her breast.

She really couldn't breathe now, couldn't move, could only hold perfectly still as his fingers skimmed over the top of the fabric, slowly circling the outer edge of her breast. She sucked in a quick gasp as his thumb grazed her tight, pebbled nipple, and she feared her knees would buckle.

His hands were so big, but his touch was soft—so damn soft—as he slid his hand under her breast and cupped it in his palm.

Her back arched just the slightest, as if her body recognized his and wanted, needed, to get closer. As if a giant magnet drew them nearer.

He pulled at the edge of her loose neckline, drawing her shirt down and exposing one taut nipple, then rolled it between his fingers. She watched, spellbound, aching with tight anticipation as he dipped his head and swirled his tongue around the hardened nub, then sucked it between his lips.

Another sharp gasp escaped her, and she struggled to keep her legs steady as flames of heat shot straight to her core. She swallowed at the dry cotton lining the back of her throat.

Dipping his hand inside her shirt, he filled his palm with her breast, squeezing and caressing as he continued to lick and tease her nipple.

Her hands tightened into fists, her nails digging into her palms as her breath came in short pants of need.

The erotic sensations of his lips and hands on her breast before he'd even kissed her had heat surging through her body and her slim grasp of control slipping.

The shadow of his light beard scraped against her sensitive skin, sending another thrill coursing through her.

He pulled back, then dragged the tank top over her head, and her chest heaved as her full breasts lay naked and exposed. A low growl sounded at the back of his throat as he gazed down at her, then dipped his head and claimed her mouth in a kiss, capturing her gasp as his big hands slid around her bare back and pulled her close.

Her sensitive nipples brushed the cotton of his T-shirt, sending waves of gooseflesh across her skin.

Demanding kisses laced with another growl trailed down her neck and across her shoulders.

Her head dropped to his chest, and she let out a low moan as his hands slid over her hips and cupped her butt. Lifting her up, he wrapped her legs around his waist. She was acutely aware of the sensation of pressing herself against his hardened bulge. Every nerve in her body was taut as she dug her fingers into his hair, the visceral need for this man almost overwhelming her.

How could her need for him be so strong, so overwhelming, when he hadn't touched her in years?

Because from the moment he'd first touched her, all those years ago, she'd given herself to him, and only him. She belonged to him.

He carried her to the bed, dropping her onto it and stopping only for a moment to tug his T-shirt over his head and toss it to the floor before he knelt above her.

His chest was so broad, the muscles hard and defined. She reached up, running her hands across its expanse, stopping to trace the few new scars that she noticed. Need and hunger filled her, overwhelming her with a desire to touch, to explore, to discover the contours and secrets of this man's body that was so familiar, yet still so new to her.

Running her hand over his muscled shoulder and down his bicep, she felt the tremble in his arms and knew he had to be fighting the same kind of control she was.

What the heck was she doing? This was crazy. She hadn't even talked to Rock in probably a year, and now within a few days of being around him again, she was ready to give herself to him, not just her body, but her heart.

Well, maybe not her heart, but at least her body.

Yeah, she was ready and willing to give that. In fact, she couldn't wait to give that.

She squirmed under him, squeezing her legs around his as she rubbed against him.

His eyes narrowed, and he tucked a stray curl of her hair behind her ear as he looked down at her. His gaze was full of hunger, and she swore she could feel the heat of it on her skin.

"Are you sure you're okay with this? You need to tell me now, because I'm about ready to rip those little shorts right off you." His lips curved into a devilish grin. "But I won't if you tell me to stop."

She shook her head back and forth, tingles of desire flooding her with his words. "Don't stop."

Those two words seemed to be all he needed to hear. He reared back, his thumbs hooking inside the hems of her shorts and her bikini panties before drawing them both down her legs.

She lay naked, exposed, her body—and what felt like her soul—bare on the bed before him.

Pushing all reasonable and sensible thoughts from

her head—like the ones that were screaming *what the hell are you doing*?—she went with the moment, letting the emotion and the pure recklessness of it take her away as he crawled on the bed and knelt above her.

Rock wasn't some stranger in a bar that she was picking up for a one-night stand. Although this might only be a one-night affair—she didn't know, and at the moment, didn't care—Rock was someone she knew, someone she had loved.

That you might still love, her heart whispered.

She pushed all of that away and just let her body feel the rough, calloused hands of a man against her skin, let herself sink into the sensation of being wanted and desired and hungered for to the absence of all rational thought.

His hand touched the curve of her hip, and heat shot through her body, making her squirm, and she held back a whimper of need.

One tiny intelligent thought made its way to the surface, and she gasped as she reached for his hand. "Wait."

"Wait?" His voice came out in strangled hesitation.

"I don't have any, you know, protection." She swallowed, trying to catch her breath. "I mean I'm on the pill to regulate my periods, but I'm not always the best at taking them exactly on schedule."

Oh geez, nothing sexier than bringing up your period when you are about to get jiggy with it. And she might as well have just admitted that she hadn't had sex in ages if the only reason she took the pill was to help with her cycle.

Rock did not seem deterred though. In fact, a grin spread across his face, and he waggled his eyebrows at her. "Don't worry. I told you I like to be prepared." He reached into the pocket of his shorts and pulled out a handful of condoms.

Her eyes widened. "You just happened to have a pocket full of condoms?"

"No, I stole them from Colt's room before I left the house. He's at work."

"Holy cow. How many did you bring?"

"I'm not sure. I was nervous. I just grabbed a handful."

She loved that he'd just admitted that he was nervous.

"We should have enough though." He opened his hand and let them fall in a cascade of plastic packets on the bed next to her. "Looks like six or eight. That should do the job."

Six or eight? Gulp.

His grin widened, and her inner minx stood up and did a cheer. *Gimme an R. Gimme an O. Gimme a C-K. Gimme a Rock, Rock, Rock, and give him to me six or eight times, and give him to me NOW!*

Settle down, girl. Just because her inner sexpot was shamelessly flinging herself at him didn't mean that Quinn had to show her hand.

She cocked an eyebrow and tried to play it cool. "Pretty ambitious, aren't you?"

He chuckled, a low, rumbling sound that only revved her engines even more, then he stood up, grabbed the waistband of his shorts, and pushed them over his hips, letting them fall to the ground.

Apparently, he'd had time to sneak into his brother's room for condoms, but he hadn't taken time to put on underwear, because he was full-on commando.

He crawled back up on the bed, giving her the full view of his naked body. And what a body. He had muscles in places she didn't even know could have muscles.

His chest was solid, and his abs were hard and defined, and those little V-shaped things that went down the fronts of his hips—oh Lord have mercy.

Grabbing one of the packets, he tore it open, and grinned down at her. "You know what I always like to say, go big or go home."

She swallowed. Speaking of big.

Oh. My. Gosh.

He covered himself and settled between her thighs, leaning over her and placing a tender kiss on the side of her throat.

His breath was warm against her skin, and she automatically wrapped her legs around him, drawing him closer and pulling him against her.

Clutching his back, she held on as he tunneled his hands through her hair, holding her head as he buried his face in her neck, murmuring sweet words of passion between hot kisses. His mouth was everywhere, her throat, her chest, her aching, tender nipples, kissing, licking, sucking, the heat of his kisses shooting straight to her sensitive core.

A growl vibrated from the back of his throat as he buried himself in her, and she clamped her lips together to keep from crying out with him.

Their bodies fell into a rhythm, almost as if they recognized each other on a primal level.

And Quinn did recognize him: she knew his smell, the sounds he made, the way he moved with her. His muscled arms might be bigger, but they still held her the same way, touched her in the same places.

Although he had learned a few new moves. A few *amazing* new moves.

She clung to him, soft moans filling her throat, and she dropped her head back, surrendering to the delicious friction.

Her center ached, filling her with rapture as he took her to the brink, her fevered nerve endings begging for release.

Another stroke, another touch, and she was gone, falling over the edge.

She gasped, the muscles in her thighs trembling as she rode the waves of pleasure.

He gripped her hips, his fingers digging into her skin as he let go with his own release, his body shuddering, then he collapsed on top of her.

Wrapping her arms around his shoulders, she reveled in the weight of him on top of her, then she couldn't breathe.

She let out a gasp and he slid off her, pulling her next to him as he lightly chuckled. "Sorry."

"It's okay." She grinned up at him. "I liked it." She curled into him, closing her eyes and snuggling against his warm body.

Her eyes shot open as a sudden thought occurred to her. "Holy crap. I should have locked my bedroom door. What if Max had walked in? Or, oh my gosh, my dad?"

"Shh. It's all right. Nobody walked in, so we're okay." He lifted his arm to release her. "But you should go lock it now."

A grin curved her lips. "Yeah?"

"Hell yeah. We've still got at least six more condoms to get through."

She covered her mouth, stifling the giggle as she climbed out of bed and tiptoed across the room to lock her bedroom door.

Turning around, even in the dim light of the moonlight, she could see him watch her walk naked back to the bed.

A man hadn't seen her naked in years, and she was tempted to try to cover herself, to cover the spots that had gone soft with childbirth and too many helpings of ice cream.

But instead, she pushed back her shoulders, ignoring the instinct to cross her arms over her bare chest, and walked confidently forward.

It had been a "what the hell" kind of night already, so why not add one more thing to it?

What the hell? Let him look.

By the sexy grin covering his face, he seemed to be enjoying the show.

Empowered by his admiring approval, her inner minx took over, and she crawled onto the bed, pressing him onto his back, then sliding her leg over him as she straddled his waist.

A naughty smile pulled at the corner of her lips as she watched his eyes widen and gleam with hunger.

Hold on to your hat, cowboy. The show has just begun.

Rock climbed out of Quinn's window and quietly eased the screen back into place.

The sun was just peeking over the horizon and bathed Rivers Gulch in golden morning light.

He hadn't meant to fall asleep, but it had felt so good,

lying in Quinn's bed with her soft body curled against him. He hadn't realized how empty his arms had been until she filled them again.

Last night had been perfect. It had bordered on freaking magical.

And he could *not* stop smiling.

He edged around the corner of the house, skimming the yard to make sure no one was around.

He just had to get to the other side of the barn, and he could slip into the side pasture unnoticed.

Taking a cautious step forward, he froze as he heard the subtle squeak of the front screen door opening.

Cringing, he turned his head, expecting to see the stern frown on the face of Hamilton Rivers.

Instead, he saw the slight figure of a woman. Her back was to him, but she wore a big sweater, leggings, and she held her sandals in her hand as she delicately let the screen door fall back into place.

He blinked, his brain trying to comprehend exactly what was going on here as the woman turned and tiptoed down the front steps.

"Mom?"

Chapter 13

ROCK'S MOUTH HUNG OPEN AT THE SIGHT OF HIS MOTHER sneaking out of the Rivers's house.

Vivi gasped, her hand clutching her chest, and she whispered, "Oh dear Lord, Rockford, you scared the pee out of me." She yanked her shoes on and scurried across the empty yard toward the barn. "I mean it. I literally peed myself a little."

"Come on, Mom. I do *not* need to hear that," he whispered back, following behind her as they hustled around the edge of the barn.

Once they were out of sight, Vivi slowed to a walk and headed toward the path through the pasture.

"Mom," Rock said, keeping his voice low as he fell in step beside her. "What in the world are you doing here?"

She offered him an impish grin and smoothed down her hair. "Would you believe that we were watching a movie and I fell asleep on the sofa?"

"Well, it's a heck of a lot better than imagining the alternative."

She let out a laugh. "Well then, that's my story, and I'm sticking to it."

"Geez, Mom." He shook his head. "Hamilton? Are you serious? You do not understand the dynamics of a feud whatsoever."

She chuckled again. "That dumb feud has been over for years."

The path dipped where a rainstorm had cut a gulley across it, and he held out his hand to help her across.

She took his hand, skipping over the ridges in the path, then squinted up at him. "Don't think I don't know what you're doing, Son. Keeping the attention on me so we don't have to talk about the fact that I wasn't the only one sneaking out of the Rivers's house this morning."

He shrugged. "I must have fallen asleep on the sofa too."

His mother's hearty laugh rang across the green pasture.

—–⌇⌇—–

Later that evening, Rock flicked his fishing pole, letting out his line with a *whirr* as he cast into the serene waters of the pond that lay between the Rivers's ranch and theirs.

The sun was just setting behind the mountains, the air had cooled slightly, and the water was alive, rippling with bugs lighting on the glassy surface. He'd already seen three fish jump, and he let his cast fall in the area he'd seen the last one.

A red-and-white-striped bobber floated on the surface, and he leaned back against his favorite tree as he kept an eye on it. The trunk of the old cottonwood was huge, and a few of its roots lay exposed, like gangly arms reaching toward the cool water of the pond.

The roots offered great places to sit, to lazily lean back against the tree, and to look across the water, the backdrop of the mountains standing tall against the brilliant blues and pinks of the Colorado sunset.

Rock let out a sigh. A good sigh, deep with

contentment. Yeah, he still felt a few effects of the concussion, and his ribs were still tender, but if he had to go anywhere to recuperate, this was the place to do it.

He could almost feel the combination of the mountains and the ranch working to heal his body and soul. There was nothing like being home.

He felt good. Really good.

A grin crept across his face. A grin that had less to do with the healing properties of the mountains and a heck of a lot more to do with the healing properties of spending a long night having wild sex with the only woman he'd ever truly loved—the woman who haunted his dreams and who made his body sore on an entirely different level.

A rustling shook the grass on the other side of the pond, and the woman he was thinking of appeared, walking through the tall stalks almost as if he'd imagined her into being.

She smiled and offered him a shy wave, and he beckoned her over.

He watched her walk around the pond toward him, soaking her in, filling his heart with the vision of her. She wore cutoff shorts and cowboy boots and a loose, short-sleeved, button-up, red western shirt. Not so loose that he couldn't see her generous curves.

Her long hair was pulled back and braided into a thick rope that curled around her slender neck, and a straw cowboy hat perched on her head.

"Hey, cowgirl," he said, offering her his best rakish grin.

She laughed and nudged his foot with her boot. "Hey, cowboy."

He patted the ground next to him. "What are you doing out here?"

She carried a thin, quilted blanket and spread it on the hard-packed dirt next to him, then sank down onto it and leaned her shoulder against his. "I just felt like taking a walk." Strands of her hair tickled his arm, and her scent filled the air around him, mingling with the smell of honeysuckle and fresh hay.

"And your feet led you straight to me."

"I didn't know you'd be here."

"Did you hope I would?"

She shrugged, trying to keep a straight face. "Maybe."

He liked this side of her, this sweet shyness that he hadn't seen in so long. The last several years, all he'd gotten from her on the few occasions that he'd run into her was sarcastic, snarky comments that were not always the most ladylike in nature.

It made him ridiculously happy to have her smiling and playfully flirting with him. It was like the same feeling he got when his team had won a championship game, like he'd just scored the winning goal and earned the trophy.

"You catching anything?" She gestured to the fishing pole that lay forgotten by his feet.

"Not yet." He leaned back against the tree, raising his arms and linking his fingers behind his head. "But I'm not too worried about it. I came down mostly for the view."

She leaned against him, snuggling into the crook under his raised arm. "It is a pretty great view."

He looked down at her and had to swallow at the sudden emotion that filled his throat. Lowering his arm, he wrapped it around her, pulling her closer to him. "I can't think of anything else I'd rather see right now."

Letting his eyes roam, he took in all of her, from her mesmerizing brown eyes to her long, tanned legs. Emotion and need stirred in him as his gaze lingered on her curves.

A long, silver necklace hung around her neck, the chain falling between her breasts. Hanging from it was a large, silver heart and a small, gold key, but the gold had rubbed off in several places.

He wrinkled his forehead. It wasn't the sort of thing Quinn would normally wear, but it looked familiar. The charms bordered on tacky, like something a teenager would wear.

A laugh bubbled up, and he pointed to the necklace when he finally recognized it. "Where the heck did you find that old thing?"

She shrugged. "I didn't have to search too hard. It was in my jewelry box, and I just felt like wearing it today."

"Didn't I give you that for Christmas my senior year?"

She nodded. "And it's always been one of my most prized possessions."

He chuckled again. "I can see why. That thing's got 'quality' written all over it."

"Hey, I love this necklace." She tilted her head, giving him a sweet smile. "I've always thought it was pretty nice for what a seventeen-year-old guy picked out by himself, and for what he could afford at the time. And I always wore it with pride."

"I can tell you with confidence that that seventeen-year-old guy's taste and spending budget has vastly improved." He reached out and lifted the heart charm into his hand. His fingers brushed against the curve of her breast, and he heard her quick intake of breath. "This was the mushiest thing I'd ever given you."

"You said it was the key to your heart."

"I remember." He gingerly set the necklace down and raised his hand to cup her cheek. "You still have it, you know. No matter where I've been, or what stupid decisions I've made, my heart has always belonged to you."

He leaned in, kissed her softly, barely grazing her lips with his.

He wanted the kiss to signify the emotion he felt, not just the lust he'd had when he'd snuck into her room the night before and tossed her onto her bed.

But then she let out one of those small, sexy sighs, and a fire lit and sparked in his belly.

She arched into him and pressed her mouth against his, deepening the kiss, her tongue skimming across his lips. Her cowboy hat fell off when she wound her arms around his neck.

Her lips were warm, pliant, and full of hunger as her hands tunneled through his hair. Her body squirmed, pressing tighter to him, and she shifted as she curled her leg around his.

So much for taking it slow. Having her legs wrapped around his and her chest pressing against him was too much. His jeans tightened as his bulge swelled against them.

She nipped at his lip, let out a soft whimper, and he almost came undone.

He twisted, ignoring the pain in his bruised ribs as he laid her back in the crook of the tree roots, keeping his arm around her to protect her from the dusty branches.

His hands skimmed up her hip, her side, the curve of her full breast. He lifted her arm over her head as he trailed a line of kisses down her neck.

What he'd originally thought were buttons on her shirt were actually snaps, and his erection swelled further as he gave a swift yank and the snaps popped free. Her shirt fell open, exposing a lacy red bra that barely contained the swell of her lush breasts.

Feeling again like he'd just scored the winning goal, he dipped his head and may have let out a low growl as he kissed the crests of her cleavage, then freed one of her breasts and dragged her taut nipple between his lips.

She let out another faint moan as he sucked and teased the tip with his tongue.

One of his hands was trapped under her as he held her, but the other was free to roam and touch, to caress and fondle, and he explored her body, pulling both of her breasts free and giving them equal attention with his lips, his tongue, and his fingers.

She squirmed and wiggled beneath him, riding the side of his leg, creating the friction she needed.

His head roared with his own need, and his fingers skimmed down her stomach, across her waist, along the soft curve of her thigh. He used his knee to spread her legs before slipping his hand up under the hem of her cutoff shorts.

He couldn't take his eyes off her. She was a goddess. Her eyes were closed, and she bit down on her bottom lip. Her one arm was still lifted above her head, and she gripped a limb of the tree in her fist.

Another moan escaped her as his fingers found her sensitive core and rubbed in gentle circles.

Her shirt was open, her breasts bare and spilling over the crumpled cups of her disheveled bra.

He shifted his hand, sliding his fingers inside her underwear. A rumble of arousal vibrated through his chest as she pressed against his palm.

It only took a few swift strokes, and she broke apart beneath him, the fingernails of her free hand digging into his arm as the spasms rolled through her.

When she stopped writhing, he pulled his hand free from her shorts. But he couldn't bring himself to cover her spectacular breasts—the view was still way too good.

Her eyelashes fluttered open, and a sly grin covered her face. She licked her lips, then her gaze flicked to the bulge in his jeans. "Your turn."

His mouth went dry, and he tried to swallow. The thought of Quinn's lips around him, of her tongue circling his...

The *whirr* of his fishing line filled the air, and he turned to see the pole pull free from where he'd jammed it in between the limbs of the tree.

Holy cow. That fish had to be a big one if it was pulling his pole toward the water.

Correction. Not *his* pole. His brother's pole. And Mason would kill him if he lost it.

He scrambled across the bank and made a grab for the rod. It slipped through his grasp and was pulled into the water.

"Shit," he yelled, making another grab for it, soaking his arms up to his shoulders.

Luckily, the pole floated, and Rock blinked in amazement as he watched it glide across the water.

He raced around one side of the pond, slipping and

dunking his foot up to his knee into the water. "Damn it." His soaked jeans and one soggy boot were heavy as he pulled it out of the water and kept after the pole.

"It's coming back." Quinn stood on the banks, doubled over in laughter as she watched him chase the pole. She'd unfortunately snapped a few of the buttons closed on her blouse.

Double damn it.

"Come over this way," she instructed, pointing toward the other side of the pond.

He raced back around, swatting her playfully on the backside as he ran past.

She shrieked with laughter as he took another misstep into the pond, soaking his foot again.

"Screw this," he said as he made his way back to her. He pulled off his boots, then unzipped his jeans and shimmied out of them. Tugging his T-shirt off, he tossed it on the ground next to his pants.

Wearing only his boxer briefs, he dove into the pond, coming up for air with a gasp as the shock of the cold water constricted his lungs.

"It's right behind you," Quinn cried, pointing over his shoulder. "Grab it."

He spun around, shaking the water from his hair, and made a grab for the pole, but it shot forward, and he splashed at the water with his fist.

"Go after it," Quinn yelled, holding her sides as another round of giggles overtook her. "You almost had it."

He turned around and sent a splash of water toward her. "You are enjoying yourself way too much, woman."

"Sorry, I'll stop laughing." She cupped her hand over her mouth and tried to look serious, but then belted out a shriek of laughter as the pole zoomed by and whacked him in the shoulder.

He swam forward, pulling his arms in hard strokes as he went after the pole, this time grabbing ahold of it when he reached out. "I got it."

Now what the heck was he supposed to do with it?

He tried to swim back to shore, hauling the pole and the fish with him. "There's a big freaking fish on there."

Scrambling up the bank, he planted his feet in the dirt and gave a hard yank on the pole. The line pulled taut, bending the end of the pole toward the water. Rock spun the handle, trying to reel in the fish as he leaned backward.

Giving the pole another swift yank, he hoped to pull the fish out of the water.

Instead, the line snapped, and he fell backward, landing hard on his butt in the mud of the bank. "Dang. I lost him."

He tossed the pole onto the bank and offered Quinn a grin. "That sucker put up a heck of a fight."

She was still laughing. "It sure did. And you look like you've *been* in a heck of a fight."

He glanced down at himself. Mud streaked across his chest and waist where he'd held the pole, caking across the purple-and-yellow bruises that had already been there. He had dirt and mud splattered up his legs and across his thighs.

Turning back to the pond, he took a few steps, then dove back into the water.

Breaking the surface, he shook the water from his hair. "Come on in. The water's fine," he called to Quinn. It really felt pretty good now that he was used to it.

She narrowed her eyes, her brow furrowing as if

trying to make a decision. Then she shook her head and pulled off her boots. "Aw hell," she said, shimmying out of her shorts.

He let out a whoop as her shorts hit the dirt.

She paused, her fingers on the few snaps that held her shirt closed, and giving her head another shake. "What did you say last night? Go big or go home?" She yanked the snaps free and peeled the shirt off, dropping it to the dirt as she ran toward him wearing only her red bra and a tiny pair of matching red bikini panties.

Splashing into the water, she let out a shriek and swam toward him. "This water is freezing," she cried as she surfaced next to him, her wet hair glistening and slicked back against her head.

"I'll keep you warm." He made a grab for her, his body already heating as he pulled her against him, her wet skin slick against his.

Twenty minutes later, they emerged from the pond, laughing and still teasing each other.

Quinn shivered, and Rock grabbed the quilt and shook it out before wrapping it around her shoulders. He rubbed her arms as the soft fabric dried the pond water from her skin.

She'd forgotten just how much fun it was to laugh and play with him. It felt good to have him back, back in her life.

Back in your bed, her quiet inner minx whispered.

Yeah. That was pretty good too.

She held out one side of the blanket. "Here, get in. You need to get dry too."

"If you insist." He offered her a flirty grin, then stepped into the circle of her arms, and she wrapped her arms around him, drying him and gaining warmth from him in the same step. The guy's body was like a furnace.

And speaking of heat.

He leaned down, and her breath caught as he captured her mouth in a kiss. His lips were cool, but his tongue was warm as he teased it between hers. His hands slid around her waist, caressing her skin and pulling her tighter against him.

Her head spun as a whole battalion of butterflies swirled through her stomach. Kissing him and the feel of his hands on her body sent a dizzy wave of sensation coursing through her.

A sensation very similar to happiness.

It was a feeling she hadn't experienced in a long time. The pure joy of being with Rock, being with the man she'd spent over half of her life in love with.

Was she still in love with him?

Had she ever stopped loving this man?

She knew that she loved this feeling. The feeling of his arms around her, of his mouth on hers. And she knew she didn't want it to stop. She wanted this feeling to last. To go on forever.

The melodic chimes of a ringtone filled the air, and Rock pulled back.

"Shoot. That ringtone is my coach. I gotta take that." He'd already pulled away, left her shivering, as he rifled through the tackle box, then held up his phone.

He tapped the screen and held the phone to his ear. "Hey, Coach." He paused as he listened to his coach's reply. "Yeah, I'm feeling good. Really strong. I was actually just doing a light workout—getting in some water therapy." He grinned at Quinn and playfully waggled his eyebrows.

She smiled back, but inside, her heart was breaking—the call just a reminder of the fact that Rock was leaving. That this wasn't going to go on forever, this wasn't going to last.

This whole thing was a temporary distraction—something for Rock to do while he was recuperating.

Cheeks burning, she turned away and quickly pulled her clothes back on, snapping up her shirt and stuffing her feet into her boots as Rock continued to talk to his coach about his recovery.

She folded up the blanket, hugging it to her chest as she picked up her hat and offered him a wave. *I'll see ya later*, she mouthed.

His brow wrinkled, and he shook his head, signaling for her to stay.

But she couldn't. She had to get out of there. Had to get away from him. Away from the reminder that he would soon be gone. That he would go back to Denver and leave her behind.

Again.

She waved off his gestures with a pretend smile that she hoped he believed.

Turning her back, she headed for the trail that led back to the ranch, tugging her hat on her head and praying that it hid the tears that were building as she walked away.

Chapter 14

THE NEXT DAY, QUINN'S MOOD FLUCTUATED FROM HAPPY TO cranky to brooding because she couldn't stop thinking about Rock and what their future did, or didn't, hold.

She'd messed up an order, adding caramel sauce to a coffee when the customer had requested whipped cream, and poured a cup to overflowing as her thoughts wandered. Her mood shifted from pensive to giddy, and she was sure she probably looked like an idiot, walking around the coffee shop all morning with a grin on her face one minute and a scowl the next.

Despite her moodiness, she was surprised at how quickly the day had flown by.

She wasn't even tired. Although she should be.

She'd stayed up late the night before, trying to focus on a book, but actually obsessively checking her phone for a message from Rock.

He'd texted her a little after eleven, telling her he couldn't get her out of his mind and he *had* to see her.

Ten minutes later, he'd been at her window and snuck into her room again. They had spent the rest of the night in her bed, and on her floor, and against the wall of her closet.

Another smile spread across her face as she thought about that first moment when he had climbed through the window and had his hands and mouth on her before she even had time to think. At least that time, she'd locked the door *before* he'd shown up.

"You sure are in a funny mood today," her coworker Carrie said as she stacked the counter with a fresh supply of paper cups to replenish the ones they'd used that morning. "You either seem kind of sad or ridiculously happy."

Quinn shrugged. "It's a weird day. Busy then slow. But I'm fine. Just trying to stay busy."

Carrie gave her a sideways glance. "Yeah, sure. This funny mood wouldn't have anything to do with a certain hockey-playing cowboy that I've heard you've been seen around town with lately, would it?"

"I have no idea what you're talking about." She playfully swatted her with the towel she'd been using to wipe the counters, then headed to the storeroom to get another box of coffee stirrers.

She came out a few minutes later and glanced at the clock, anxious for the last ten minutes of her shift to be over. Her car had been giving her fits again, and Rock had offered to pick her up after her shift ended.

Her body tingled at the anticipation of seeing him again.

The coffee shop was practically empty. An older couple sat by the window, quietly chatting, and one of their regulars had her laptop and a stack of notebooks spread across her normal corner table.

The only other customer was a dark-haired guy who had been at the same table for several hours. He wasn't a local, at least not one she recognized, but his hipster outfit pegged him as a city guy. Not many of the men in Creedence wore skinny jeans, a vest over a V-neck

T-shirt, and loafers with no socks. His hair was cut in a current style and had product in it, and the stylish frames of his glasses looked expensive.

The shop was one of the few places in town that offered free Wi-Fi, so it wasn't unusual for customers to spend a few hours at a table with their computers. But something seemed up with this guy. He'd been to the counter for a refill three times already, and he'd ordered a different pastry each time, which wouldn't have been so unusual if she hadn't seen him sneak one of them into the trash after taking only one bite.

Maybe he was a picky eater or hadn't liked the pastry, but he'd also kept sneaking furtive glances at her, and she'd seen him cozying up to Carrie, chatting like old friends with her coworker.

He did smell good though, she noted as he approached the counter again and held up his empty cup. "Any chance I could get another refill?"

"Of course," she said, taking his cup. "I haven't seen you around before. Are you new in town?"

"Nope. Just visiting. But I am intrigued with the local sights." He offered her a flirty grin.

Uh. Was that some kind of pickup line?

"Colorado is a beautiful state."

He leaned his hip casually against the counter. "And it's got some beautiful women."

Yep. That was definitely a pickup line—not a very good one, but a line just the same. And how was she supposed to respond to that? Say thank you?

Best to ignore it.

She passed him the refilled cup. "Here ya go."

"I'm Gavin, by the way." He held out his hand.

She took it, noting that his handshake was firm and confident. "Quinn."

"Nice to meet you, Quinn. I've been watching you the last few hours."

Watching her? Um, creepy.

"Not in a weird sort of way." He cocked one eyebrow in a way she assumed was meant to be suave or debonair. "But you know, in an interested sort of way. I've bought three pastries from you while I tried to figure out how to meet you and invite you out for dinner."

"Oh. Well, I…"

"Don't worry. I won't embarrass you by making you turn me down. I heard that you're already dating someone." He glanced at Carrie, who had obviously been listening but was now completely absorbed in cleaning the coffee machine.

"Thank you." What the heck was she thanking him for? She didn't know what else to say.

"Hey, you can't fault a guy for trying, right? Although it sounds like the guy you're dating isn't someone I want to mess with. He's big, right? A hockey player?"

She glared at her coworker.

Blabbermouth.

"He plays for Colorado, right? What's his name? Stone? Rock? James? I think I heard somewhere that he lived up in this area. He got hurt recently, didn't he? How's he doing?"

A funny feeling tingled at the base of Quinn's spine. This guy was suddenly asking a lot of questions. Her body stiffened, and she took a small step backward. "Where did you say you were from again?"

Before he could answer, the object of his inquiries walked in the door.

Quinn's breath caught. Rock had on jeans and a light-blue T-shirt that emphasized his tan skin and stretched across his broad, muscled chest. He wore cowboy boots and looked hot as hell as he sauntered into the coffee shop, a flirty grin on his face. A grin just for her.

But the easy grin fell away when he saw the dark-haired guy standing at the counter. Not just fell, but plummeted. It was replaced by a look of anger, and he drew his shoulders back, making him appear taller and even bigger than he already was as he strode toward them.

What the heck? She didn't see Rock get angry very often. And the sudden shift of mood caught her off guard.

Was he jealous?

The guy must have seen the change of expression on her face, because he turned his head, but instead of looking scared or terrified, which would have been any normal person's reaction if they saw a huge, pissed-off guy stalking angrily toward them, he almost seemed excited to see Rock.

His eyes gleamed, and his cheeks appeared to flush slightly. In fact, the way he looked at Rock showed a heck of a lot more interest than he'd just shown in her when he was talking about asking her out to dinner.

What was that about? Seriously, the guy was practically salivating.

"Hey, Quinn," Rock said, his body tense as he eyed the other man suspiciously. "What's going on here?" His voice was hard as steel, his shoulders were pulled back, and his broad muscles strained at the seams of his shirt.

His eyes flashed with fury as he glanced between her and the other man.

Was he angry at her?

Her back stiffened. "I was just serving this gentleman a refill on his coffee."

"Gentleman, my ass."

"Rock." Her voice came out in the same tone she used with Max when he said something that was impolite.

The man held out his hand. "Hi. I'm Gavin. I'm a big fan."

A big fan? What?

Rock ignored his outstretched hand. "I know who you are. And I've got nothing to say to you." He glared over at Quinn. "And I hope you don't either."

Gavin didn't seem bothered by Rock's rude behavior. "You look pretty good, Rock. How are you getting along with your injuries? When do you think you'll be back with the team?"

Rock disregarded the comment and gave Quinn a callous glare. "Have you been talking to this guy?"

"What?" What in the world was going on? Why was Rock acting like this? And how did he even know who this guy was? "What do you mean? Of course I've been talking to him. I made him his coffee. He's a customer."

"He's no customer. He's a reporter. Works for the *Denver Herald* or something. And I guarantee he's not here for the coffee."

Dang it. A reporter. She should have known. She knew something was up with the guy.

The reporter wasn't fazed by Rock's behavior at all. He kept asking questions, like a dog with a bone. "That was a pretty big hit. Are you pressing charges against the guy?"

Rock didn't answer, his lips pressed tightly together as he glared down at the smaller man.

"Come on, man. Give me a break here. You gotta tell me something."

Rock flexed the muscles of his fingers as he took a step closer, towering over the reporter and glaring down at him. "I have plenty of things I want to tell you, starting with what you can do with your questions, but I'm going to stick with 'no comment' and ask you to leave."

Gavin looked around the mostly empty coffee shop. "It's a free country. And like your friend said, I'm a customer."

Rock's hard stare flicked between the reporter and Quinn. "I'll be in the truck," he growled, then stomped from the shop, letting the door slam behind him.

"Geez. What's his problem?"

"His problem is creeps like you who follow him to his hometown and try to trick the people he knows into giving you some dirt on him. Our business here is done." She pulled her apron over her head and tossed it on the counter.

"My shift is over, Carrie," she said, turning to her coworker, who was acting busy wiping the counter, but who Quinn knew had been hanging on every word of the whole conversation. "I'm going home. I have nothing to say to this cretin, and I'll assume that you don't either. Right?"

Carrie shook her head. "No, of course not. I won't say anything. I'm sorry. I didn't know he was a reporter. I just thought he was interested in asking you out."

Quinn rolled her eyes. "I don't need your help in finding a date either. And you can make it up to me by not giving this guy any more information about me or anyone in this town." She grabbed her purse from the cabinet under the counter and snatched a blueberry muffin from the bakery case. "And I'm taking this. Put it on my account."

She turned back to the reporter. "We're done here. Neither one of us has anything else to say."

He glanced between the two women as if weighing the chances of getting any more information out of either of them. He must have realized that chance was zero, because he set his cup down on the counter and offered them a shrug.

His friendly features morphed into hostile ones as his lips curled into a sneer. "Okay. Suit yourself. But for the record, I wasn't really interested in taking some Podunk country girl out to dinner. And the coffee here sucks."

"Oh wow, now you've really gone and hurt my feelings. I really wanted to go out with a slimy little worm like you, but I'll just have to settle for going to dinner with my hot as hell, rich and famous, hockey-playing boyfriend."

He smirked.

Shoot. She'd just called Rock her boyfriend. Stupid reporter. Had he deliberately baited her?

Anger boiled up, not just at the arrogant little weasel, but because his comment about her being a Podunk country girl had hit a little too close to home.

She glanced down at the cup of coffee on the counter and considered tossing the remains into his smug, smirking face.

But that would only add more fuel to the fire, and she didn't want to give him any more ammunition.

Instead, she pressed her shoulders back and held her chin up as she marched out of the shop.

Rock was sitting in the truck, his face a stony mask

of fury as she grabbed the handle and yanked the door open.

The cab practically radiated fury as he hunched over the steering wheel, the veins in his neck protruding and his leg bouncing on the floorboard in an agitated tempo.

"Were you talking to that guy?" He practically spat out the words. "Giving him a story? About me?"

He was scary mad, but she wasn't afraid of him. She knew he would never hurt her. Not physically. He had *hurt* her, of course. He'd broken her heart into a million pieces when he'd broken up with her to go off and have his fancy, big-shot career. When he'd left behind the simple country girl, who Gavin from the *Denver Herald* had just reminded her she was.

She glared at Rock as she crammed the seat belt into the buckle. Her own anger and humiliation of being duped and insulted bubbling up in her. "Hell no. I didn't even know he was a reporter. And it pisses me off that you think I would talk to someone about you."

"Well, it pisses me off to come to pick you up from work and see you talking to a reporter. I hate reporters."

"Welllll, I hate it when a guy acts like a jerk and accuses me of doing something I wasn't even doing."

"Maybe you didn't know you were doing it. Those guys are slimy. They get you to answer questions and give them information without even knowing that you're doing it. What did you say to him?"

"Nothing." A tiny sliver of guilt rippled through her. She had called him her boyfriend. But Carrie had pretty much already confirmed that fact before the guy had even said a word to her. "I didn't say anything about you. I didn't even know he was interested in you until right before you walked in the door."

"What does that mean?"

"It means that he acted like he was interested in me." *Acted* was the right word, since he'd made it clear that it would be ridiculous for him to be interested in a hick girl like herself. She tried to shake it off, but the words, and the memories of Rock leaving her, still stung.

"Interested in you, how?"

"You know, interested in asking me out."

Rock's knuckles turned white on the steering wheel, and he reached for the truck handle. "Well, that little…" he growled.

She reached out and grabbed his arm. His bicep was hard as a rock, taut with his tightened muscles. "Rock, don't. Leave it alone. If you go in there and slug him, you'll only give him more of a story."

His hand stilled on the truck's handle, but his body remained tense. "What did you tell him?"

"I said yes. We've got plans for Saturday night." She couldn't help herself. What did he think she would say?

His head whipped back toward her. "What?"

"Geez, Rock. Do you seriously think I'd agree to go out with that guy? With *any* other guy? After the last few days with you? What the hell do you think I told him?"

He glared at her, his lips set in a tight line. "I'm sorry," he said quietly through gritted teeth. "I just really hate reporters."

"So you said. Repeatedly. I'm not a dumb-ass. I get it," she said, her voice too loud for the small cab of the truck and still carrying the tone of anger.

"So how did you leave it? After I left? Was he still trying to get a story?"

"No, he insulted me and our coffee, and I called him a slimy worm and told him he was nothing compared to you, and I stormed out." She held up the pastry. "And I grabbed you this blueberry muffin, you jerk."

His eyes widened, and a tiny smirk pulled at the corners of his lips. "I don't know which pleases me more, that you called him a slimy worm or that you thought to bring me a baked good."

She sat back against the seat, the tension in her shoulders easing as she set the pastry on the seat between them. "Just eat your muffin and drive."

He let out a low chuckle and picked up the small cake, stuffing it into his mouth in two big bites. "It's good," he said around the bite in his mouth. "Blueberry's my favorite."

She crossed her arms over her chest. "I know."

He grinned, a tiny crumb of muffin clinging to the corner of his lip. "Thanks," he said, then put the truck in gear and headed for the ranch.

Rock's temper had eased on the drive home, and he turned to Quinn as he pulled up to her house and turned off the engine. "I'm sorry, darlin'. I overreacted."

Her arms were still crossed, and her bottom lip pushed forward in a slight pout. "Yeah, you did."

"You're right to be angry. I could have handled that better." He took a deep breath and let it out slowly. "I just hate those guys. They're always in my business. I used to try to be nice to them, give 'em quotes and interviews, but I've been burned too many times when they've misquoted me or taken bits and pieces of what I said and turned it into something else. The press likes to portray me as this asshole brawler who's some kind of womanizing playboy."

She arched an eyebrow at him.

"Okay, so I might be a brawler, and I've been known to be an asshole on occasion, but I'm no womanizer. I have the utmost respect for women." He offered her the smallest of smiles. "One woman in particular."

"That's just because you know your mama would track you down and beat you with a wooden spoon if you didn't."

He let out a laugh. "Yes, she would." He nudged her leg. "I really am sorry, Q. I should have known that you wouldn't talk to a reporter about me. Not on purpose, anyway."

"I didn't even know he was a reporter."

"I know. That's what I meant by not on purpose. All I'm asking is that in the future, you be wary when someone starts asking too many questions about me."

She nodded and uncrossed her arms. "I hear you. I'm not used to this."

"I know. And it sucks. And I hate that being associated with me puts you in contact with skuzzballs like that guy."

"It's okay. I can take it. I'm pretty tough."

"I know you are." He did know it. Her sassy mouth had taken him to task more times than he could count. But it was also one of the things he loved about her.

He loved that she could hold her own in a fight. He had at times riled her up just so he could see the spark in her eyes, and right now, looking at her pouty red lips, all he could think about was capturing her feisty mouth in a hard kiss.

She jutted her chin out. "But I need you to believe that I would never purposely tell someone about your personal business."

Or *our* personal business. If things kept going with Quinn the way they had been, she may get more than she bargained for in the way of the nosy public.

"I do believe you. And you're the first person I'd pick to be in my corner during a fight." He leaned across the seat to set a tender kiss on her lips — not the kind of kiss he wanted to give her, but the best choice for in the cab of his truck, in broad daylight, in her family's driveway.

A grin curved the corners of her lips as he pulled back and tucked a stray strand of her hair behind her ear.

"You taste like sweet talk and blueberries," she said.

"You taste like heaven."

Butterflies swirled in his stomach as her face broke into a smile.

Damn, but he did love her smile.

She shook her head and reached for the door handle.

He jumped out, ruminating on how many things he'd just pitched around in his mind that he loved about her. And he didn't usually toss around the word *love* lightly.

It wasn't really a big shocker. Heck, he'd been in love with Quinn since before he even understood what being in love meant.

But he didn't remember it being like this. Teenage love was all-consuming, the only thing he could think about, dream about. It took over his mind and his heart and every moment of his day. She was all he could think about, wondering what she was doing, what she was eating, and when they were together, his limbs ached to constantly be touching her.

Ah, dang. Considering how he'd been mooning around over Quinn the last few days, maybe it was just like that. Maybe he was just like that lovestruck teenager who would have done anything for the girl he loved.

Well, anything but take her with him when he left for the greatest adventure of his life.

He let out a sigh.

It was no use going back. They couldn't change the past.

But maybe, for the first time in years, he let himself believe that they just might have a future.

She was out of the truck before he could get around to help her out, but she paused on the porch steps, shading her eyes with her hand as she peered back at the faded blue sedan that sat in the driveway. "I wonder whose car that is."

It had a crack just starting on one side of the windshield and was covered in dust.

Another roar of anger rumbled through his chest. "It better not be that reporter. I'll throw that guy out on his ass."

"I'll help," Quinn said as she opened the door and marched into the living room.

He followed in her steps, then almost ran into her as she stopped in the middle of the room.

He heard her quick gasp of breath, saw the color drain from her face, and his gaze darted around the room, trying to assess what was happening.

Dark tension filled the room, and he knew something was wrong.

Logan stood by the stone fireplace, his arms crossed, his legs slightly apart as if in a fighter's stance. His eyes were cold and hard as he stared at the man sitting in the chair in front of him.

The man's back was to him and Quinn, and he didn't recognize him. All he could see of him was his pressed western shirt and a dark head of hair.

But Quinn recognized him.

He could tell by the way she stood frozen in place, her posture rigid and her eyes giving off that deer-in-the-headlights look.

Her arm was pressed against his, and he could feel her trembling. What the hell was going on? His protective instincts kicked in, and he took a step forward.

But she held her arm out, stopping him. Not saying anything, just stopping him with the pressure of her hand.

A child's laugh filled the air, and he realized Max was sitting on the floor in front of the man, his face tipped up, his expression rapt.

The boy must have seen his mom though, because his eyes lit, and he scrambled up off the floor and ran toward her. "Mom, look! Look who's here! It's my dad! He came to see me!"

Ho-ly shit.

Chapter 15

It was Rock's turn to stand frozen in place as the dark-haired man stood and turned around.

Monty fucking Hill.

He couldn't believe it. What the ever-loving hell was he doing here?

It was clear from Quinn's expression that she didn't have a clue either.

His gaze snapped to Logan. Had he had something to do with this? Had he brought this guy here to keep Quinn from being with him?

Quinn's brother glared at Monty's back. No, he obviously hadn't had anything to do with it either.

Had Max somehow contacted him? Or had his questions about his father somehow conjured him out of thin air?

Monty ducked his head. "Hey there, Quinn. Long time, no see."

Rock watched the muscles tighten in her jaw as she looked from Hill to Max, obviously fighting to hold back what she really wanted to say.

And he was sure she had a lot to say.

"What are you doing here?" she finally choked out.

"I was passing through and thought I'd drop in to see my boy." He wrapped an arm around Max's shoulder, and Rock wanted to knock it away. In fact, he wanted to punch the deadbeat in the throat. Then kick him in the nuts, then punch him in the face. And he would just be getting started.

My boy?

Shee-it. Why was he here all of a sudden, claiming Max was his?

Rock ignored the clawing in his gut that reminded him that Max really was *his* boy.

"You look good, Quinn. You haven't aged a bit." Hill offered her a smile that was a cross between friendly and flirty.

Rock's hands curled into fists. After he punched him, he was considering running him over with his truck.

She didn't return the smile. Her lips pressed into a flat line, and a vein pulsed in her neck.

Monty held out a hand to Rock. "Monty Hill. You're Rock James, right? I think we played football against each other in high school."

Hill knew damn well who he was.

For the second time that day, Rock ignored a snake's outstretched hand.

But this was a different kind of snake than the reporter. The press guy was an annoying garter snake that wound its way through the grass and caused a fright when it slithered next to his foot. Hill was more like a rattler—a coiled-up predator full of venom that no one knew when it would strike. Or who it would hurt.

Well, screw that. He knew how to take care of a rattler. He stamped on its mouth with his boot heel or chopped its head off with a shovel. That was the only way to keep it from hurting someone, and Rock wasn't going to let that snake hurt Quinn or Max. Not his family.

He took a step forward, then stopped in his tracks, his knees threatening to buckle underneath him.

Quinn and Max *weren't* his family.

He didn't have any claim to them at all.

In fact, Max was Monty's son, so they were Hill's family.

That thought sobered him quickly, especially when he looked down and saw Max's sweet face as he looked up to him with adoration.

Shit. Max also looked at Monty that way. Like that asswipe hung the freaking moon. Quinn had told him that she had been careful never to talk poorly of Monty around Max, because she didn't want to give him any more issues—it was enough that he had been abandoned by his father; she didn't want to add in that Monty had rejected him as well.

So instead, Max was acting like Hill was some kind of hero who had just swooped in to save the day.

And how could he wreck that impression? How could he take that away from Max—one of the sweetest kids he'd ever met. A kid he had already fallen in love with.

His head pounded, the headache back with a vengeance as indecision tore through him.

What the hell was he supposed to say? To do?

Should he stay here and support Quinn or back away and let them have time to figure out what was going on? He wanted to be here for Quinn, but he wasn't sure he had that right.

He tried to gauge what she was feeling, what she wanted, but for once was at a loss.

Her face was pale, a blank mask void of emotion. Her shoulders were tight, and she stood with her legs planted in a stance of fight or flight.

Although he knew she'd never pick flight, she'd never abandon Max or walk away from him. No. Leaving was Rock's department. And, apparently, Monty's.

Bile filled the back of his throat at his comparison to this slimeball guy who had abandoned his family, who had walked away from the people who needed him the most.

Pain seared through his head, and he gave it the smallest shake, as if to clear the idea that he had done the same thing.

He couldn't feel Quinn trembling anymore, and he realized she'd taken just the barest step *away* from him instead of toward him.

Maybe that was the answer he was looking for. Maybe she didn't need him at all.

She could fight her own battles—had been fighting them on her own for years, without his help or concern.

But he hadn't been back in her life like he was now. Maybe she needed him now. Maybe this time he could do something.

A hard notion hit him. Maybe she wanted Monty to be back in Max's life. Maybe she wanted Max to have his dad around. She'd told him that Monty had walked away, but she'd never really said if she'd wanted him to stay.

He needed to talk to her, to get her away from this situation so he could find out what was going on in her head, what she needed from him, what she needed him to do or *not* do.

Somehow, he didn't think she'd approve of his idea to punch the guy in the throat and kick him out on his ass, at least not in front of Max.

The front door banged open, and Hamilton stormed in, his face a mix of fury and concern as he headed straight for Monty. He towered over Hill and glared down at him. "What the hell are you doing here?"

"I came to visit my son," Monty said, his voice hard as he stared back at Ham, as if daring him to throw a fist.

That was not a dare that any sane man would make. Ham might be in his fifties, but the guy was hard as steel, his body lean and muscled, and Rock had seen him wrestle a steer twice the size of Monty to the ground just last week when they were branding.

Hamilton Rivers defined the word *tough* in *tough as nails*.

He held his ground, staring Monty down with eyes that were glinty and hard. His jaw was set, and a vein pulsed next to his eye. The cords in his throat strained against the skin of his neck, and his hands clenched in tight fists at his sides.

The air crackled with tension as the group held their collective breaths, waiting to see what Ham would do.

"Grandpa?" Max's small voice broke through the silence.

This was it. This moment would tell Rock what Quinn was feeling. If she would let her dad do the thing that Rock, and most likely Logan, wanted to do. Would she let her dad sock this guy in the face? Would she let him kick him out?

Quinn stood next to her dad, her gaze darting between Ham, Monty, and Max. Without saying a word, she held out her hand and placed in on Ham's arm, a silent message that shouted "stand down, soldier."

And that was all it took.

All that Rock needed to know. She didn't want them to throw Monty out.

At least not in front of Max.

He should go. This was obviously a family thing, and he was obviously the outsider. Everyone else in the room was related to one another in some regard.

Except for him.

He opened his mouth to tell Quinn that he was going to go, but before he could speak, she took a step forward, a step closer to Monty.

"Could I speak to you a minute? Alone?" Her voice was a tight blend of anger and control.

And broke Rock's heart.

Monty tore his gaze from Ham's and took a step back, surrendering his stance of power. "Sure. No problem."

She gestured toward the den off to the side of the kitchen, and Monty turned and headed in that direction.

Rock didn't know their whole history, but the guy must have been around enough to be familiar with the house. He obviously knew the layout as he opened the french doors and stepped through.

Quinn followed behind him, her steps heavy, her shoulders slumped, as if she were headed to the gallows instead of into the study.

She turned, and Rock waited to see where her gaze would fall. Who would she look to for support? He held his breath as he prayed for her gaze to turn toward him, to glance his way, to seek his encouragement.

But she didn't.

Avoiding anyone's eyes in the room, she kept her head down and pulled the doors shut behind her with a resounding click.

———∽∿∾———

Quinn swallowed, her throat dry as she tried to think of something to say.

She had plenty to say, but somehow didn't think covering him with a river of violent swear words would be the best way to get the conversation off on the right foot.

Leaning her hip against the side of the desk, she took a deep breath and unclenched her hands. "Okay, Monty, it's just us. Now you can tell me what the hell you're really doing here."

Okay, maybe not a river of swear words, but she couldn't hold back at least a small trickle of a stream.

"I told you. I'm here to see Max." His shoulders slumped forward. "And to apologize to you. I probably could have handled the way I took off a little better."

"Oh, you mean when you used me at that party and then acted like nothing ever happened between us? Or do you mean when I told you I was pregnant and you denied that Max could be yours? Or do you mean when I sucked up my pride and offered to let you be part of Max's life after he was born, and instead, you took off, and I had to hear from Melinda down at the Burger Barn that you'd left town and never even told me, or your son, goodbye?"

"Yeah, that would pretty much be what I meant." He offered her a shrug and a coy smile that she assumed he meant to be charming.

It wasn't.

That charismatic bad-boy charm wasn't going to work on her. She'd fallen for it before. She wasn't about to fall victim to it again.

She narrowed her eyes as she studied him. He looked different, not unrecognizable, but older, and not exactly the cool teenage bad boy she'd first met. He was still good-looking, but he'd cleaned up; his jeans were neat and minus the trademark holes and tears that used to be a constant part of his wardrobe.

The night she'd met him, he'd been wearing a faded T-shirt with the sleeves cut off, his significant adolescent muscles on full display. His hair had been just a little too long, as if he hadn't had time to get it cut versus he wore it that way on purpose. The real truth had been that he couldn't afford to get his hair cut, couldn't afford new jeans that didn't have rips and faded fabric thin from wear.

He'd had a green John Deere hat, the kind with the mesh in the back, which he'd always worn back then, giving him that cute plowboy look.

Today, he had on a pressed, button-up western shirt, although the visible creases made it clear it had just come out of the package. His jeans also looked new, along with the fresh haircut. But his boots were scuffed and worn, and his hands seemed calloused and dry. A thin line of dirt or grease ran under the length of his thumbnail.

He'd obviously worked hard to give the impression that he was doing fine for himself, but his watch—a cheap knockoff with a faded band—gave him away.

"Why now? Why after all of these years of not even recognizing that he was your son are you suddenly here wanting to see him?"

"I get why you'd be confused. I've been a jerk. I know that. But I've made some significant changes in my life, and I swear, I'm here to make amends."

"What kind of changes?"

"It all started when I got into some trouble down in Texas."

"That doesn't sound like much of a change."

He shrugged. "I deserve that. But I'm telling you, I have changed. I'm not like that anymore. As part of my sentence, I had to join this men's group and attend it and counseling once a week. It changed my life. These guys are the real deal, and they've shown me the error of my ways and the real path to the truth and the light."

Quinn almost choked. She was a firm believer in the power of prayer and had seen the hand of God work in mysterious ways, but she'd been fooled by Monty before and had a hard time believing his arrogance would yield to a complete one-eighty of his earlier beliefs. Plus, his words held the slightest tone of drama, like he'd memorized the lines and was putting on a performance.

She narrowed her eyes, studying him as she tried to discern if he was truly being sincere and really had been touched by faith. "Are you serious right now? You're telling me you are back, that you traveled all the way here from Texas and are now ready to recognize Max as your son because you suddenly found Jesus?"

He cringed, and she *almost* believed her words had hurt him. "It's not a joke. I know I used to give you a hard time for going to church and believing in all of that stuff."

Gave her a hard time? Was that what he called it? She remembered when she'd called him to tell him she was getting the baby baptized at the same church where she'd grown up, where she and her brother had been baptized.

Monty had chastised her and informed her in no uncertain terms that he would *not* be taking part in some foolish tradition with a bunch of judgmental hypocrites who thought handing out casseroles and sprinkling some water on a baby's head would grant them access to heaven. Which was another thing he'd expressed disbelief in.

"Monty, you told me once that you would rather go to hell in a limo with Satan as the driver than set foot in a church. So yeah, I have a hard time believing you."

"Believe it. It's true. I know I wasn't the most supportive when you used to talk about wanting to go to church and to raise our kid there, but I finally understand what all this faith stuff is about."

She wrinkled her nose, as if his words, the bullshit he was selling, carried a bad scent.

She didn't know what to believe. This had to be a con, a scam. There had to be more to his story than he was letting on. She knew faith could change a person, but she'd never known Monty to be real susceptible to change. "So what do you want from us?"

"I just want a chance to get to know my son."

She cringed every time he called Max his son. Even if it was true, he had denied it for so long, the words carried a false note. "What does that mean, exactly?"

"It means that I moved back from Texas. I'm staying with one of my brothers, and I'd like to be able to spend some time with Max. Get to know the kid. And get to know you again."

Well, that damn sure wasn't happening. She had no interest in getting to know him again. He was a bygone that would stay a bygone, as far as she was concerned.

She wasn't going to be sucked back in by an old flame that had burned the hell out of her.

Although that's exactly what had been happening the last week. She'd been getting sucked in by not just an old flame, but a full-on forest fire, and a fire that had not only burned her, but left her heart seared and scarred.

Rock.

She'd given Rock another chance.

But Monty wasn't Rock. She'd never been in love with Monty. Never given him her entire heart.

And this guy was nothing like Rock.

Still, he had told her he wanted a second chance, that he had changed, just like Monty was saying, and she had given him a chance.

Except with Monty, it wasn't just giving him a chance to hurt her; she was opening up the possibility that he could hurt her son. And she wouldn't let anything happen to Max.

But what if Monty was telling the truth? What if he really had had a life-altering experience and had truly changed and was trying to make a fresh start? Last week's sermon had been about how all things were possible with God, but she had a hard time believing even God could change this man.

A hard thought struck her—one that twisted her gut and had the acid churning in her stomach.

What if by keeping Max away from Monty, she was hurting him more?

She'd always tried to shelter Max from learning what

kind of man his father really was, but what if he was old enough now to judge for himself?

And what if Monty really had changed, and she was keeping her son from having a chance to get to know and have a relationship with his father?

She chewed at the loose cuticle on the side of her thumbnail, weighing her options, then let out a sigh. "Fine. You can see Max. But only for short visits, and I'm always going to be there."

Monty's face lit with what appeared to be a genuine smile. "That's fine. That's great even. Let's get started."

"Slow down there, slugger. We need to establish some ground rules first."

"Rules? What kind of rules?" His tone darkened for a moment with an obvious disregard for authority.

She narrowed her eyes in a glare, and he backed off.

"Okay, yeah, sure. Some rules are fine. Like what?"

Except for that one moment that his expression slipped, he still seemed altogether too agreeable. She didn't like it. And she still didn't trust him. But she'd give him a chance. For Max's sake.

"No keeping him up past his bedtime, no feeding him sugar and caffeine without asking me first, no undermining my parenting, and no daring him to do anything stupid that could get him hurt."

Monty nodded. "That sounds reasonable."

"In fact, he's not allowed to do any kind of activity that could involve him getting hurt."

This time he pulled a face. "Come on, that seems a little unreasonable. He could get hurt walking across the driveway. Or just in normal roughhousing."

"Max doesn't do much roughhousing."

"Why not? Is there something wrong with him? Is he sick? Is there something you've been keeping from me?"

"Geez. No. He's not sick. He just doesn't play like that. He's not into wrestling and horseplay."

"What is he into?"

She shrugged. "Bugs and dinosaurs and books. He loves to read."

"Books? What about sports? Doesn't he play baseball or football?"

Quinn let out a laugh. "No. He doesn't. My dad tried to get him to play T-ball one year, and that was a bust. And just a few weeks ago, I heard Logan try to get him to go outside and play catch, and Max politely declined."

Monty wrinkled his forehead. "What kind of kid doesn't want to play catch?"

She let out a sigh. This wasn't going to be easy. "The kind of kid that Max is. You said you wanted to get to know him."

He held up his hands. "Okay, you're right. I just want a chance to hang out with him. Does he have some time now?"

Another sigh escaped her. "I guess so, sure." She opened the doors of the den.

Her dad, brother, and son all sat morosely in the living room.

Rock was gone.

Her heart stuttered. He hadn't even waited around to tell her goodbye or see if she was okay.

Was she okay? She had no idea.

That's not true. She would be okay. She had to be. She was a mom. That's what moms did. Or were supposed to do. Moms made everything okay.

She pasted on a smile, avoiding her dad and brother's gaze. "Well, it looks like Monty is going to be sticking around for a little bit." She couldn't bring herself to say *your dad*. "Would you like that, Max?"

Max's eyes widened, and he jumped off the sofa and ran to her, throwing his arms around her legs. "Thanks, Mom. You're the best." He turned and offered a shy smile to Monty.

Monty returned the smile and bent down to Max's level. "I brought an old football with me to toss around if you want to go outside and play a little catch?"

Hadn't he heard a word she'd said?

"Sure," Max answered. "That sounds fun."

Wait—what? *That sounds fun?* Who was this kid and what had he done with her son?

"Come on." Max took Monty's hand and led him out the front door.

She offered an incredulous look to her father and brother, who both looked just as dumbfounded, then followed them out the door.

Monty really had brought an old football with him, and he carried it into the front yard and lobbed a gentle throw at the small boy.

Max completely missed the ball, the oblong shape slipping through his hands. But instead of getting upset, he giggled and laughed like his blunder was the funniest thing he'd seen all day.

His toss back to Monty was clumsy and woefully short of its mark, and Quinn waited for Monty to reprimand him or give him a hard time for his terrible throw. But he didn't.

He was surprisingly patient with Max as he recovered

the ball and offered the boy tips on where to hold it and how to throw it.

Max butchered throw after throw, but he didn't lose his determination, and Monty kept his cool.

Quinn sat on the porch steps, watching them play, but zoning out as Monty regaled Max with tales of his high school glory days on the football team of Franklin High. She didn't recall those days as being all that glorious.

But Max seemed enraptured with every word out of Monty's mouth. His energy never waned as he continued to try to master the art of catch. And his skills did seem to improve.

"Good job, champ," Monty said as he caught one of Max's better throws.

Her son beamed with pride at the compliment.

She tried to keep her eyes from rolling.

Was she making the right decision here? Should she let Max spend time with Monty? What if he hurt him? Not if—when? Because she had no doubt in her mind that Monty would end up hurting her boy.

The only problem was she didn't know what she could do about it.

She wasn't a coward, so she wouldn't run away or hide.

Killing him seemed out of the question—but only marginally so.

For now, all she could do was keep on her toes and keep a watchful eye on Monty. He claimed he had changed, and maybe he had, maybe he did deserve a second chance, but she wasn't about to let her guard down.

Not for one minute.

—∿—

Quinn was putting the finishing touches on supper later that night when she heard her father come in the front door, followed by the sound of small footsteps running down the hall.

She heard Max greet Ham, then listened as he regaled him with stories of all the things he'd done with Monty that afternoon.

Thankfully, she'd put a roast in the Crock-Pot that morning, so all she'd had to do was boil a few ears of corn and throw together a salad. She put the last of the meal on the table, then slumped into her chair as Ham and Max washed their hands and joined her.

Her dad had barely finished the blessing when Max started up again.

He filled his plate as he talked, using his spoon to dump a large mound of butter next to his corn. His small hand shook the pepper shaker, black flakes raining down onto the bright-yellow butter. "And then he showed me how to put my fingers between the laces to throw the football. He said I'd get a better spin on it then. My dad—he's a real smart guy."

Oh yeah. He's a smart one all right. Quinn's gaze was fixed on her son's plate, seemingly transfixed as she watched him shake the salt, then stir the butter mixture together before swirling his corn through it.

Her father was doing the same thing, absently spinning his corn in his own butter, salt, and pepper mixture as he listened to Max talk. She wondered if her forehead held the same crease of concern that was evident on Ham's.

Logan was filling in at The Creed tonight, so it was just the three of them. Well, four, if you count Monty, who, although he had driven away an hour ago, still seemed to be present in the room with them.

Her dad didn't say much throughout the meal. Neither did she.

She figured they were both trying to keep their mouths shut as Max chattered on—and on—about how great his dad was. A little sliver of pain sliced through her heart, and she tried not to wince every time he said *my dad*, as if Monty were getting equal billing in this parenting gig, even though she'd done all the work the last eight years.

"Mom? Mom?"

Max's voice cut into her thoughts. "Yeah, baby?"

"I was telling you about how my dad is a famous bull rider. He told me he's been in hundreds of rodeos. Did you know he rode bulls?"

"I know he's full of bull," she muttered, then wished she could take it back as her son's thin shoulders drooped and his small brow furrowed.

"What's wrong? Why are you being so mean?"

Dang. How was she supposed to answer that?

She let out a sigh. "I'm sorry, Max. I've just had a long day."

"You're acting like you're mad. Did I do something to make you mad?"

"No, of course not."

"Aren't you happy that my dad came to see me?"

She swallowed back the cutting remark forming in her mind and tried to soften her tone. "Yeah, sure I am, buddy."

Max looked down at his plate, his own voice dropping a degree in volume. "I'm sure glad. I've been wishing and praying that he would come. And now he's here, and I feel so happy, like my heart is gonna bust out of my chest. But you just seem mad and kinda sad, and that makes me feel bad about being so happy."

Oh. Ouch.

She took a deep breath, pushing down all of the negative feelings she had toward Monty, and forced a smile. She could do this. She could pretend for Max's sake. She could do anything for Max's sake.

Even spend time in the company of the low-down snake who had slept with her and then had always denied even being Max's father.

"I'm not mad. I'm just tired," she said, trying her best to sound genuine. Hell, she *was* tired. That wasn't a lie. "I'm glad for you that you are getting a chance to meet your father." She tried not to choke on the word *father*.

"I'm glad too. Super-duper glad. I like him. I think he's pretty great."

Of course you do.

Another stab to her heart.

It's easy to seem great when all he had to do was show up one afternoon and toss a football and a few compliments around. He wasn't the one who had to set a consistent schedule, and wipe a snotty nose, or clean up vomit, or say no to more television or computer when it would be so much easier just to give in and say yes.

No. All of those things were what she'd had to do, what she still had to do, alone. Sure, her dad and her brother helped, but the majority of Max's parenting came down to her. Success or failure fell squarely on her shoulders.

"Why don't you help me clear the table, then get cleaned up?" She looked over at her dad. "I'll wash these dishes if you can find him some clean pajamas and get him started with the shower."

"Sure," Ham said, already pushing his chair back and lifting his plate to carry it to the kitchen. Max followed suit with his plate and glass, then tore off down the hallway toward his room.

Ham brought in the last of the dishes as Quinn filled the sink with water, squirting in a healthy dose of liquid detergent. Her dad prided himself on being frugal and had never seen the need for a dishwasher, and on nights like tonight, the menial task of washing the dishes was just what she needed.

Being in the kitchen alone, she sang along to the country music station on the radio as she let the hot water and the chore of scrubbing the dishes take her mind off the problems of her son, her newfound relationship with her old boyfriend, and the unexpected arrival of Monty Hill.

She finished washing the last pan and was just wiping down the counters when her dad stepped back into the kitchen.

He leveled her with a steely stare. "Just what in the Sam Hill do you think you're doing?"

Chapter 16

QUINN BRUSHED THE CRUMBS FROM THE COUNTER INTO THE sink. "I'm cleaning the kitchen. What does it look like I'm doing?"

"You know darn well what I'm talking about. What the hell do you think you're doing letting that dirtbag Hill back into your and Max's lives?"

"I didn't *let* him do anything. He just showed up today."

"You didn't call him? I know Max has been asking about him a lot lately."

"Hell no, I didn't call him. I don't even have a number for him. I didn't even know where he was living. I'm just as surprised as you are to see him."

"Why is he here? And better yet. What does he want?"

She shrugged. "I don't really know. He said all he wants is a chance to get to know Max."

"Horse pucky. I don't believe it. There has to be something else to it."

"He claims that he recently found religion." She picked up the dish towel and dried her hands.

"He's about to find my size-12 boot up his ass." He snatched the toothpick holder from the counter, shook one out, and clamped it between his teeth. "And I don't buy that story for a minute. Surely you're not falling for this guy's line of bull?"

"No, I'm not falling for anything. I'm simply giving my son a chance to get to know his father."

Ham shook his head, gnawing the toothpick flat between his teeth. "I swear, I don't know what you're thinking lately. First, you start up again with that no-good James boy—"

"Oh brother. Dad, you've known Rock since he was a kid." Her head was spinning. How had this conversation just switched from her letting Monty back into Max's life to her starting back up again with Rock?

"Yeah, well, I also know that he left you high and dry and brokenhearted when you two were kids, and I know that I've never seen you cry over anything as hard or as much as you did over that boy leaving. That's a hard thing for a father to forget. And to forgive."

Wow. That was the closest thing to an emotional sentiment that she'd heard from her dad in a long time.

"Well, it's not your cross to bear or your offense to forgive. It's my burden, my broken heart, and my choice. If I've learned anything over the last eight years, it's that holding on to old hurts doesn't do anyone any good. Holding a grudge doesn't help anything or anyone. And what am I teaching my son if I tell him he should forgive people who show genuine remorse and say they're sorry if I'm not willing to do that myself?"

Ham grunted and switched the toothpick to the other side of his mouth. "I guess I can concede that. With Rockford, anyhow. At least he comes from good stock. I know his mama taught him better."

She raised an eyebrow and waited to see if he could hold a straight face while talking about Vivi. Rock had told her about his mom sneaking out of their house the other morning. It hadn't surprised her. She'd suspected something between the two for years.

The subject of Vivi must not have been enough to hold his attention right now, because he switched back to Max's father. "But I have a harder time accepting any kind of forgiveness for this idiot Hill. Rock was a kid when he left, and he took off to have a career. Hill is a man, and not only did he abandon his kid and his responsibilities, he's spent the better part of my grandson's life denouncing that he even existed. His own flesh and blood. That's a much worse crime in my book."

A hard ball of anger and hurt built in her stomach, but she fought to give it any kind of leverage. She needed to stand her ground. "I agree, and I'm not arguing that point. I'm just saying, what kind of person does that make me if I tell my son to do something I'm not willing to do myself?" She still held the dish towel, and she twisted it in her hands. "Did you hear him at supper tonight? He's so excited that Monty is here. He thought I was mad at *him*."

Ham let out a weary sigh. "Yeah, I heard him."

"So, how am I supposed to deal with that? I can't punish my son for the sins of his father. And I can't let Max think I'm upset with him when I'm really pissed as hell at his father. And what if he really has changed?"

Her dad arched an eyebrow at her. "I find that highly unlikely. But I see your point. And as hard as it is to bear, it's probably better that Max sees for himself what kind of man Hill really is." He pinched the end of the toothpick between his fingers and snapped it in half. "But I swear to you, if he hurts that boy, I'll kick his ass all the way back to Texas or whatever the hell rock he crawled out from under."

She tossed the dish towel on the counter. "Not if I get to him first, 'cause then there'll be nothing left of him to kick."

The next day, Quinn was still wrestling with the decision to let Monty come back again as she emptied the dish drainer.

It was already well after noon, and Max was waiting on the front porch for his father to show up. She could hear the scrape of his boots on the hard wood as he pushed the porch swing back and forth.

The *thunk* of the swing hitting the house coincided with the pounding of her headache.

She pulled out her phone, checking the time. Again. He was almost twenty minutes late.

What if he didn't show up at all? What would she tell Max?

This whole thing had been a bad idea.

She tucked her phone back in her pocket, ignoring the pinch in her chest at the display not showing any kind of message or communication from Rock.

Why had he left the day before without even saying goodbye?

She'd waited all night, thinking he'd call or send her a text saying he was sorry for bailing out on her or checking to see if she was okay. But he hadn't done either. And the later it got without any word from him, the angrier and more depressed she got.

What had she expected?

She'd expected him to call, that's what. Or come by. Or something.

The sound of an engine drew her attention, and she looked out the open kitchen window to see Monty's piece-of-crap car speeding down the driveway.

Slow down, idiot. Didn't he realize there were animals and a kid around this farm?

No. But he probably realized he was late.

At least he'd shown up. She just wasn't sure if that made her happy or not.

Max jumped off the porch steps and raced around to Monty's side of the car. She cringed as she waited for her son to hug the guy, but he stopped short, suddenly shy as Monty stepped out of the car.

"Hiya, champ," she heard Monty say as he offered Max a high-five. "Sorry I'm late. But I brought you a present."

Oh great. What kind of present had he brought?

She took a deep breath and stepped out of the kitchen as Max came flying into the house, the screen door slamming behind him.

"Mom! Mom! Look what my dad brought me! A present!" His eyes shone with excitement as he held up a cheap-looking toy car.

Monty stepped into the house and gave her a nod of greeting.

She tried to keep her features neutral as she peered at the toy. "Wow. Very cool." Monty must have really gone out of his way for that thing. He probably picked it up at the gas station on the way over.

No worries though. A two-dollar toy car totally makes up for the years of no child support.

Inhaling a deep breath, she tried to calm down. Max was a sensitive kid, and he was far too good at reading her emotions, as evidenced by his comments at dinner the previous night. It wouldn't help anything for him to think she was upset again.

"Can I show my dad my room, Mom?"

"Sure." She cringed as Max took Monty's hand and led him down the hallway toward his bedroom.

"This is all of my stuff," Max declared, opening his arms wide as he gestured around the room. He pointed to his bookshelves, then his dresser, as he introduced each thing, like a grade school tour guide. "These are my books. This is one of my favorites. It's about dinosaurs. I also like books about robots. This is my favorite rock that I found when we went to Rocky Mountain National Park. Mom only let me bring home five, and this one is the best. This is my bank. It has lots of money in it. I saved up for my Sunday school class, and I'm going to buy something cool. I don't know what yet. But it will be cool. And this is my favorite LEGO robot. My uncle helped me build it."

Monty nodded and made little remarks about each thing, using the word *cool* to describe most of Max's treasures.

Quinn had to give it to him though. He seemed interested in everything Max was showing him and listened to the descriptions of all of his favorites. Her eyes had already glazed over. But she'd already heard about all of these things.

Max led Monty toward his bed, where three stuffed animals lay against the pillows. "These are my pet puppies. They're not real dogs; they're just stuffed animals. But Mom won't let me have a real dog till I turn ten. Even though I told her I'd be real responsible. I'd feed it and take it for walks and everything. But Mom says I gotta wait."

"Ahh, that's too bad. I'm sure you would be real responsible. It seems like all boys should have a dog growing up. I know I always wanted one."

Max's eyes widened. "You did? Did you get one? Like when you were ten? Or before?"

"Like never. I never did get one. My dad wouldn't let me have one at all." A funny expression crossed Monty's eyes, just for a moment, like a cloud passing in front of the sun.

She was sure Max didn't notice, but Quinn caught it.

"Well, that should about wrap up the tour of Max's room," she said, her voice a little too bright. She really needed to find some aspirin. The headache was pulsing against her temples. "We should probably head out for lunch."

"Yeah, sure," Monty said. "I was thinking we could grab some burgers at The Creed."

Her mouth watered at the thought of a burger. At least her headache hadn't affected her appetite. Maybe she'd feel better after she ate. "Sounds fine."

"I'm starving," Max said. "I'm going to eat ten hamburgers." He galloped down the hall and out the front door.

Quinn grabbed her purse and followed her son and Monty, pulling the front door shut behind her.

Monty stepped off the porch and headed toward the large garage set off to the side of the house. He peered in, his forehead wrinkling with perplexity.

What was he doing? Did he want her to drive?

He spun around, craning his head toward the barn.

"What are you looking for?"

Shrugging, he offered her a sheepish grin. "I was just thinking maybe we could take your new car."

New car? Her car was on its last legs and barely running. "What are you talking about?"

He leaned his head to the side, as if still searching the property. "I heard you got a fancy new convertible."

Oh really? Wonder where he heard that little piece of gossip.

Freakin' Len Larson and his big fat mouth.

It had to be Lennie. She remembered now teasing him and asking him how he liked her new convertible. But how the heck had that already gotten back to Monty?

"My car's in the shop," she answered flatly, or at least it should be, so her answer was close enough. "We'll have to take yours."

His shoulders slumped, and he let out a weary sigh. "Oh yeah, sure. No problem." He headed for the car, sliding into the driver's side, leaving her to get Max buckled into the back seat.

His car was an older model sedan, but at least it was fairly clean inside and devoid of trash. Although it did have the stale scent of greasy fast food and a hint of cigarette smoke, which did nothing to help her headache.

She fastened herself into the front seat, feeling like she was buckling in for more than just a ride into town.

Rock took his hat off as he stepped into the cool interior of The Creed.

Colt had told him he was covering the day shift and

had offered to buy him a burger if he came down to the pub for lunch. It was after one, and Rock was hoping to avoid the majority of the noon-day crowd.

He slid onto a stool at the bar, setting his hat down on the counter next to him, then motioned for his brother to pour him a cold one.

Colt brought him a soda instead.

Rock sneered at the glass. "What's this?"

"It's the middle of the day, Bro."

"Who's the big brother here?"

Colt grinned and offered him a shrug, then held up a laminated menu. "You wanna see this?"

"Nah, just order me a cheeseburger with the works. And some fries. No, wait, make it some onion rings." A few onions wouldn't matter today—it's not like he was going to be kissing anyone anyway. He pulled his phone from his pocket and glanced at the display for about the hundredth time since he'd walked out of Quinn's house the day before.

The display was the same. No missed calls. No notifications of text messages. Nothing from Quinn.

He sighed and shoved the phone back into his pocket. What did he expect? He hadn't called her either. He was trying to give her time, to let her come to him if she needed him.

Obviously, she didn't need him.

"So, are you planning to mope around all day or just for the better part of it?" Colt asked, leaning against the edge of the bar. The tavern was fairly empty, and Rock was the only customer sitting at the bar.

"Shut up," Rock growled. He'd told his family about Monty showing up the day before as they'd sat around the breakfast table that morning. They'd all been surprised at his return.

But none of them had been surprised at Rock's reaction. They knew to stay out of his way when he had a good sulk going on. But they also only let him sulk for so long.

Colt held up his hands. "Hey, I get it. This whole thing would rile me up too. But what I don't get is why Quinn would even let that guy into her house."

"You would have too if you had seen Max. That kid acted like Hill was freaking Santa Claus on Christmas morning. He was so excited, running around like he was gonna wet himself with joy. What was she supposed to do?"

"Tell him to go to hell."

Rock let out a chuckle. That's what he would have liked to see her do as well. "I think she was in shock. She didn't really say anything." Or if she had, he hadn't stuck around long enough to hear it.

"That doesn't sound like the Quinn I know. That girl's never been afraid to speak her mind."

"Yeah, that's what I would have thought too. But she couldn't. Not with the way Max was carrying on, like having Hill show up was like the arrival of Christ himself."

"More like the Antichrist."

His brother's comment earned a slight grin. "You should have seen the guy too. Acting all friendly, like he'd just dropped by for Sunday tea." Rock shook his head. "What a douche."

Colt looked up as the door of the Tavern opened, and he tipped his head toward the entrance. "Looks like the douche just walked in."

"What?" Rock spun in his chair, letting out a groan as he watched Hill holding the door for Quinn and Max. *That's just great.*

"Rock!" Max's face lit up as he saw him, and he ran toward the bar, scrambling up onto the seat next to Rock. "Guess what? My dad came to see me again today. And he is taking us out to lunch. And he said maybe we could get ice cream after. And he brought me this."

Max held out a small red car. It was made of cheap tin, and the bar between the wheels was already bent. It looked like the kind of junk toys they sold at a dollar store or a gas station. "Isn't it cool?"

Rock nodded, biting his tongue to keep from giving his actual opinion.

It was obvious Hill hadn't spent any time talking to Max. The boy had no interest in toy cars. It took only about five minutes of listening to the kid talk to know that he loved dinosaurs and bugs and books. He was smart and had the kind of mind that was always trying to figure things out, to fathom how things worked.

If the guy had any sense of the kid, he would have brought him a book on dinosaurs or a set of LEGOs or something to build. Not a cheap tin car.

"Hi, Rock." Quinn bit out the words, her lips set in a tight line, her eyes wary as she approached the bar.

Damn. He should have called. Or texted. Or anything.

Their whole relationship had changed in the last several days, but this felt like the old Quinn. Like the way she used to act over the last several years when she saw him out in public and was forced to interact with him. The same cold shoulder, the same icy, flat tone of voice.

"Hey, Q." He hated the way she winced at his

greeting, as if the old nickname caused her physical pain. He nodded at Monty.

Max turned to Hill, a proud smile beaming from his face. "You remember Rock? He's my friend. He took me and my mom to the drive-in movies. And he has a car with no top on it. And he's a famous hockey player. We watch him sometimes on TV."

Oh really?

Rock glanced at Quinn, an inquisitive eyebrow raised, a tiny smile playing across his lips as he hoped to draw her into the joke.

She didn't return his smile. Instead, she rubbed her palm across her forehead as if she had a headache. "Come on, Max. Let's let the famous hockey player eat his lunch."

"Okay." He crawled down from the barstool, then looked up at Rock, his eyes full of hopefulness. "What about ice skating? You're still taking us skating tomorrow, right? Right? You promised."

Oh crud. He'd forgotten about the ice skating.

"Max, that was before your—" He choked on the word *dad*, not able to bring himself to say it. "Before Monty showed up. I don't want to take away your time from him."

"What does that matter? He can come too. We can all go together." He turned to Monty and his mother. "Can't we all go skating together tomorrow?"

Monty glanced around the bar, anywhere but at Max, as he tugged on the collar of his shirt. "Yeah, that's cool. I can go. Let's all go skating. Together." He narrowed his eyes at Rock as he said the last word, almost as if daring him to say no and disappoint the kid.

Awesome.

There was nothing in him that wanted to go ice skating with Monty Hill. But he had promised Max. And he was not one to renege on a promise.

Maybe he could find a way to "accidentally" check Monty into the boards of the ice rink.

"Sounds great," he said. "We'll all go."

He glanced at Quinn again, hoping for a positive reaction, but her crossed arms and the annoyed sigh she let out were unmistakable signs that she still wasn't a happy camper.

Great. His own sulkiness settled back in his chest. "See you tomorrow then. You want me to pick you up?" he asked, giving it one more last-ditch effort.

"No, that's fine. We'll meet you at the ice rink," Quinn answered. "Around two? Is that good for you?"

"Sure. That's fine." What would really be good for him was if he could get her to smile or nod or uncross her dang arms. Anything to get that look off her face, the one that was a cross between pissed off and hurt.

He hated that look and hated it worse that he was partly responsible for putting it there.

Him and the asswipe he was going ice skating with tomorrow.

"Okay, we'll see you tomorrow." She took Max's hand and led him to a booth on the other side of the restaurant.

"See you tomorrow," he grumbled, turning back to the bar, not wanting to watch the little family as they settled in at a table for lunch.

Colt set his plate on the bar in front of him, and Rock picked up his cheeseburger and shoved a bite into his mouth.

"Sounds like you've got a play date with Hill tomorrow. That oughta be fun," Colt said, the corners of his mouth turning up in an amused smirk.

"Yeah, I can't wait," Rock muttered, keeping his voice low as he spoke around a mouthful of burger. Not that they could hear him from across the bar, but he didn't want to give Quinn any more ammunition in her things-that-piss-me-off-about-Rock arsenal.

"You sure you want to do that?" Colt kept his voice quiet as well, leaning casually against the bar.

"No. But what am I supposed to do? I promised the kid."

His brother shrugged.

"Besides, I can't begrudge the kid wanting to know his dad. If anyone knows what it's like to grow up without a dad, it's us."

"Yeah, but our dad died. He didn't walk away from us on purpose."

Rock took a gulp of his soda, washing down the bite that had just gone tasteless in his mouth. "I know. I've been thinking the same thing. But now the guy is back. And what if he really has changed? Hell, I'm not the same guy I was back in high school. Maybe this guy isn't the same punk-ass twat he used to be either."

"Maybe he is."

That's what Rock was afraid of.

"Yeah, maybe he is. But I don't know. And who the hell am I to judge? I've screwed up enough stuff in my life that I sure as heck can't judge someone else's." Especially because most of those screwups involved the way he'd treated the blond cowgirl sitting in the booth across the room from him.

But Quinn had given him another chance. Had let him try to make up for the mistakes he'd made. She'd put her pride and humiliation aside and had been working to forgive him. Wasn't he a big enough man to do that for someone else?

Especially when an innocent kid was involved? He could do this. For Max's sake.

He'd been selfish before—had hurt someone because he put himself and his career over the feelings of someone who meant the world to him. Everything might have been different if he'd only tamped down his arrogance—only let go of his pride and selfishness.

And he had a chance to do that now. A chance to put his wants and needs aside and let a little boy have a chance at a relationship with his father, a chance at a family.

He wouldn't stand in the way of that. Wouldn't make trouble for Quinn or Max. He knew he needed to step back and let them have this time. No matter how much it hurt or pissed him off.

So he would give Quinn time, let her come to him if she needed him. He'd meet them tomorrow and teach Max how to skate, but other than that, he'd leave them alone. Give them time to see if they could create a family.

He dropped the rest of his burger on his plate, his appetite gone. "I'm gonna head out," he told his brother as he stuffed one last onion ring in his mouth and crammed his hat on his head. He tossed a twenty on the counter. "See ya, Bro."

Keeping his eyes on the door, he walked out of the bar. He could tell himself that he needed to give them space to be a family, but he dang sure didn't need to watch it happen.

Chapter 17

QUINN LISTENED WITH HALF AN EAR AS MAX TOLD MONTY about the kinds of plants one of his favorite dinosaurs liked to eat.

Their lunch had arrived, and she'd been picking at her meal, taking small bites of her burger and nibbling on a few of her fries as her thoughts kept drifting to Rock and the way he'd walked out of the bar.

He'd looked almost sad, and she'd wanted to text him to ask if he was all right. She didn't know what was going on with him. In the last few days before Monty had arrived, he'd texted or called her several times throughout the day, but since her ex had shown up, she hadn't heard a single thing from him.

Was the memory of her being with Monty too much for him? Or was he just trying to give her some space? Or had this whole thing reached a new level of complicated and he'd decided he didn't want any part of it?

"You folks ready for some dessert?" the waitress asked, breaking into Quinn's thoughts.

She shook her head. "No, I think we're good."

"I'll just leave this here then." She set the check on the side of the table.

Monty reached in his back pocket, then frowned. "Aw crap. I must have left my wallet on my dresser at my brother's house."

Really?

She leaned back in her chair, waiting to see how he would spin this as she mentally calculated how much the bill would total. She had her tips from the day before in her purse and probably had just enough to cover it.

He pulled his phone out. "Let me give him a call and have him run it over here." He paused. "Although it will probably take him a good thirty minutes to get it here." He tapped the phone on his lips as if in deep thought. "And I'm not sure if he's working today."

She sighed and reached for her purse. "It's okay. I think I've got it."

"No. You don't have to do that. I'm sure I can get someone in my family to drive my wallet over here."

She was tempted to let him try just so she could watch him attempt to get one of his lazy-ass family members to find his wallet and make the fifteen-minute drive over here, but she knew it would be an exercise in futility.

"I can pay for it," Max said. "I have money saved up."

That did it. She couldn't very well force Monty's hand now. Not after her sweet, generous eight-year-old son had offered to pick up the tab.

"It's all right, Max. I can pay for it," she said, pulling out her wallet. "You keep your money."

"Sorry about that," Monty told her. "I'll get the next one."

Great. She couldn't wait.

And she'd just started to think that maybe he had changed.

Max wanted to stop at the park on the way home, and as tired as she was, she was glad to have him run off some of his extra energy.

"You guys go ahead," she told them as she sank onto a park bench next to the playground. "I'll just watch."

At least her headache had gone away.

And it was a nice summer day to sit on a park bench. Although she would prefer it if she wasn't sitting here watching her son run around the playground with the man who had walked out of their lives and, up until a few days ago, had decided he didn't want anything to do with them.

After about half an hour, she waved them over and told them it was time to go, that Max needed some downtime. She could tell when he started getting too silly or giggly that it was time for a break and to slow things down.

Plus, she'd had about all the family bonding time she could handle.

As much as she wanted to give her son a chance to know his father, it was hard to watch him idolize the man who had ignored him for the past eight years. Especially since Max was acting like Monty freaking walked on water.

Maybe she should've handed him her bottle of water and let him turn it into wine. Now, that was a skill that would make the time spent hanging out with her ex worth it.

She still couldn't figure Monty out. She studied him as he drove them back to the ranch.

He did seem different. He was being surprisingly patient with Max and hadn't bailed on him yet. He'd patiently pushed him on the swings and spent way too long — in her opinion — searching the stream next to the park for perfect specimens of rocks. But it was easy to be patient for a few hours over the course of a few days.

Although he did seem to be genuinely interested in spending time with Max. Of course, Max was still acting shy and on his best behavior around him. Monty hadn't had to deal with a too-tired meltdown or a bout of vomit.

Monty pulled up in front of the house and got out.

Hmm. She had assumed he would just drop them off, but he seemed determined to continue the day. Maybe he needed a real challenge.

Although spending twenty minutes searching for rocks had been a pretty good one. And he'd done fine with that.

"Max needs to take a break. We usually spend a little time reading in the afternoon, if you want to read him a book." She was sure he'd be ready to leave after reading one chapter of a middle-grade book.

"Sure. I can do that," he said. "You want me to read you a book, Max?"

"Yeah." Max raced for his room, and she and Monty trailed after him.

Max pored over his extensive selection of books and finally settled on one of his favorites. "This one. It's about these four kids who travel through time and solve mysteries." He handed the book to his father.

"Sounds good."

She was thankful Monty had pulled up the rocking chair next to Max's bed. She didn't think she could handle it if she had to watch Max curl up next to him as he read.

Although that's what he'd done with Rock earlier that week.

But it was different with Rock.

Wasn't it?

The thought of Max curled up next to Monty as he read to him filled her with unease and wariness, yet when Rock was reading to him, it filled her with something very close to happiness. Maybe because way down in her secret heart of hearts, the scene with Rock was the one she wished were true.

The scene that portrayed the three of them as a family. A real family.

Emotion flooded her throat, and she stepped out of Max's room and into the hallway. Flattening her back against the wall, she slid to the floor, listening as Monty read the book to her son, *their* son.

She let out a weary sigh and dropped her chin to her chest. Closing her eyes, she tried to focus on taking some deep, cleansing breaths. She could get through this.

It took only five minutes to read a chapter. She could get through another five minutes.

She cocked an ear as she heard Monty get to the end of the chapter. Maybe now he would go home.

Nope. He started the next one. Geez. Was he going to read the whole book?

Apparently so.

Thirty minutes later, he emerged from Max's room, his eyes widening when he saw her sitting on the floor in the hallway.

"What are you doing out here?"

She shrugged. "Just listening."

His brows knit together for the briefest of seconds, then he quickly smoothed his features back into a pleasant smile.

Or maybe they hadn't. Now she wasn't sure. It had happened so fast. Maybe she was just imagining his reaction—projecting her assumptions of how she thought he would react. She'd anticipated that he would be bothered by her constantly keeping an eye on them, but maybe he wasn't.

Maybe he really had changed.

"He fell asleep," he told her.

"You read to him for a long time. I was surprised you lasted that long."

He lifted one shoulder. "It was an interesting book. And he seemed to really be involved in the story."

"He loves that one." She pushed up off the floor, stretching her sore muscles as she walked toward the front door. "Thanks for coming by."

"No problem. It was fun." He put his hand on the screen door, then turned back to look at her. "I really have changed. I just want a chance to get to know my son."

Then where have you been the last eight years? She bit back the response that she really wanted to say, too tired to get into an argument now. Plus, he did seem different. She wanted to believe him. To believe in him. For Max's sake. "I hope so. Because he's a really great kid."

"I know." He glanced down the hallway toward Max's room and looked as if he were going to say something else about him, then changed his mind. "See ya tomorrow. Ice skating, right?"

"Yep."

Another day of family fun. She couldn't wait.

———⁓———

The next day, Rock gripped Max's hand as they stepped out on the ice.

He hadn't been on skates in over two weeks, but the feeling of the hard surface under the blades of his skates felt like coming home.

So did being on the ice in his hometown rink. *And* having Quinn watching him from the bleachers.

But having a large banner on the wall with his name on it was new. And seeing it still made him feel a little funny, giving him a feeling that was a mixture of pride and humility.

Thanks to him, the rink had gone through some major updates, getting some much-needed renovations and a new sheet of ice a few years ago. It was the least he could do. This rink and the pond in their pasture were the places he'd learned to skate, where he had spent hours practicing his skating and stick-handling skills.

It had been old then, the ice buckled and the boards uneven in a couple of spots, but it was the best they had, and he'd always told himself that if he ever made it big, he'd fix up the old rink for the next generation of skaters.

And that's what he'd done. When he'd signed a new contract a few years ago, he'd donated a large portion of the money it took to make the renovations.

And today, leading Max out onto the ice for the first time made every penny worth it.

The boy's face shone with excitement and terror as he clutched Rock's arms, wobbling forward and trying to keep his balance.

Rock chuckled, skating backward with ease, his feet and legs as at home on the ice as if he were wearing a pair of sneakers. "Broaden your stance and bend your knees. Don't feel bad about putting your arms out for balance," he told Max.

"Like this?" Max held one arm straight out.

"Yep, you got it." He guided the boy around the rink a few times, then over to a pair of five-gallon buckets stacked on top of each other. The buckets were a common tool used in ice skating lessons, giving the kids stability as they learned the feel of the skates.

"You can hold on to the buckets and skate behind them at your own pace," he instructed. "I know it feels funny, and your feet might hurt a little, but I tied your skates so tight so you would have ankle support. It will help, I promise."

"They aren't too tight. They feel good."

He'd been tempted to bring an old pair of his skates from when he was a kid, but he wasn't sure if they would fit and wanted Max's first skating experience to be a good one. Part of the rink's renovation project had involved ordering in new skates in both the figure skating and the hockey skating styles, so Rock was sure they would have a pair for Max to use.

"I think I'm getting it," Max said, a smile beaming from his face.

Rock loved the kid's enthusiasm. Nothing shook him.

"Take it slow. And don't be afraid to fall." He glanced up to where Quinn and Monty were sitting in the bleachers.

Monty had declined to skate, claiming he had a bad ankle from an old football injury.

Yeah, right. Rock thought he just didn't know how to skate and didn't want to look like an idiot. But it was fine with him that the guy offered to just watch from the bleachers.

Or at least it had been until Quinn said she wasn't

going to skate either and would just sit in the bleachers with him.

Why would she choose sitting out with Monty over skating with him and Max?

Maybe the guy really had changed, and she was starting to see the good in him.

Wasn't this what Rock wanted? The whole reason he was backing off and giving her space—so Max could get to know his real dad, and she and Max could have a whole family?

Forget about that, he told himself, turning his attention back to the boy. This was about Max and teaching him how to skate. Not about him and Quinn.

He refocused on Max, offering encouragement and all of the lessons his coaches had taught him when he was a kid.

Max soaked it all up, following every piece of advice Rock offered. And he was doing great, really starting to get the hang of it.

And Rock was having fun, celebrating his small victories and laughing with Quinn as she called encouragement from the stands.

"He's doing awesome," he called out to her, offering her a smile and hoping for one in return.

"I know. He's totally getting it." She laughed and applauded as a grin split her face. A grin that felt like the moment the clouds drifted away on an overcast day and let the sun shine in.

"He's a natural." He pulled the bucket along, and Max skated behind it, barely needing the rim of it for balance.

"You're doing good, champ. You don't even need those stupid buckets," Monty called.

"Ignore him," Rock said, holding Max's eye and fighting the slimy feeling running down his back at Monty's fatherly endearment. "It's fine to use the buckets until you get the hang of this. Skating can take time to learn, and for some things, it's okay to go slow and take your time."

He wished Monty would shut up. It was hard enough for a kid who was used to spending more time reading than running to pick up the skills, without having his newfound dad make him feel like he was not picking it up quickly enough.

The ice rink was slow that afternoon. Only a few other people were skating, and most were figure skaters who stayed in the center, practicing turns.

Rock had Max in the corner by himself as he worked on keeping his balance.

"You guys look great," Quinn called out. "Keep it up, Max. You're doing amazing. You got this."

Memories of a teenaged Quinn cheering him on from the sidelines flooded his thoughts, memories so vivid they hurt his chest. That girl had meant everything to him. And he'd been such an idiot for letting her go.

He knew he should stay focused on Max, but the need to hear her cheering for him again was too strong. He skated backward, doing a quick circle and hitting Max's legs with a small spray of ice as he maneuvered a hockey stop.

Max giggled and laughed, and Quinn let out a cheer. "Nice moves, Rock." Her laughter and teasing spurred him on, and he knew he was showing off for her. Just a little. But his skills had improved since she'd last seen him skate.

It wouldn't hurt anything to give her a tiny show. And if it made Monty jealous in the process, then it would be even better.

He grinned down at Max. "You want to see how fast I can skate?"

The boy's eyes lit up, and he nodded. "Yeah."

"Hold on to the bucket. I'll be right back." He skated backward for a few feet. "You watching?"

Max grinned and bobbed his head.

Rock spun around and took off, circling the ice, his feet flying as he crossed his skates to glide through the turns. He rounded the last corner and did another hockey stop, this time sending a spray of ice shooting toward Quinn and Monty.

He was rewarded with laughter from Quinn, applause from Max, and a scowl from Monty. *Perfect*.

"Do it again," Max cried.

He had to admit, the speed skate felt good. He felt good. His blood was pumping from the expended energy and the attention of Quinn.

"Okay, one more time. But this time, I'll go backward the whole way." He scissored his feet, gaining momentum as he sped backward around the ice. On the far side of the rink, a young girl had strayed from the center, and he slowed to go around her, spinning in a circle around the girl and earning a giggle from her.

Was Quinn watching?

He glanced from the girl to the bleachers.

But Quinn's attention was on the other side of the rink. He frowned as she stood up, a look of alarm on her face. "Be careful, Max," he heard her call.

He whipped his head back just in time to see Max,

one hand on the bucket and one on the wall as he pushed off from the side in order to gain momentum.

Monty had come down from the bleachers and was egging him on. "You can do it," Rock heard him call.

Max was attempting to cross one foot over the other, just as Rock had done.

But his feet tangled, and his arms pinwheeled as he tried to keep his balance.

As if in slow motion, Rock watched the buckets tip and the boy fall forward, hitting his face on the rim before the buckets shot away from him.

Max held out his hands to break his fall but still hit his chin, sending a bright-red spray of blood across the white sheet of ice.

Chapter 18

ROCK HEARD MAX'S CRY OF PAIN, FOLLOWED BY QUINN'S shriek of fear as she scrambled out of the bleachers.

Max was curled in a ball, crying and cradling his arm.

Rock's skates bit into the ice as he raced toward the boy.

He was fast, but not fast enough.

Monty had run out onto the ice and got to Max moments before Rock skated up to them.

He fell to his knees, not caring about the tears in the denim. He wasn't showing off now. He cared only about getting to Max.

Blood covered the bottom half of the boy's face, and Rock wasn't sure if it came from his nose or his chin.

His heart stopped, and fear filled his chest.

He'd seen guys bleeding on the ice, seen them spit a knocked-out tooth into their glove, but nothing had ever affected him like seeing the blood on Max's small face.

Quinn ran onto the ice, her feet slipping and sliding as she raced to her son, then pulled him into her arms, cradling him to her chest.

He cried out as she touched his arm.

She pulled back and gingerly held his arm. "He went down pretty hard on his hands. He might have broken his arm. We've got to get him to the hospital."

Rock was at a loss. He scrubbed a hand through his hair. "I'm so sorry."

He fumbled with his laces, trying to get them untied, but Monty stepped in and took the boy from Quinn's arms before Rock could even get his first knot untied.

He knew it would take precious extra minutes to get his and Max's skates off. He waved them on. "You guys go on. Don't worry about his skates. I'll take care of everything here. Just go."

Monty was already heading for the door of the ice rink. Quinn hurried ahead, holding the door open, her thoughts focused only on her son.

Rock's heart was heavy as he watched them go.

Damn it. This was his fault. He should have been paying attention to Max instead of showing off and trying to impress Quinn.

Once again, his selfishness hurt someone he cared about.

Stepping off the ice, he sank onto one of the bleachers. Tearing at the laces, he yanked his skates off and crammed his feet into his boots.

In her haste to get the boy to the hospital, Quinn had left her purse next to Max's jacket and his sneakers. Crap. She was going to need her wallet and identification to get Max seen. Plus, he was sure her health insurance cards were probably inside.

He stuffed Max's things into her bag, noting her phone was also in her purse, and tossed his skates into his own bag. Grabbing it all, he hurried to the counter and explained about the skates and promised they'd return them.

The kid behind the counter gave him an indifferent shrug. "That's cool. I know who you are."

Small towns.

He only hoped that small-town mentality was working for Quinn as well and the fact that she didn't have her wallet wasn't holding up Max being seen by a doctor.

Rock floored the gas pedal of the truck, spitting gravel as he pulled out of the ice rink parking lot and headed toward the hospital. There was only one in town, so it wasn't hard to figure out where they'd gone.

His cell phone rang, and he hit the button on his steering wheel, not even checking the display to see who was calling. "Quinn?" he said into the cab of the truck.

"No, it's Mom." Vivi's concerned voice came through the speakers. "What's wrong?"

His mom could always read his moods, even through one word. "Max fell at the ice rink, and he might have broken his arm. Quinn took him to the hospital, and I'm headed there now."

"Okay, I'll get Ham, and we'll be there in ten minutes." His mom disconnected before he had a chance to argue. It didn't matter. He didn't have time to worry about what his mom was doing. He needed to get to Quinn and Max.

He pulled into the parking lot of the hospital, spotting Monty's piece-of-crap sedan. Grabbing Quinn's bag, he hurried across the lot and through the emergency room doors.

He noted the empty waiting room as he charged up to the reception counter.

"Hey, I'm looking for Quinn Rivers. She brought her son in here a few minutes ago. I've got her bag." He held up the purse, as if he needed proof of his story.

The nurse smiled and nodded. "Yes, they just went

back to the exam rooms. I'll have someone let them know you're here. What's your name, sir?"

But he was already pushing through the doors, ignoring the women's call of, "Sir, you can't go back there. It's only for family members."

Screw that.

Quinn was his family. No matter what happened between them, in the past or the future, she would always be like family to him.

The emergency room was fairly slow. He passed an old man lying in a bed, his arm hooked up to an IV and his wife calmly sitting in a chair next to him, a paperback book open on her lap.

Hearing Quinn's murmured voice, he pulled back the curtain of the last room to reveal Max propped up on the examination table. A young nurse wearing purple scrubs was sponging the blood from his face, and Quinn was standing next to the bed, a worried expression on her face. Monty stood behind her, his face an ashen shade of gray. He looked like he might either vomit or pass out.

They all turned toward him, Quinn's eyes widening in surprise.

He held up her purse. "You forgot your bag. I thought you would need your wallet and your insurance cards."

"Thanks," she mumbled, then turned her attention back to Max. Her face was pale, her lips pinched and her brows drawn together with worry.

Max offered him a small smile, but the blood that was still on his face turned Rock's stomach sour. Poor kid.

Now that he was here, he didn't know what to do. Standing at the foot of the bed, he twisted the strap of

Quinn's bag in his hands, his knuckles turning white against the brown leather strap.

Monty took a step between him and Quinn, a scowl forming on his face. "Thanks for bringing the bag, but we got this." He held his hand out for the purse. "They only allow *family members* back here, so you're gonna need to wait outside."

"Ma'am, you can't go back there," a nurse called to Vivi and Ham as they hurried toward the exam room.

Apparently, his mother wasn't any better at listening than he was.

"We got here as quickly as we could." She leaned forward, clutching her stomach as she caught her breath. "How is he?"

"Hi, Grandpa," Max said, talking around the sponge the nurse was still using on his face. "I fell down at the ice rink. I get to have stitches. And maybe I'll even have a scar."

A tiny smirk passed across the nurse's face, but Rock felt anything but amused. His heart ached that this sweet boy's face was going to carry a permanent scar because of his stupid neglect.

"We'll have to get some ice cream to celebrate," Ham said, obviously trying to keep his tone light for Max. He tilted his head toward Rock and lowered his voice. "What in the hell happened?"

"I can tell you what happened," Monty said, pushing around Quinn and getting in Rock's face. "You weren't paying attention. That's what happened. You were too busy showing off what a big shot you are, and you let Max get hurt."

His temper flared, and Rock's back straightened as he

spit back, "You were the one pushing him to let go of the buckets and try to skate faster."

"That's because you were trying to treat him like a little kid with those stupid buckets."

"He is a little kid," he snarled through gritted teeth, his hands clenching into fists.

"Simmer down now," Ham ordered. His brow furrowed, and a scowl formed on his mouth as he turned to Rock. "Tell me what happened. Did my grandson get hurt because of your negligence?"

Vivi stepped in between Rock and Ham. "Of course not. Rock would never let anything happen to Max."

Rock hung his head, emotion building in his throat.

"He sure as hell did let something happen to him. He shouldn't even be around Max," Monty said, his eyes narrowing at Rock.

His words were like arrows to Rock's heart, each one a sharp point that slashed open another wound. His head told him it was Monty's goading that caused Max to let go of the buckets, but his heart ached with guilt at the part he'd played in it.

He should never have left Max's side.

"Maybe *you* shouldn't be around Max," Vivi shot back, then lowered her voice to a whispered hiss. "You've done more damage to him than anyone in this room."

"Maybe you should all calm down," the nurse said.

"It wasn't Rock's fault," Max said, raising his small voice to be heard above the others. "I just fell down."

The whole group stopped talking at once, as if Max's voice was a reminder to all of them that their conversation wasn't meant for his ears.

Rock appreciated Max sticking up for him, but his

faith in him wasn't enough to prevent the guilt that washed over him in giant, crashing waves.

"Hey, what's going on in here?" A man in a white lab coat, presumably the doctor, stepped around the curtain.

He shot them all a disapproving look, then offered Max a smile. "Hello, young man. I'm Dr. John. I'm guessing from all the blood that you're the patient."

"Yep," Max answered. "I was ice skating, and I fell down and hurt my chin and my arm."

"You did? Well, that's no good. Why don't I take a look at you and see what I think?"

Rock, Vivi, and Ham took a step back to let the doctor pass into the room. Monty inched closer to Quinn.

Dr. John performed a cursory exam, then turned to Quinn. "Are you this young man's mother?"

Monty puffed up his chest. "Yeah, and I'm his father."

Quinn ignored Monty, her gaze trained on the doctor's face, her eyes brimming with tears. "Is he going to be okay?"

"Oh, sure. It looks like he's going to need a few stitches in his chin, and I have a feeling he might have fractured his wrist, but he's going to be fine. We'll get him all taken care of, and he'll have a cool cast to show his friends."

Quinn nodded but didn't say anything.

He grinned down at Max. "I'm going to put a couple of little stitches in your chin, then we'll send you over to get an X-ray of your wrist. That part won't hurt a bit. It's just like taking a picture. Then we'll know for sure if it's broken or not. If it is, you can pick a cool color for your cast. How does that sound?"

"Okay. I think I want blue. Do you have blue?"

Max asked, apparently focused on the color of the cast and not yet comprehending what getting stitches actually entailed.

The doctor chuckled. "Yes, I'm sure we've got blue." He raised an eyebrow at the group of people standing around Max's bed. "Now, I'm going to have to ask all of you to step out to the waiting room. Not just because I need the room to work, but because you're upsetting the receptionist, and I'm more scared of her than of you."

"I'm his father," Monty said, standing his ground.

Yeah, we all heard you the first time, idiot.

The man's words felt like fingernails on a chalkboard, grating down Rock's spine. This guy hadn't even been around for the last eight years, and now he's coming in and acting like he has a right to be here?

Guilt swirled in his gut. Wasn't he doing the same thing?

He hadn't been there for Quinn and Max either. And now, after spending the last week with them, he was acting like they belonged to him as well.

But they didn't belong to him. And even if they did, he didn't deserve them. Especially Max. Not after what he'd done.

His chest hurt, and he felt like he couldn't breathe. A pulse pounded hard in his temples as the headache that had started as he'd left the ice rink rose to a crescendo. He had to get out of here.

He pushed past Ham and strode out the exam-room doors. He could feel his mom at his heels.

It wasn't until he was almost to the door of the hospital that he realized he was still clutching Quinn's bag. He turned around, and his mom almost crashed into him.

He thrust the purse into her hands. "Here. Give this to Quinn. She left it at the ice rink."

"Rock, wait," Vivi said, reaching for Rock's hand.

"You wait," he answered, pulling back his arm. "I've got to get out of here. Text me and let me know how the X-rays turn out." He let out a sigh, then leaned down and pulled his mom into a quick hug, mumbling an apology into her hair before he pushed through the hospital doors and headed for his truck.

Slamming the door, he leaned his forehead against the steering wheel and punched his fist into the dashboard. His eyes burned, and his head throbbed with pain and anger.

How could he have been so stupid?

Pull it together, buddy. Falling apart isn't going to help anybody.

He leaned back in the seat and inhaled a deep breath. Starting the truck, he pulled out of the parking lot.

A spark of color caught his eye as he drove down Main Street, and he flipped on his turn signal and eased into a parking space in front of the bookstore.

If Max was going to be laid up with a busted arm, the least he could do was get him something to take his mind off the pain. He'd find him a great book, or two, or five. Whatever it took to help.

A bearded man in a faded flannel shirt sat on the sidewalk between the bookstore and the drugstore, a mangled cardboard box at his feet. Four fluffy, brown-and-white puppies scrambled over one another, whining as he approached them. A handmade sign leaned against the side of the box that read FREE OR BEST OFFER.

"What offer is better than free?" Rock asked as he leaned down to scratch the head of one of the puppies.

The man shrugged. "I'll give you a pup for free, but I wouldn't turn down a donation if you wanted to offer one." He winked and offered an impish grin. His teeth, or what remained of them, were stained yellow from tobacco and neglect.

You had to admire the man's thought process. And it made a certain kind of sense.

The puppies *were* adorable.

A reddish-brown dog lay next to the man's leg, her attention divided between him and her puppies. She was a true mutt, a mix of retriever and maybe Australian shepherd.

The man rubbed her neck with a calloused and weather-worn hand. "I didn't even know she was carrying pups until she had 'em. Scared the crap out of me. They're cute little buggers, but I can barely feed me and her. I can't handle another four mouths to feed."

She was a medium-sized dog, and she seemed sweet, but who knew what breed of dog she'd mated with. Or what kind of temperament the father had.

For just a moment, Rock debated grabbing one of the puppies for Max but was pretty sure the happiness it would bring wouldn't be worth the wrath he would incur from Quinn. She'd already told him she wanted Max to be older before he got a dog. And besides, there was something special about getting to pick out your first dog by yourself.

He reached in his wallet and handed the guy a twenty. "I can't take a pup, but this should help feed all of you for tonight."

"I'm much obliged to ya." The man nodded at Rock, then slipped the bill inside his shirt pocket.

"Good luck." Rock was sure the guy wouldn't have a hard time getting rid of the puppies. They were cute little things.

Forgetting about the dogs, he pulled open the door of the bookstore and stepped inside.

The quaint store had been around for years and had expanded since the last time he'd been there. It now carried stationery, cards, and an assortment of journals, and had a small coffee-shop counter at the back of the store.

The children's section was in one corner and had several stacks of books and a spattering of educational toys. Searching the shelves, Rock found a large, colorful book on dinosaurs, an equally huge one on bugs, and a LEGO set that had three different robots to build. Max would love them all.

Rock approached the counter, knowing he would buy the whole store if he could, if it would take even one ounce of Max's pain away.

Or even one smidgen of his guilt.

Quinn kept her arms crossed, as if holding on to herself would keep her from completely falling apart as she watched the nurse finish smoothing the bright-blue cast on Max's thin arm.

The X-ray had shown a small fracture in his wrist, and the doctor had explained that it was a very common break and should heal quickly. The fracture was minor and had missed the growth plate and would require Max to wear the cast for only three or four weeks.

They'd already made an appointment to come back in three weeks to check it out.

"Mom, want to sign my cast?" Max held up his arm and offered her a toothy grin.

Gosh, she loved that kid. Loved him so much it caused a physical ache in her chest.

He had a way of finding the best in every situation, of finding a way to smile even in the darkest moments.

Pulling on all of her inner strength, she forced a smile and nodded her head. "Of course, baby. I'll sign it."

"Do I get to sign it too?" Monty asked, wiggling Max's sock.

She'd taken the skates off him and left them in Monty's car. Her brain was muddled with all of the information and everything that happened, and she had no idea where Max's shoes even were. She knew Rock had grabbed her purse, so she was thankful for that, and she assumed he would have picked up all of their things.

Rock.

He'd looked so forlorn and miserable when he'd been in here earlier. She knew he was blaming himself for Max getting hurt. She'd wanted to comfort him, to tell him that it wasn't his fault. But all of her focus had been on her son, and she hadn't had time to try to offer him comfort too.

Truthfully, she could use his broad shoulders to comfort her right now. Being a single mom was hard, especially on days like today, when she had to keep it together and appear strong for her boy.

But inside, she didn't feel strong—didn't feel strong at all.

Rock wanted to be her friend. Well, she could use a friend right now. And she was anxious to get out to the waiting room to find Rock and let him know that she still needed him—to tell him that this wasn't his fault, and neither she nor Max blamed him.

She finished filling out and signing the rest of the paperwork. Then they were told they were free to go and gathered their things.

She held out her arms, and Max scrambled into them, snuggling against her neck but still mindful of his injured chin. The doctor had put in two small stitches and covered it with a cartoon Band-Aid.

Quinn pressed a kiss to her son's forehead. He smelled like shampoo and little-boy sweat and the faint, coppery scent of blood. The nurse had washed the majority of it from his face, but it still dotted his clothes, forming speckles of hard, crusted, brown stains.

Her own shirt was smudged with dried blood as well, and she just wanted to get home and get them both cleaned up and into fresh clothes that didn't reek of injury and pain.

"Let's go home, buddy."

"You want me to carry him?" Monty offered.

She shook her head. "I've got him."

Monty had been surprisingly helpful, and she was shocked that he'd stayed with them this whole time, only leaving Max's side when he was taken in for the X-ray.

He hadn't spoken much, but he'd offered his silent support just by being there, and she'd noticed.

Still, as nice as it was for Max to have his dad there, Monty wasn't the one she wanted. He wasn't the one she needed by her side, and he wasn't the one she wanted to have wrap her in his big arms and tell her everything was going to be okay.

She held her breath as they pushed through the

emergency-room doors, praying Rock would know what she needed.

Her eyes scanned the waiting room as Ham and Vivi rushed toward them, but the rest of the waiting room was empty.

Her chest tightened when Ham took Max from her. She heard him asking about his cast, and she felt Vivi pull her into a warm hug and say something about having her purse and Max's shoes.

"Where's Rock?" she asked, her voice barely above a whisper as she spoke into Vivi's ear.

"I'm sorry, honey. He already left," Vivienne said as she squeezed Quinn tighter.

Quinn held on to her, clutching her back, her heart breaking into a thousand tiny pieces. The heart she had thought was broken, but that Rock had been slowly knitting back together, until this moment, when he had crushed it again.

Chapter 19

IT WAS TIMES LIKE THESE WHEN QUINN MISSED HAVING A mother, a woman to comfort and soothe her, to brush back her hair and tell her everything was going to be all right.

Vivi was the closest thing she had to a mom, but she wasn't *her* mom; she was Rock's mom. Just as Quinn's would be to Max, Vivi's allegiance would always be to her son.

Pulling away, Quinn took a deep breath. She was on her own here. She and Max.

Vivienne James might not be her mother, but she'd modeled the behavior of a strong woman for all the years Quinn had known her. Vivi was tough as nails on the outside, but her heart was still as soft as butter. If Vivi could run a ranch and raise three boys on her own, so could Quinn.

She had to. Because the only person she could really count on was herself.

She pushed her shoulders back and stood a little taller. *I can do this.*

"They need a copy of my insurance card and ID. Let me take care of that real quick, then let's go home," she said.

"I can drive you," Monty offered.

She shook her head. "You've done enough today. I really appreciate you being here, but you don't have to stay with us."

"I want to. Really."

"I'll bring them home," Ham said, his tone conveying that the topic wasn't up for discussion.

Monty's face fell, and his shoulders slumped forward.

The guy genuinely seemed to want to still be with them.

Not like a certain other guy who had already left.

Again.

"You know what would really help, Monty? If you could pick up Max's prescription and bring it out to the house. That way, we don't have to make the extra stop and wait for it, and we can head straight back now and get Max settled."

"Sure. I can do that."

"Great. And the doctor suggested we get some children's ibuprofen, like Motrin. Can you get that too? I'll write down what I usually get."

"Yeah. Sure." His features formed into a grimace, as if he'd just tasted something sour. "Shoot. Maybe I can't. I'm a little light on cash right now, and my debit card's been acting up. This move back here to be with Max has really tapped my finances."

She took her purse from Vivi and dug for her wallet. "Oh. Of course. I wouldn't expect you to pay for it."

Why would you pay for a couple of bottles of medicine when you haven't paid for a single item of your son's care yet?

Stop.

The guy's been patiently sitting with us all afternoon, she reminded herself. He'd been kind and had even found her a cup of water from the nurse's station.

She handed him three crumpled five-dollar bills, the

last of her tip money for the week. "We use the drugstore on Main. They have Max's information on file, and they can call me if they need my permission to release his medication to you. But you shouldn't have any trouble."

"I'll head over there now." He patted Max on the leg. "I'm gonna go pick up your medicine for you, but I'll be out to the house in about half an hour. Okay?"

Max nodded, his eyes starting to droop as he rested his head on his granddad's shoulder.

It took Quinn only a few minutes to furnish the receptionist with her insurance information and finish clearing up the paperwork. Ham and Vivi took Max out to the truck, and he was already asleep by the time she crawled into the back seat of the King Cab.

She rested her hand on his head as her dad put the truck in gear and headed toward the ranch.

He woke up when they pulled up to the house, but Ham still carried him inside.

"Why don't you bring him in the bathroom, and I can get him cleaned up and into some fresh pajamas," Quinn suggested.

"I'll find something to make for supper for you all while you do that," Vivi said, already on her way to the kitchen.

Quinn filled the bathroom sink with warm, soapy water, and Ham set Max gingerly on the side of the counter. They carefully peeled off his soiled T-shirt, then Ham held his casted arm up while Quinn soaked a washcloth in the water and rinsed the remains of the dried blood from his neck and chest.

She gently washed his face, keeping the area around the Band-Aid dry. Her dad stayed with him while she hurried into his bedroom and got him a pair of pajamas. She picked the softest set, and Ham helped her maneuver Max into the shorts and T-shirt set.

The three of them walked down the hall just as Vivi was setting a plate of pancakes down on the table.

"It's simple, but it's comfort food, and it's quick. I made the first stack for you, Max." She smiled up at Quinn and Ham as they helped the boy into his chair. "I've got some scrambled eggs frying up too. They'll be done in a minute."

"Thanks, Vivi," Quinn said, dropping into a chair and picking up a fork. "Want me to help you, honey?"

"No." Max took the fork from her. "Geez, you guys. I broke my arm, not my whole body. I can eat by myself. I have another hand."

His comment earned a chuckle from all of them.

"You're right," Quinn said, leaning back in her chair with a sigh. "I'm just being a mom."

Vivi disappeared back into the kitchen. She dished up plates for Ham and Quinn and set them on the table. "Should I make a plate for Logan?"

Ham shook his head. "Nah. He's down in the southern part of the state, picking up some cattle and a few supplies. He won't be back for another few days."

She nodded. "Well, there's enough for Monty when he shows up as well. I made a plate for him and covered it, so it should stay warm."

Ham raised an eyebrow at her. "Aren't you eating?"

"No. I'm gonna head home and feed my crew. Mason and Colt were working the back pasture this afternoon, and they'll be coming in soon and hoping to be fed."

Quinn noticed she conveniently left out Rock's name.

Although she was sure he'd be sitting at his mother's table as well.

Ham pushed back in his chair. "Let me give you a ride home."

"You'll do no such thing. Sit back down. Eat that food I just made you while it's still hot. I have two perfectly good legs, and I can find my own way home. Besides, I could use the walk." She pressed a kiss on top of Max's head. "You were very brave today. I'm proud of you."

He wrapped his arms around her waist, his fork still clutched in one hand. "Thanks, Vivi. And thanks for the pancakes. They're awesome."

She laughed and gave Quinn a one-armed squeeze. "Hang in there, honey. Boys get into scrapes. If this one is anything like mine, it won't be the last time you wash blood out of his clothes. But he's a strong boy. He'll be fine."

"Thanks. And thanks for making supper. I really appreciate it."

"Think nothing of it. I was happy to do it." She offered Ham a wink and headed for the front door. "I'll check in with you tomorrow."

"I'll give a call to let you know how Max is doing," Quinn said as Vivi stepped through the door.

"Sounds good. Night." She let the screen door shut behind her.

The rest of them quietly turned back to their plates and dug into their pancakes.

The sound of an engine drew their attention a few minutes later.

"That must be Hill. It's about time he got here with the medicine," Ham grumbled.

Quinn was sure it was Monty as well, but she couldn't help secretly hoping it was Rock. She let out a breath she didn't realize she was holding when she saw Monty approach the screen door. "Come on in. We've got some pancakes for you."

He pushed open the door, a plastic drugstore bag in one hand and a broad grin on his face. His jacket was zipped up and bulging out in the front. "I've got something for you too," he said, his voice high with excitement.

The front of his jacket moved, as if something squirmed inside of it, and a tiny yip emitted from his collar.

Oh, hell no. He didn't.

He wouldn't.

Not after she'd just told him the day before that she wanted Max to wait until he was older.

"What is it?" Max said, his own voice climbing higher.

Monty unzipped the front of his jacket, letting the brown fuzzy head of a puppy poke over the top.

"A puppy!" Max shouted and scrambled off his chair to race toward Monty.

"Max, be careful of your arm," Quinn admonished.

"Oh my gosh. Oh my gosh. Is he really for me?" Max peered up at Monty with disbelief and pure unadulterated joy on his face.

"He sure is, champ. He's all for you." He passed Max the small dog, then peered up at Quinn. "That is if your mom says it's okay."

Seriously? Did he really just say that?

That is just beautiful. Well played, Mr. Hill.

There wasn't a chance in hell she was going to tell Max that he couldn't have that puppy, and he damn well knew it. But it hadn't stopped him from putting her in this ridiculous spot.

Max carried the wriggling puppy over to Quinn. "Oh, Mom, can we keep him? Please? I promise I'll take care of him. I'll feed him and walk him, and he can sleep on my bed. Please, Mom?"

She tipped her head up so Max couldn't see her expression as she glared at Monty. "Where did you find this puppy?"

"I know a guy." He puffed out his chest. "It cost me a pretty penny too, but it was worth every cent just to see the happiness on my boy's face."

Interesting. Especially because earlier he didn't have enough money to pay for aspirin, but now he had enough to buy a dog.

Max giggled as the dog licked maple syrup from his face. "He likes me. He already likes me."

"Of course he does," Monty said.

"So can I pleeeaaassseee keep him, Mom?" Her son gave her the most pitifully sad eyes she'd ever witnessed.

"Having a dog is a huge responsibility. He'll have to be fed and watered every day. And dogs have to be brushed and bathed and taken care of."

"I will. I will take care of him. And I'll feed him every day and change his water every single hour."

She let out a heavy sigh. What choice did she have? Monty had put her in a terrible position. If she said no, she'd look like an unfeeling bitch. No matter what she said, he was still going to come out of this deal smelling like roses.

She glanced at her dad, who offered her one of his trademark stalwart shrugs. "It's up to you."

Fat lot of help he was.

"I guess we can keep him for tonight and see how he does," she relented. Although she knew once she caved, that there was no turning back. They were getting a new puppy.

"Yes!" Max shouted for joy. The puppy wiggled in his arms.

He set it on the floor, and it toddled across the hardwood, then squatted and peed on the rug.

Which seemed an entirely fitting response to the way her day had been going.

———⟋⟍⟋⟍———

Rock stepped out from behind the barn and studied the Rivers's house. Disappointment filled him that Monty's car was still in the driveway.

He'd spent the last few hours debating if he would even bring the gifts over to Max, but decided it wasn't fair that the kid had to suffer just because he was ashamed to face his mom.

The night was still warm, and a full moon filled the sky, lighting his way as he'd walked across the pasture. He carried the books and the LEGO set under his arm.

Cautiously approaching the porch, he heard the sound of laughter coming from inside the house and crept up the stairs to peer through the big bay window in the front of the house.

The scene inside tore his heart in two.

Quinn, Max, and Monty were seated in a circle on the floor, laughing and giggling as they played with a little brown-and-white fluff ball of a puppy. The puppy clambered around on the floor, scrambling between them and sending Max into fits of hysterical giggles.

He recognized the puppy as one of the litter that had been outside of the drugstore.

But he couldn't imagine Quinn had taken one on a whim, especially not with Max's arm being broken. It would be too easy for the puppy to inadvertently hurt him.

No, Quinn wouldn't take a chance on that happening. Besides, she'd been adamant about him not having a dog until he turned ten. They'd just talked about it a few days ago.

The dog had to have come from someone who had a blatant disregard for the rules of a mother and for the consistency of a child's routine.

Which meant it had to have been Hill.

Rock stood in the shadows of the porch, and something inside him broke as he watched the three of them playing with the dog.

Despite how the puppy came to be at the house, and despite the fact that Max had a bright-blue cast binding his arm and a Band-Aid covering the stitches in his chin, they looked like they were having a great time.

They looked happy.

They looked like a family.

A terrible realization hit him. No matter how much he loved Quinn, and he did love her—he always had and he always would—it didn't matter. Because he loved her enough to let her go.

Not let her go like the last time.

The last time, he'd walked away because he was a stupid teenager, and he was being selfish.

This time he had to walk away because he was trying to be *un*selfish.

Because as much as he couldn't stand Monty freaking Hill, the guy had shown that he wanted to be in Max's life and wanted to get to know him. He hadn't cut and run today at the hospital, at the first sign of trouble.

And he didn't know if he and Quinn had a chance to patch things up and work it out between them—heck, he didn't want to think about it if they did—but he knew they didn't stand a snowball's chance in hell if he stuck around.

If he weren't here, then maybe they'd have a chance at creating a real family, a whole family.

And he owed that to Max, to the sweet little kid who took everything in stride, who always saw the good in everyone, even in assholes who didn't deserve it. Like the man who had walked away from his mom, and the one who had walked away from both of them.

Hill might still be an asshole—the jury was out on that one—but Rock knew he didn't have to be. He could do the right thing, for once in his life. He could do something that didn't benefit him.

He could give them up. Give them a chance to build something, to build a life. Together. To let Max have a dad.

He took a step back and slipped from the porch, leaving the books and the LEGO set outside the door.

His chest ached, and he clenched and unclenched his fists as he strode purposefully across the driveway.

As soon as he rounded the barn, he took off, sprinting across the field, running as hard as he could, running away from the woman and the child he'd fallen in love with, running away from the hardest decision he'd ever made.

He blew out his breath, huffing as he pumped his legs

harder. His thighs burned, but he kept running, driving himself, pushing harder as he ran toward his house and away from the only person who felt like home.

———✻———

"Did you hear something?" Quinn asked, cocking her head. "I thought I just heard something on the porch."

"I'll check," Monty said, groaning as he stood up from the floor. The puppy toddled after him, sending Max into another fit of giggles. "I'll let this guy out for a minute while I'm out there."

Quinn cleared the table and loaded the dishwasher with their few supper dishes while Monty was outside. She could see Max was fading on the sofa as he struggled to keep his eyes open.

She was fading as well but knew her night was far from over.

Besides the dishes and laundry that still needed doing, she knew she was in for a long night with a new puppy that hadn't ever spent a night away from its mother. Which wasn't going to be good for her son, who needed his rest after the trauma his body had gone through today.

She also knew that Max was going to beg her to let the pup sleep in his bed, and there was no way she was going to let that happen without giving that little dog a good bath.

Monty might have deemed himself a hero in Max's eyes by bringing him a puppy, but she was the one who was in for the real work. He hadn't thought to purchase anything else, like food, or a leash, or even a dog bowl for it to eat out of.

So a trip to the pet store and another hit to her dwindling bank account were now on her agenda for the morning.

The front door slammed, and Monty walked back in, the puppy in one hand and balancing a box of LEGOs and two books in the other. He brought with him the distinct scent of smoke, and Quinn guessed that his trip outside had been more than just a thoughtful gesture with the puppy and more about sneaking a quick cigarette.

"Look what I just happened to find on the front porch," he said, setting the puppy on the floor and handing the things to Max. "You like LEGOs, right?"

Max's eyes widened, and he jumped off the sofa and threw his arms around Monty's waist. "Yes. Thank you. This has been the best night of my entire life."

Quinn perched on the corner of the sofa, drying her hands with a towel as she peered at the new things. The books were good-sized, and the LEGO set was huge, and all of it looked expensive. She knew from trying to buy LEGOs at Christmas how much a set like that would have set Monty back, and she had a sneaking suspicion that he was taking credit for another man's gift.

He hadn't come out and said he bought them, but he hadn't denied it either.

There was only one person she knew who would buy such thoughtful and generous gifts for her son and not be concerned about getting credit for their purchase.

But if Rock had bought them, why hadn't he come in to give them to Max himself? To check on him to see if he was all right?

She let out a sigh. If Rock couldn't bother to come in, then maybe he deserved to have Monty take the credit for his gifts. Besides, she had more pressing issues to worry about right now than the guy who hadn't bothered to call her since he'd left the hospital.

He'd sent her one text with the words I'm so sorry. She'd texted back that it wasn't his fault, but she hadn't heard from him again after that.

He must have been thinking of them, of Max at least, if he'd gone to all the trouble to find the toys he knew her son would love.

She tried to put Rock out of her mind—she didn't have time to think about him right now. She had a dog to bathe and medicine to dispense and laundry to fold.

A gnawing feeling twisted in her gut though as she watched the respect and admiration grow in her son's eyes for a man she wasn't entirely sure deserved it.

Chapter 20

THE NEXT MORNING, QUINN STRETCHED HER ARMS OVER HER head, her back already aching, and it was only lunchtime.

Her morning had been spent making and cleaning up breakfast, sewing a button back on one of Max's shirts, calling to make a vet appointment for their new addition, and listening to Max go through a million names as he tried to come up with the perfect one for the new puppy.

Plus, it took close to an hour to figure out a way for Max to take a shower without getting his cast or his chin wet, which meant she, and the puppy, both ended up soaking wet as well by the time he'd finished.

This was all making memories, she'd reminded herself. Every moment of chaos and laughter were building blocks in the images of Max's childhood.

She'd finally found time to take her own shower and get out of her pajamas. After dressing in a pair of khaki shorts and a simple white T-shirt, she'd twisted her damp hair into a braid. Figuring it would be an on-the-run kind of day, she'd stuffed her feet into a pair of comfortable sneakers.

On a whim, or so she told herself, she'd pulled on the heart and key necklace that Rock had given her as a teenager and dropped it inside the V-neck of her shirt. She'd been wearing it every day for the last week, trying not to think too much about it when she put it on, but maybe subconsciously hoping that Rock would notice and know she was still thinking about him.

She absently fingered the necklace now as she listened to her dad and Max debate another round of names for the puppy.

Max had already thrown out the more common names, like Fido and Buddy. He wanted something special and unique for his dog. He was taking the picking of its name very seriously.

"You want to give him a good name that he can live up to. Something smart or tough, like Einstein or Rocky," Ham was saying. "Or how about a strong, presidential name? You could call him Ford or Reagan."

"Or George Washington," Max offered with a giggle. They were sitting at the kitchen table, and he had the puppy cuddled in his lap.

Ham chuckled. "That's kind of a long name to call when you want him to come to you."

"Yeah, good point." Max wrinkled his nose. "Who was your favorite president, Grandpa?"

"Well, I don't know that I was partial to any particular one over another, but my dad was always a big fan of Harry Truman. He'd always admired the way he'd stepped in to the role of president after the real president passed on—always thought of the guy as a real hero. So that would be a fine choice. You could call him Harry or Truman."

"Truman's a cute name," Quinn weighed in as she finished stacking grilled cheese sandwiches on a platter.

Max held the puppy up and stared into its small face. "Is your name Truman?" The puppy licked his nose, and Max let out a giggle. "I think he likes it."

"Well, there you have it," Ham declared.

"Yep. There you have it. His name is Truman." Max peered over at his mom. "Mom, we need to get Truman some puppy food and a collar and a leash so I can take him for a walk."

She pointed to a sheet of paper on the kitchen counter. "Yeah, I've been working on a list of all the things he'll need. I made him an appointment to get checked out at the vet clinic tomorrow morning. But I was hoping I could talk your grandpa into running you into town to pick up this stuff after lunch."

"I could probably do that. I've got a couple of things to do in town anyway."

Quinn nodded at Max as she set the sandwiches on the table. "Put the dog down for now and come over here and let me help you wash your hands. Dad, you want to pour him some milk and grab those carrots out of the fridge?"

Max relented to her assistance in washing his hands, then sped through his lunch, anxious to get to the store.

Ham told him he had a few chores to finish up in the barn before they could leave, but he and Truman could come outside and keep him company while he worked.

It took Quinn only a few minutes to wash the noon dishes and put the kitchen back together. Vivienne had dropped off a pan of brownies a few days earlier, and she nibbled on the corner of the last one as she added another item to the list.

Washing up the pan, she figured she might as well run it back over to Vivi. She could use the walk and the fresh air to clear her head.

And if she happened to run into Rock while she was

over there, then so be it. Maybe she could finally ask him what the hell was going and why he was avoiding her.

She scribbled a quick note to her dad, then grabbed the pan and headed for the far side of the barn to the path that connected the two ranches.

Just because she'd stuffed a piece of gum into her mouth and swiped on a little lip gloss didn't necessarily mean she was hoping to see Rock. She could have just wanted fresh breath and glossy lips while she walked.

Walking briskly along the path, she imagined all the ways she might "accidentally" run into Rock, but her gait slowed as she drew closer to the James's house.

What if he didn't want to see her? What if he wouldn't talk to her at all?

Forget that. She'd spent the last eight years avoiding this man, and she was through with that route. He'd made it clear that he wanted to be in her life again, so why the sudden one-eighty? Why was he now avoiding her?

Besides the obvious fact that her son's biological father had suddenly come back into the picture. But they could work through that.

They just needed a chance to talk.

Without distractions.

Crossing through the pasture, she could hear music and banging coming from the barn, and she walked across the drive and peered through the barn doors.

Her breath caught in her throat at the sight of Rock, bare chested, wearing only jeans and boots. His back was to her, and the muscles across his broad shoulders bunched and flexed as he swung a hammer to pound a nail into the side of a two-by-four.

His deep voice rose through the barn rafters as he sang

along to the country song booming through the speakers of the radio. He belted out the lyrics, matching not just his baritone to the singers, but his emotions as well.

The song was one of her favorites and spoke of missed chances and lost love, and her heart broke as she stood in the doorway of the barn, listening to him sing.

His voice was as familiar to her as her own. Memories coursed through her like water trickling down the creek. Memories of being with Rock, his arm around her shoulder as they cruised down a dirt road, not going anywhere in particular, just driving and singing along to the radio.

The images in her mind were as clear as if they'd happened yesterday.

They might be older, and their bodies might look a little different, but their hearts were the same. And she still loved him. Had always loved him. Would always love him.

He reached for another board and saw her standing there. The hammer fell from his hands, and he reached to turn down the radio.

"Q. What are you doing here?"

She held up the brownie pan. "I was just returning this pan to your mom. Then I heard the music."

"How long have you been standing there?"

"Long enough to hear you giving that country star a run for his money." She offered him a timid smile and took a tentative step forward. Then another, until she'd closed the gap between them. "Actually, returning the pan was just an excuse. I really came to see you."

A thin sheen of sweat covered his chest, and more images of them together filled her head. But these weren't from the distant past, they were from several nights ago when they'd been in her bed, tangled together, both of their bodies heated and sweaty from passion.

Rock held up his hand. "Don't." His T-shirt lay across the side of the workbench, and he grabbed it and pulled it on over his head.

Her mouth went dry at his warning and at the way he'd backed away. As if he didn't even want her near him.

A scowl formed on his lips, and his eyes were downcast, his expression reminding her of someone who had lost their only friend. But she was his friend, and he hadn't lost her.

Not yet.

"Rock. What is going on?" She implored him with her tone, beseeching him with her eyes. "Just talk to me."

"How's Max?"

She shook her head, as if trying to clear the sudden topic change. "He's fine. I mean, he broke his arm, and he has a couple of stitches, but he'll be fine. He's already bragging about how cool his cast is."

He'd cringed when she said he broke his arm, and now his mouth was set in a tight line. "It won't be so cool a few weeks from now. Then it will just be itchy and smelly and a pain in the ass." He leaned back against the workbench, his shoulders slumped. "I'm awful sorry, Quinn. I never should have skated away from him like that. I should have been there."

She closed the distance between them, clenching one hand into a fist and gripping the brownie pan in another as she resisted the impulse to reach out and touch him.

He looked so sad, so broken. This wasn't the same guy she'd been hanging out with the last week.

"It wasn't your fault. It was an accident."

He pounded his fist on the workbench, making both her and the tools jump. "It *was* my fault. I was the one on the ice with him. I should have been watching him. Instead, I was being an idiot, careless, only thinking of myself and my ludicrous attempts to impress a girl." He glanced sideways at her. "Sorry. Woman."

A grin tugged at the corners of her mouth. "It was just an accident, and accidents happen. You broke your arm as a kid, and you survived."

They'd been about twelve years old and had gone down to the pond after school. It was a cold day in the middle of winter, and Rock had wanted to shoot some pucks. He'd broken his arm when he'd skated over a stone and fallen into the net. He'd been skating too fast and had been too focused on the shot to stop in time.

"Yeah, I did. And if I remember correctly, that happened because I was showing off for a girl too. The same girl."

She did reach out now and laid a hand gently on his arm. "He'll be okay. And no one is blaming you."

"Except me," he said, shaking off her hand.

"Then stop it." She picked up his hand, held it tightly in hers. "Why don't you tell me what's really going on? Why you're avoiding me and not answering my calls or texts."

He stared at the floor. But he didn't pull his hand away. "Because I can't. I can't do this." His voice shook as if holding back his pain.

"Why the hell not?" Her voice rose with the temper building inside her, and she threw the brownie pan against the workbench and planted her fist on her hip. "Huh? Answer me, Rockford James. Why the hell not?

You didn't seem to have any trouble doing this the last week. You didn't seem to have any trouble doing this when you were sneaking into my bedroom in the middle of the night and sending me all of those texts."

He winced and slowly shook his head, his gaze still trained on the floor.

This was not the Rock she knew. The one whose temper often got him in trouble on and off the ice. The one who could easily pick a fight with a reporter or egg on an opponent into throwing a punch.

"Talk to me, damn it. Tell me what's going on. Tell me why you're running hot and cold with me. Why one minute you want me so bad you're crossing the pasture at midnight, and the next you won't answer my calls and can't stand to even look at me. Is this all just some kind of game to you?"

His head whipped up, and his eyes narrowed. "This is no game. At least, not one I have any chance of winning. I'm not running hot and cold, Quinn. I'm running pure hot, all the time. Hot with need and hunger. And anger at the situation. The problem is not that I don't want you. I want you so bad, it hurts. Like nothing I've ever felt before. My heart aches like an actual wound has torn open inside me, and every time I see you, it tears a little bit more, ripping through my chest and taking my breath away."

Her body stilled, and her anger flooded away with the sincerity and pain in his words. She knew what he was feeling, had the same bone-deep ache in her own chest.

She reached out, picked up his hand, and held it to her cheek. His arm tensed, but he didn't pull away.

She fought to control the tremor in her voice and the

tremble of her lips. "But I'm right here in front of you. All you have to do is reach out and touch me. You don't have to pull away. I'm not. I'm standing right here. I'm not going anywhere. Not this time. This time I'm not letting go. I love you, Rock."

His brow furrowed, and he gave her a long, pained look.

Her breathing slowed, her lungs constricting.

Maybe this was what was going on. Maybe this was the real problem. Maybe he didn't love her anymore.

Or didn't love her at all.

He tried to speak, his mouth opened then closed.

His palm tightened against her cheek, and he took a deep, shuddering breath. "I love you too, Quinn. I always have. And I always will."

Her breath rushed from her chest, and she reached for his shoulder, clutching the fabric of his T-shirt in her fingers.

"I have always loved you too. And I've been trying to show you that. That's why I'm wearing this stupid seventeen-dollar necklace with the tarnished silver heart. To show you. Show you that my heart, my body, my soul, has always belonged to you." She swallowed, the emotion filling her throat.

"Do you still want to be with me?" she managed to whisper.

His eyes squeezed tightly shut then opened, and he stared into hers with an intensity that had a million sparks of heat licking at her spine. "I want to be with you with every fiber of my being. I want to hold you and kiss you. Hell, I want to tear your clothes off right now and take you against the wall of this barn."

Heat, warm and molten, surged through her veins. She wanted him too. And this time, she was going after what she wanted.

She hadn't stood up for herself before.

All those years ago, Rock had left, but she had let him walk away. She hadn't gone after him. She'd reacted in defense and tried to hurt him back instead of digging in her heels and fighting for him.

She pushed back her shoulders, narrowing her eyes as she stared deep into his, trying to convey the depth of her emotion. There was no tremble in her voice this time.

This time, her words came out not as a request, but as a command. "If you still want me, then take me."

He stared at her, indecision clouding his eyes, then the hand holding her cheek skimmed down and around her neck at the same time his other hand slid around her waist. He pulled her to him, yanking her against his chest as his lips crushed hers, taking her mouth in a passionate assault.

Her arms wound around his neck, and her fingers tunneled through his hair.

The tiniest of moans escaped her lips, and she arched her back, pressing into him, giving herself to him. Giving him everything.

His one hand clutched her neck, and the other moved roughly over her back and down her hip, cupping her butt and pulling her tightly against him.

She felt his groin harden, and she pressed closer, aching for the delicious friction.

His tongue pushed between her lips, pillaging her mouth as he feasted on her, tasting her, devouring her.

And she loved it. Wanted it. Wanted him.

Her body responded to his with its own desire, her nipples tightening and her breasts swelling with need. Her legs threatened to buckle, and she melted against him, holding on as if she were drowning and he was the only thing that could save her.

He could have done anything he wanted to her—could have peeled off her clothes and taken her on the barn's workbench or laid her down on a bed of hay in one of the empty stables.

Instead, he'd stripped her bare, laid open her soul as she'd confessed her feelings for him, then he pushed her away.

Gasping for air, he held on to her shoulder, holding her away from him as his face contorted in pain. "Stop. I can't. We can't. We can't do this."

What?

"Why? What's wrong?"

Suddenly, a thought hit her, slammed into her like a Mack truck flying down the highway at seventy miles an hour. A terrible, awful thought.

She tried to speak but couldn't say the words.

Pulling back, she let his hand drop from her arm. Her mouth had gone dry, her throat constricted. She swallowed, then choked out, "Is there…is there someone else?"

His shoulders fell forward, slumping in defeat as he hung his head.

His voice was barely a whisper. "Yes. There is."

Chapter 21

Q<small>UINN'S HEART FELT LIKE IT HAD STOPPED BEATING.</small>

Frozen in place, all she could do was blink as his words burrowed through her shocked brain. There was someone else? But then why did he...? How could he...?

Before her mind went to all the dark places of who this other woman was and what she and Rock had done the past week, Fury stepped in, pushing the hurt defensively behind her as she championed for Quinn. "Are you fucking kidding me?" she spat. "You've been sleeping with me while you're committed to another woman?"

His expression softened. "Geez, Quinn. No, of course not. It's not like that. It's not another woman. I wouldn't do that to you. But there is someone else. Someone I'm thinking of. That I'm *trying* to think of. Someone who deserves something better."

She was so confused. Her emotions were tumbling like they were being spun in a mixer. "What are you talking about? Who?"

"Max."

Her breath caught, and she brought her hand up to cover her mouth, a shudder of emotion ripping through her chest.

Max?

Not another woman. But her son?

"Max? Why? What does my son have to do with this? I thought you liked him."

"I do. I love that kid. I know that sounds crazy. He's not mine, but this last week, spending time with him, with you both, I completely fell in love with the little guy. He climbed right into my heart, and that's why we can't do this. Why *I* can't do this. I can't do this to him."

She shook her head. "I don't understand."

"No. You wouldn't. That's because you're not a young boy that's had to grow up without his dad."

Her eyes widened, and she shook her head, feeling his words like a slap to the face.

"I'm not saying you haven't done a great job. Max is an amazing kid, and so much of that is attributed to you and how you've raised him. But he has a chance to have his dad in his life, and I can't be the one to screw up that chance."

"His dad? What are you talking about? This is about Monty? Rock, you're not making any sense."

"I saw you, okay. I saw you through the window last night when I brought the books and the LEGOs for Max."

"I knew they were from you."

"Who else did you think they were from?"

"Max assumed that Monty brought them, and he didn't do anything to correct that assumption."

A muscle twitched in Rock's clenched jaw. "It doesn't matter."

"It does matter. Those were really thoughtful gifts, and Max loved them. Why didn't you give them to him yourself?"

"I was going to. But then I saw you through the window. You were all three sitting on the floor, playing with the dog. I could hear Max giggling, and you…" He paused and swallowed. "You were laughing too. You looked like a family, a real family, and it struck me, in that moment, that that's what you would look like if I weren't around."

"But you are around."

"Not really. Not all the time. I have this whole other life. My career. I don't even live here. I still have the team, and I'm gone all the time. I'm not even home long enough to have a dog. I've made a lot of selfish decisions in my life, things that affected not just me, but other people around me, people I cared about. People I loved. And I don't want to be that guy anymore. I don't want to be that selfish guy who only cares about himself."

"But what about me? Do I even get a say in this matter?"

"No." His voice was soft but stern. "Because your say *doesn't* matter. The only one who matters is Max." He dragged his hand through his hair. "I know. I know what it's like to grow up without a dad. And I don't want Max to know what that feels like."

"But what about us? What about everything that's happened between us the past week?"

"This last week has been amazing. And maybe things would have been different if Hill hadn't shown up when he did." He reached his hand out, as if to touch her, then changed his mind and let it fall. "Hell, I know they would have been. But he *did* show up. And he's here now, and he's making it pretty clear that he wants to be in Max's life. So, it doesn't matter what I want, or even what you want. It matters what's best for that sweet kid."

How could she argue with his logic? He was making perfect sense. To her head. But all her heart heard was that he was leaving. That he was walking away from her again.

"We can work this out."

"I am trying to work this out. I've been thinking about this for days. And this is the answer. The only answer. The thing that is best for Max. He's a great kid, Q. You've done an amazing job with him. You're a great mom. But a kid needs a mom and a dad. And Hill is stepping up and trying to be there. And as much as I can't stand the guy, my opinion doesn't matter. So far, he's proven he wants to be a father to his kid."

She rolled her eyes. "After eight years of ignoring him."

"I hear you. But he's here now."

"He's only been here for a few days."

He pounded his fist onto the workbench again. "Damn it, I'm trying to think about someone besides myself. I'm trying to be a better man than I've been in the past. Don't make this harder on me than it already is."

She winced and tried to take a step back, but he reached for her, pulled her to him, and held her in a tight hug. He pressed a kiss to the side of her head, then drew his head back and looked down into her face.

He touched her cheek, laying his palm tenderly against her skin. His voice was low, gruff with emotion, and his pain shown evident in his eyes. "I love you, Quinn. I always have. I always will. But it's not enough to tell you that. I've said it before. This time, I'm trying to show you. Show you that I love you and your son enough to let you go."

He tilted his head and pressed a soft kiss to her lips. One sweet, tender, beautiful kiss that left Quinn's body aching for more. Then he did what he said he would do.

He let her go.

He turned and walked out of the barn, leaving her

standing—heartbroken and stunned—next to the work-bench, disregarded and abandoned. Both her thoughts and his tools were jumbled, spread in disarray, the only sounds in the barn the hushed flutter of the swallows in the eaves and the sad country song playing softly on the radio.

The walk back across the pasture was spent crying over and cussing at Rockford James. He made a crazy sort of sense, and Quinn tried to see it from his point of view. But that's what kept sticking in her craw. It was all from his point of view. She didn't even get a vote.

Well, screw him.

She didn't need him anyway.

She didn't need anyone. She'd taken care of herself and her son just fine over the last eight years. It was time to quit pining over a guy she'd loved when she was a teenager.

So what if she still loved him and he said he still loved her? Sometimes things didn't work out. That was life. Shit happens.

She still had to get out of bed in the morning and face her day and take care of herself and Max. No one else was going to do it for her.

Pushing her shoulders back, she wiped her cheeks with the back of her hand as she rounded the corner of the barn. She didn't want Max or her dad to see her crying. Didn't want to have to explain that she and Rock were through.

But she didn't have to worry. Her dad's truck was gone. The only car in the driveway was Monty's beat-up blue sedan.

Great. Just what she needed. More humiliation.

It was bad enough that Rock no longer wanted her, now she had to face Monty, the man who'd made no secret of the fact that he hadn't wanted her all those years ago.

His car was empty, and she didn't see him in the living room or kitchen as she climbed the porch steps and peered through the front windows.

Is this how it had been for Rock the night before? When he'd seen them through the window, laughing and playing with the puppy?

How they must have looked like a perfect, happy family to him.

Where *was* Monty?

She scanned the outbuildings. He must be in the barn or walking around the farmyard.

Maybe she could slip quietly into the house, and he wouldn't even have to know she was there. Then maybe he'd drive away, and she wouldn't have to face him at all.

The last thing she wanted right now was to make small talk, or any kind of talk at all with her ex.

All she wanted to do was crawl back into her bed— the bed where she'd made reckless love to Rock only a few nights before—pull the covers over her head, and lick her brokenhearted wounds.

She stepped into the house, catching the screen door so it didn't slam behind her.

A makeshift gate of blankets and chairs had been stretched from the wall to one side of the kitchen island. She could see Truman asleep on a blanket next to the refrigerator, most likely comforted by the steady hum of the appliance.

The note she'd written still sat on the kitchen table, but it had been flipped over, and her dad had scrawled another note back, telling her he'd taken Max into town to pick up the things for the dog.

She jumped as a noise sounded from down the hallway, like a clink of metal against plastic.

Grabbing a chunky candle from the center of the table, she held it up, her first instinct to reach for a weapon, ready to clobber a burglar. Not that a cupcake-scented candle was much of a weapon, but at least it was something.

Taking a deep breath, she tried to slow her pounding heart, laughing at herself as she realized it probably was *not* a home invasion, but more likely Monty. He must have decided to wait for Max in his room.

She quietly approached the door to her son's room—just in case—but the laughter died on her lips when she saw Monty standing next to Max's bed, dumping out the contents of his savings bank and stuffing the bills into his pockets.

"What the hell do you think you're doing?"

Monty's head whipped up, his eyes round, his gaze searching the room as if desperate to find a plausible explanation for why he could possibly be stealing from his own son.

"This isn't what it looks like," he stammered.

Quinn could see the sheen of sweat on his upper lip. "Oh, really? It's not? Because it *looks* like you're stealing the money from Max's savings bank—the money he put aside to give to his Sunday school class and to save for something special. But if it's *not* what it looks like, then by all means, please enlighten me."

He had the gall—and the arrogance—to look offended. "I'm not *stealing* it. I'm just *borrowing* it. Just until my next paycheck."

"Paycheck? What paycheck? You never even mentioned that you had a job."

His face changed, like a mask shifting into place. His features went from slack guilt to contempt, his lip curling into a disdainful sneer. "You think you're so much better than me."

She cringed, drawing her head back as if he'd thrown something more at her than his scornful words. "What are you talking about?"

"You walk around, acting all holier than thou, with your schedules and your expensive car and your filthy rich boyfriend."

She let out a harsh laugh. "Who? Rock? He's not my boyfriend. And I don't have an expensive car."

He crossed the room in two large, foreboding steps and pressed her back against the wall. His eyes narrowed in hatred, and she could smell onions and stale cigarettes as his hot breath grazed her cheek. "Don't lie to me. I see the way he looks at you. The way you look at each other. I don't know what kind of game you're playing, but you're not fooling me."

"I'm not trying to fool you. Or anyone. Why would I? I don't care what you think of me."

"You should care. Because I know things. Things that could tear your perfect little life apart."

What the heck was this guy talking about? "Are you threatening me?"

He offered her another scornful sneer. "Not threatening. Just letting you know that you're not holding as many cards as you think. I didn't realize what claiming Max as my son could do for me before, but I do now."

"What did you say? You didn't realize what claiming Max could *do* for you?" Fury built in her, forming a swirling ball of heat in her gut and spreading out through her limbs. This man was in her son's bedroom, stealing money from his piggy bank, and he had the audacity to tell her that he just realized what Max could do for him, like her child was some kind of commodity. And then to threaten her?

No. This shit was not going to fly.

She pushed back against him, summoning up all of the bravery she could muster. "Get the hell out of here. I knew this was a mistake, letting you in here. I want you out of this house and out of Max's life."

He laughed, a hard, mean huff of a sound. "Or what?"

"Or I'll throw you out."

"Yeah? You and whose army? I don't see anyone here but us."

Shit.

He was right.

Heart pounding, she realized the desperateness of her situation.

She was alone.

Even if she screamed for help, no one was around to hear her.

This is what she'd just been thinking on her way back from Rock's. She was on her own. In this room and in her life. The only one she could really count on was herself.

She tried not to panic. Her gaze darted frantically around the room, looking for a weapon, anything to defend herself.

She still had the chunky candle in her hand. It might smell like vanilla cupcakes, but it could do some damage if she smacked it against the side of Monty's head.

His gaze followed hers, and his lip curled in contempt. "I hope you aren't getting any crazy ideas in your head now, Quinn. You might think you're tough, but you're not. You're nothing."

Anger simmered in his words, in the barely controlled tremor in his voice, in the pungent smell of his sweat. His body tensed, his muscles quivered, and she knew she was in trouble.

Before she had a chance to even raise the candle, he struck. His movements quick, like a snake striking its prey.

With one hand, he grabbed her arm, and with the other, he seized her collar, twisting it in his fist and hauling her tighter against him. The chain of her necklace popped and slid from her neck, and the sound of fabric ripping tore through the air.

But all she could feel was the tight grip that he had on her upper arm, the intense pressure of his fingers digging into her tender flesh.

"Drop the candle," he ordered.

She bit down on her lip, trying not to cry out from the pain. His knuckles were pressing into her windpipe. It's not like she could use the stupid jar candle anyway. She'd have to think of something else. A different kind of weapon. Like her brain.

That she could do. She might not have made it to college, but she could outsmart this idiot.

She opened her palm and let the candle fall to the floor. It hit the carpet with a thud, but didn't break.

He let go of her shirt, releasing the pressure against her throat, and she sucked in a deep breath.

His other hand still held her arm in a death grip, but he pulled back a few inches. Just enough for her shirt to fall back and for her to realize that the ripped fabric left her bare and exposed.

He realized it too. His gaze fell to her chest, to her lace bra now visible beneath the torn shirt, and the dark look in his eyes changed from anger to a greedy lust. "We are all alone out here. We shouldn't be fighting, Quinn. Not when we could be using this time for better things. Like making us another Maxie."

The tone in his voice was lecherous and threatening, and her anger slipped away, replaced by cold, stark fear.

Sweat broke out on her back, and she struggled to stay calm. To think.

He dipped his other hand, sliding it down her neck, then cupping her breast and holding it firmly in his grasp as he bent his head closer to her ear. "Remember the night we made Max? You were so easy that night, so desperate to get back at your stupid boyfriend, you practically begged me for it." He tightened his grip, squeezed her breast painfully. "Well, I'm here now. And I won't even make you beg. Not much anyway."

He offered her a vulgar chuckle—a laugh mixed with crudeness and threat.

Bile rose in her throat. "Get your filthy hands off me." She tried to raise her leg to knee him in the groin, but he blocked her with his thigh.

He still had her pressed against the wall, and his body was strong, his grip on both her arm and her breast tightening further. "Oh, she's getting tough. That's good. I like a fighter." He twisted her around and threw her down on Max's bed.

She scrambled backward through the array of coins and bills that lay scattered across the bed. Grabbing the plastic bank, she threw it as hard as she could at Monty's face.

He howled when the bank hit him in the cheek before it fell to the floor.

A red mark flamed on his cheek, and he pressed his fingers against the spot. His anger intensified, his eyes narrowing into tight slits as he reached for her legs. "You're gonna pay for that, bitch."

She kicked out, trying to use the strength in her legs, trying to connect her feet to anything that would cause him pain and keep him away from her. Trying to think of anything to say that would stop him. "Don't do this. My dad's going to be back any minute now. And you know if he catches you here like this, he'll kill you."

He paused, for just a second, as if digesting her words.

"And my brother is supposed to be home anytime now too." She grabbed the loose bills left on the bed and tossed them toward him. "Just take the money. That's what you came here for. Just take the cash and get out."

He stood glaring at her, his arms held out at his sides, his chest heaving.

She held her breath, desperately praying he would either take the money and leave or that her dad or brother would arrive home any second.

Either the lure of the money or the threat of Ham and Logan must have tipped the scales, because he scooped up the money and shoved it into his pockets.

He pointed a finger at her, and she stared at it, noticing the thin line of grease still under his nail and that the cuticle was torn and bleeding. "This isn't over. Not by a long shot. I tried it the easy way. Now you're gonna pay."

Backing out of the room, he left her with one more threat. "And so is Max."

She heard his footsteps moving quickly down the hall, and she scrambled from the bed, slamming the door shut and leaning her back against it.

Her heart racing, she held her breath, listening as the front door slammed, followed by the sounds of a car door and an engine starting. She heard the gravel as his wheels spun and he tore out of the driveway.

Letting out her breath, she sank to the floor, her back still against the door.

Spying her broken necklace on the carpet, she crawled toward it. Clutching the chain, the key, and the heart pendant in her fist, she curled in a ball and let loose a sob.

She gave herself a few minutes, a few minutes to let the terror and the anger of the situation out in her tears, then she pulled herself together and stood shakily to her feet. She didn't want Max or her dad to see her like this. Logan wasn't really supposed to be home until tomorrow. That one had been an empty threat. But her dad really could drive up at any minute.

She pulled the bedroom door open and walked down the hall, hoping Monty hadn't done any other damage on his way out of the house.

Her mouth felt full of cotton, her throat parched and dry. She needed a drink of water and to wash her face.

Still clutching the necklace in her hand, she headed toward the kitchen.

Her heart froze as she saw the makeshift gate had been thrown apart, the blankets and chairs tossed to the side.

Oh no. Oh, please no.

Running toward the mess, she wildly searched the floor for the puppy. She knew before she saw the empty kitchen, knew Monty had carried out his threat of hurting Max.

The puppy was gone.

Chapter 22

SHE COULDN'T BELIEVE IT.

Couldn't believe someone would do something so cruel.

Why would Monty take the dog?

Quinn's heart ached as she stared at the empty kitchen floor.

What the hell was she supposed to do?

Her purse lay on the kitchen counter, her phone next to it. Without thinking, she picked it up and tapped the screen, calling the first person, the only person, who came to mind.

The one she'd always needed.

He hadn't always been there for her in the past, but she sent up a silent prayer that he would be there now.

"Hello."

He *was* there.

The sound of his voice caused her shoulders to slump forward, and she leaned against the side of the counter for support. "Rock." She breathed out his name, a whisper that was a cross between a cry and a weep.

"Quinn. What's wrong? Where are you?"

"I'm here. I'm home. But he's gone. He took him."

"Took who? Quinn, take a breath and talk to me."

She took a deep, shuddering breath. "The puppy. Max's puppy. He took him."

"Who did?"

"Monty. He was angry. He took the puppy to hurt me. To get back at me."

"Stay there. I'm already in my truck. I'll be there in two minutes."

The phone went dead.

She tried to catch her breath, to think. But all she could focus on was the bone-deep ache in her heart. This would kill Max. And it would be her fault.

This was all her fault for letting that man back into their lives.

The sound of a truck engine broke through her thoughts. She ran out onto the porch to see Rock's pickup tearing down the driveway.

He pulled to a stop in front of her, gravel flying as his tires skidded across the dirt. Opening the door, he growled, "Get in."

She flew off the porch and scrambled into the truck, pulling the door shut behind her.

Rock's face was a mask of stone, his mouth set, his brows drawn tightly together. But his eyes widened as he turned his head to look at her. "What the hell happened to you?" His lips formed a tight line, and he spoke through gritted teeth. "Did that fucker hurt you?"

She looked down at her torn shirt, at the bruises forming on her arm, at the broken necklace still clutched in her hand. Opening her fist, she held it out to him, her voice faltering as she whispered, "He broke my necklace."

He spoke his next words slowly, enunciating every syllable. "I'm going to break his fucking neck."

After such vehemence in his words, she was surprised when he reached out and tenderly touched the red marks

on her arm. And even more surprised at the tears that
welled in his eyes.

He drew his arm back, squeezing his eyes shut and
drawing the back of his hand across his cheek. "Put on
your seat belt," he ordered, then put the truck in gear and
sped out of the driveway.

He didn't speak as they drove toward Monty's
brother's house, and she didn't push him. The muscles
corded in his forearms, and his knuckles were white as
he gripped the steering wheel. His eyes stayed focused
on the road, his jaw set, his teeth clenched together, fury
radiating off him so strongly she could almost feel it, as
if it filled the cab of the truck, pushing her back against
the seat.

The distance between the two towns was close to
twelve miles, but Rock tore up the highway, pushing
the truck, and she was afraid to look at how fast they
were going.

"They still in that shitty dump just east of town?" he
finally asked, still not taking his eyes off the road.

She swallowed. "Yes."

He spotted the broken-down farmhouse and slowed
the truck as he turned into the drive. Monty's car was
parked next to the house.

He hit the brakes, and dust and gravel went flying.
"Stay in the truck," he ordered as he slammed the door
and strode toward the house.

"The hell I will." She clambered out after him, suddenly terrified that Rock really was going to kill Monty.

He raised his fist and pounded on the front door.
"Open up, Hill. I know you're in there." They waited
a few seconds, then he turned the knob and pushed

the door open, barging through the front door of the house.

Monty stood next to the sofa, his cell phone gripped in his hand. "You can't come in here. That's trespassing."

"Not if we're invited," Rock said. "And I swear I heard you say 'Come on in.' Didn't you hear him say that, Quinn?"

"Yep. Sure did. Clear as day." Her bravery had returned as she stood next to Rock.

A whimper sounded, and her gaze shot to the corner of the room where Truman's furry brown head poked over the corner of a liquor store box.

Monty took a step toward the puppy, but Rock moved faster, holding out his arm and fixing the other man with a steely stare.

He picked up the box and handed it to Quinn. "Take the dog out to the truck. Wait for me there."

She took the box and backed toward the door, the puppy crying and climbing up the sides, its nails scratching the cardboard as it tried to lick her face.

"You can't take that dog. That's stealing." Monty held up his phone. "And I already called my brother. He's a cop, you know. He's on his way."

"Good. We can show him the bruises you put on Quinn's arms and neck."

Monty's face paled, then returned to his scornful sneer. "I didn't touch her. And she's lying if she says I did. If she's got bruises, they're probably from you. I know you've got a real bad temper. I've seen you on TV, always getting into fights."

I thought he said he didn't know who Rock was. The thought flitted through her mind, then disappeared as

Rock turned to her, his features hard and angry. "Take the dog out to the truck. I need to have a word with Hill. Now, Quinn."

She stood frozen, indecision holding her in place. She didn't want to leave Rock alone with Monty, but she also wanted to make sure they had possession of the dog by the time his brother showed up. If he really did show up.

"Okay." She backed through the door and onto the porch, clutching the box to her chest.

Panic filled her as she saw Rock slam the door behind her and heard the dead bolt slide into the lock.

Rock turned from the door to face Hill, his fists already clenching at his sides, aching to drive them into Monty's stupid face.

Hill held up his hands as Rock walked slowly forward. "You can't touch me. My brother's a cop."

"I don't give a shit who your brother is. You don't ever lay a hand on Quinn again. In fact, I don't want you to even look at her. Her or Max. You had your chance. And you blew it. Now you're going to leave."

"Oh yeah? Are you going to make me?" He acted tough but scooted behind the table as Rock advanced toward him.

"Oh please, just give me *one* reason. I'm already planning to punch you in the throat for laying your hands on Quinn. All I need is for you to say one more thing—give me one more reason to smash my fist into your disgusting face."

Monty held up his hands. "Hold on. Nobody needs to punch anybody."

Rock laughed. He wasn't going to let Hill get in a single punch.

"You want me to leave?" Monty stammered. "Fine, I'll leave. You just gotta make it worth my while."

"Worth your while? What the hell are you talking about?"

"You got plenty of money, Mr. Big Shot Hockey Player. You have what it takes to get me out of Quinn's and Max's lives. What do you think I came back here for? I know that guys with cash will pay to keep me out of the lives of the women they love. But I won't go for so cheap this time. Ham's measly ten thousand bucks didn't last very long. So if you want me gone, it's gonna cost you fifty."

Ham's measly ten thousand bucks? Hamilton had paid this guy off to leave Quinn and Max alone? No wonder he was so pissed at having him back. Ham could barely see straight when Monty was around. Hell, he'd probably been waiting to get him alone so he could punch him in the face too. Just wait until he saw the bruises Hill had put on his daughter.

Rock could probably leave now without laying a hand on him and it wouldn't matter. Ham would track him down and kill him later.

But then he'd miss out on the satisfaction of feeling his flesh collapse under his fist. And of spilling the man's blood who had dared to harm Quinn and was now demanding a payoff to disappear again.

"Fifty thousand dollars?" Rock asked, regarding the man with scorn. "That's what your child is worth to you?"

Max and Quinn were priceless to him.

The very idea that someone could put a price tag on their son's head was repulsive.

It wouldn't matter if someone offered him fifty thousand or fifty million. He would never consider giving away his family for money.

"You better take me up on it quick, before I change my offer and make it sixty," Monty threatened.

Rock shook his head, both at the absurdity of the fact that this guy was bartering his family away and that he had considered for a moment paying him the money just to make him disappear. "You know what you're going to get from me, Hill? Fifty thousand fuck yous."

A sarcastic sneer played across Monty's lips. "Are you sure about that? Sure you don't want to change your mind?"

"The only thing I'm changing my mind about is the fact that I had decided earlier that I'd let you keep your teeth."

Hill's face paled, but he wouldn't stop, wouldn't shut up. "You can threaten me all you want, but I hold all the cards, James. Because Max is *my* son, and I've only gotten started with him. You don't want to pay now, but I guarantee you're going to wish you would have."

That was all it took, the final straw to tip him over the edge. Fury boiled in his blood at the threat to Max, and Rock couldn't hold back.

He took two giant strides and kicked the chair out from in front of him before swinging his fist into Monty's face.

The feel of Monty's bone cracking under his knuckles did little to appease his anger. Neither did the anguished cry or the blood that spurted from his broken nose.

Rock wanted to hurt him, wanted to cause him pain. Pain that would last a long time—that would remind him with every throb of agony that he shouldn't have touched Quinn, shouldn't have threatened Max, shouldn't have messed with Rockford James, or his family.

His fist swung in a wide arc, and he landed another punch into the side of Monty's cheek, splitting the skin under his eye.

"Rock, stop it!" Quinn screamed, running toward him from the kitchen.

He heard Quinn's voice, but it sounded far away, barely discernible over the rush in his ears. She must have gone around and come in the back door of the house.

She grabbed his arm, trying to pull him back from Monty, who now lay crumpled in a ball on the floor, his hands covering his head in defense. "You have to stop. We need to go. I heard the sirens. Monty's brother is on his way. We have to get out of here."

Taking another step back, he shook his head to clear it as he tried to focus on her distressed face. "No. He hurt you, and I can't let that stand. I don't care if his brother shows up. He deserves this."

Quinn glanced down at Monty, and her lips pulled back in a sneer. "He deserves a lot worse than this, but not from you. Not right now. Please, Rock. Think of your career. Think about Max. He's still his dad."

That comment stopped him in his tracks, and he let his fists fall to his sides. This asshole had just offered to give up that privilege for fifty thousand dollars, so he wasn't stopping for Monty's sake, but for Max's. For the little kid who wouldn't understand why he'd punched his dad in the face.

"Please," Quinn begged. "We have to leave."

She grabbed his hand, and he let her lead him out the front door and toward the truck. The wail of sirens filled the air, the sound finally getting through to Rock, and they raced to get in the vehicle and get out of there.

Quinn had put the box on the floor of the cab, and she scooped up the puppy and held him to her as he sped down the highway and away from the direction of the sirens.

Rock held out his arm, and she scooted across the seat and pressed against him as he curled his arm around her shoulders. She leaned her head on his chest and slid her arm around his stomach, holding onto him and cuddling the puppy between them.

He kept his eyes on the road but pressed a kiss to the top of her head and felt her tense muscles relax against him. That was all he needed for now.

They didn't talk as they drove back to the ranch. They didn't need to. It was enough to just take comfort in holding on to each other.

Pulling up in front of the house, Quinn sat up and looked around the driveway. "I can't believe my dad isn't even back yet. They're probably sitting in the café, blissfully eating apple pie and vanilla ice cream." She shook her head. "I guess it's really only been a few hours, but it feels like a lifetime since I left your house and came back here to find Monty in Max's room."

"What the hell was he doing in Max's room?"

"That's what I asked him. He was stealing Max's money from his piggy bank."

"What?"

"Yeah, that's what started this whole thing. I caught

him stealing money from his own son—money that Max had saved for church."

"I would have kicked the guy out on his ass."

"That's what I tried to do. That's when he attacked me. I didn't realize until just now that I haven't even told you about it. I got so caught up in getting the dog." The puppy had fallen asleep, and she lifted him from her lap and set him down gently in the box so as not to wake him.

"I didn't need to know everything that happened. All I saw were the bruises on your skin and I…" He took a deep breath, knowing it wouldn't help to rehash it. "Do you want to tell me about the rest of it now?"

She nodded, then leaned back against his arm, which was still resting along the back of the seat. His hand moved to her shoulder, to offer comfort as she told him what had happened in Max's room. He had a feeling she was leaving out some of the details. But what she did say was bad enough.

Rock's teeth clenched, and he struggled not to put the truck in gear and drive back over to Monty's to finish the job he'd started.

He pounded his fist against the steering wheel. "I'm sorry, Quinn. I didn't know. Hell, maybe I did. But I didn't want to know—didn't want to be right. For Max's sake. For that sweet little kid, I wanted Hill to have changed—to have turned into a decent guy."

"I wanted that too. I swear, I wanted to believe him. Believe in him. I don't know what I'm going to tell Max. How I'm going to break it to him. He thinks Monty hung the moon."

"It's going to be tough." He pulled her into a hug,

burying his face in her shoulder and holding her tightly. Pulling back, he brushed her cheek with the back of his fingers and looked into her eyes, hoping she saw the sincerity there. "I'll help if I can. I'm here for you."

He dipped his head, unable to hold back, and pressed his lips to hers in a tender kiss.

She melted into him, clutching the fabric of his shirt in her fists as she deepened the kiss. A soft sound escaped her lips, a cross between a moan and a sigh, and he wanted to pull her onto his lap, to hold her and protect her. And to peel her clothes off and lay her down on the seat of his truck.

Slanting his mouth across hers, he cupped her cheek, holding her face with both hands as he tasted her lips.

She kissed him, hard, balling her hands into fists, then pushed him away. "No. Stop. You can't do this to me. You say you want to help, that you're here for me. But you're not. You weren't."

"I know. I'm sorry. But I'm here now."

She scooted back, away from him. "I can't. I can't take it again. You left me back then, broke my heart and left me behind. And I thought I'd die of it. Instead, I made a stupid choice and wound up a single mom. And I swore I would never trust another man. Not after you left me, then Monty left me."

She shook her head, a tremor sounding in her voice. "But I did. I trusted you. You came back and seduced me with your sweet words and your thoughtful gestures. You made me believe in you again. Believe in love again. Then just when I thought we might really have a chance at this thing, you turned tail and ran. Again."

"I didn't run."

"Oh no, you're right. You *let me go*. Isn't that what you said? Some bullshit about loving me enough to let me go?"

"It wasn't bullshit. It was real. And it was the hardest thing I've ever done. But I was trying to do the right thing—do what was best for you. And for Max."

"Well, that's what I'm doing too. And I think what's best for me and for Max right now is for my son to see that he has a strong woman for a mom. A woman who doesn't have to depend on a man. Who can stand up for herself, on her own two feet."

"He's already seen that. You've been doing that for years."

"Not really. Not totally. Because in my heart of hearts, I always hoped—always prayed—that you would come back. Come back and save us. And then you did. You came back to me, but you didn't save us. You didn't make things any better. You did for a very short time when I thought you had really come back, when I thought we had a future, and I could see you getting close to Max and filling up my heart again. But then you left once more. I know what it's like to love you, Rock, and then have you walk away. And I can't let that happen to my son. I can't let his heart be broken the way mine has been."

Her words were like shards of broken glass piercing his heart. He knew he'd hurt her, knew he'd screwed up when he'd walked away the first time, but damn it, this time he'd been trying to do the right thing. The best thing for all of them.

"Quinn. I'm sorry I hurt you. I never wanted to do

that, and I never want to hurt Max. I love that kid. If we could just—"

She held up her hand, cutting off his next words. "Don't. This is hard enough as it is. You say you don't want to hurt us, then don't." She opened the truck door and slid out of the seat.

Picking up the box with the puppy inside, she stood next to the cab and lifted her chin as she looked him square in the eye. "You said you wanted to let us go. So do it. Let us go. It's not like it's going to be that hard—you're going back to Denver anyway. As soon as you recuperate, you'll go back to the team, back to your life. Your *real* life. You can look back on this time as a momentary distraction and get back to the business of being who you really are— Rockford James, team legend, hockey superstar."

"That's not fair." He leaned forward, reaching out his hand, afraid that the best thing in his life was slipping away from him and he couldn't do a thing to stop it.

Quinn shook her head and let out a hard breath. "No, it's *not* fair. None of this is fair. It's not fair that you came back and let me fall in love with you again. It's not fair that you're leaving and going back to the life you have without us. But that *is* life. And life's not fair."

Her bottom lip trembled as she spoke, breaking Rock's heart further.

He knew this was hard on her, and it was killing him, but what she said also hit a nerve. He did have a life in Denver, did have a career that he was going back to, a team that was counting on him. He didn't live here. He lived an hour and a half away.

But it might as well be twenty hours away or a hundred, because even though his house was in Denver, he was hardly ever there. He was always at the rink or on the road, traveling with the team.

"You know what I'm saying is true," she said, tears welling in her eyes. "I can see it in your face. You know you're going back as soon as you're well enough to play. So go back. I'm not asking you to stay. I'm asking you to do what you said you would do this morning. Let us go."

She took a step back, shut the door of the truck, then turned and ran up the porch steps and into the house.

Rock sat in the truck, feeling like he'd been punched in the gut. No, not punched. Stabbed. Like someone had ripped a hole in his stomach, then reached in and pulled his insides out.

Nausea swelled in his throat, and he leaned his head on the steering wheel, fighting the urge to open the door and throw up.

He rubbed his chest, trying to quell the pain in his heart. Pain that burned his throat, that made his bones sore, his soul ache.

He'd been in hundreds of fights in his career, on the ice and off. He'd been punched and kicked and toma-hawked with a hockey stick. He'd had his teeth busted and his eyes blackened and more stitches than he wanted to count, but nothing hurt or felt as painful as watching Quinn walk away and knowing there wasn't a damn thing he could do about it.

Because everything she'd said had been true.

Chapter 23

QUINN PICKED AT THE FOOD ON HER PLATE THE NEXT NIGHT as she tried to listen to the story Max was telling her. It had been a long day, and she'd sought to stay busy to keep her mind off Rock.

She'd cleaned the house from top to bottom, done several loads of laundry, paid the bills for the ranch, and had made a big supper of spaghetti and homemade meatballs. Anything to keep her hands and her mind busy, so she wouldn't have time to think about her heart.

Her brother had come back late that afternoon with a load of cattle and supplies, and Rock's brother Mason had been over, helping him unload. Logan had invited him for supper, and although she'd always loved Mason, it seemed that everything he did tonight—his mannerisms, the way he talked, the way he laughed, heck, even the way he held his dang fork—reminded her of Rock.

The only blessing she'd had that day was the fact that she hadn't heard anything from Monty. She wasn't sure what she was expecting, but she'd felt an odd sense of tension throughout the day, as if she were waiting for the other shoe to drop. She knew he wouldn't quietly disappear. She just didn't know what he would do instead.

It had been hard watching the disappointment in Max though. Watching as he stood at the front windows, looking down the driveway, hoping Monty's car would appear. He hadn't ever called before. He'd just shown up. This was the first day they hadn't seen him, and she could sense the frustration and hurt in Max.

Her son was usually so easygoing, but today he'd been moody and cranky.

Ham must have sensed something was going on as well, because he spent most of the day outside, in the barn and the pastures. She hadn't told him what had happened the day before, but he knew her well enough to know that if she started a cleaning spree like the one she was on today, that it was best to make himself scarce.

"So what do you think about that, Mom?" Max asked, his fork held up in the air as if punctuating his question.

She blinked, trying to form a plausible answer out of the few tidbits of the story she'd heard him talking about. "I think that sounds reasonable."

He gave her a funny look but accepted the answer.

"I think it's about time you got ready for bed, young man," her dad said. "Why don't you take your plate into the kitchen and go get your pajamas on."

Quinn offered Hamilton a thankful look. "Don't worry about your plate. I'll get it this time. You just worry about getting all that spaghetti sauce off your face. And I mean with a washcloth, not with Truman licking it off."

Max giggled and slid from his chair. He headed down the hall toward the bathroom, the puppy bounding at his heels.

"That was a delicious meal," Mason said, setting down his napkin and pushing back from the table. "Thanks, Quinn."

She smiled over at him. *He is not Rock*. "You know you're welcome anytime."

A knock sounded, and she looked up to see Len Larson filling the frame of the screen door.

"Come on in, Lennie," her brother called.

Len opened the door and took off his hat as he stepped into the living room. He hung his head and shuffled forward. "I'm sorry to disturb your supper. I'm looking for Quinn."

What the heck was wrong with him? The guy was normally cheerful and easy to laughter. But something was up. His face was pinched, and he twisted his hat nervously in his hands. He looked like either his dog had just died or his underwear was too tight and causing him some degree of discomfort.

"You don't have to look too far, Lennie. I'm sitting right in front of you," she said, failing to keep the sarcasm out of her voice. Her patience was already thin, and she had a bad feeling about what was causing Lennie to act so out of the ordinary.

He dipped his head and wouldn't look her in the eye as he reached into his pocket and pulled out an envelope. "I'm real sorry about this," he said as he held the envelope out.

Logan grabbed the envelope and looked at the front of it before passing it to Quinn. "It's a summons. What the hell is going on, Len?"

The big man shrugged. "Like I said, I'm real sorry. I'm just doing my job."

Quinn tore open the envelope and scanned the pages inside. She couldn't believe it. *That son of a bitch*. "It's from Monty. He's filed a petition with the courts for custody of Max. Claiming that he's in danger. This is a summons to appear in court tomorrow. It's to meet the judge for a first appearance to determine if Max is safe."

"Tomorrow?" Logan asked, looking from Quinn to Lennie. "What is going on? What do you know about this, Lennie? Spill it."

Len swallowed. "Apparently, he ended up in the emergency room yesterday and ain't too happy about having to get his eye stitched up. He told me he pulled these forms from the internet and filed 'em with the county clerk yesterday. He said the courts have been quiet this week, and you know his brother's a cop, and I guess he helped him get the case on the docket for tomorrow because of the urgency of the situation."

"What urgency? And what does him having to go to the emergency room have to do with us?"

Len stared down at the floor, his face going another shade of red, like his drawers had just gotten even tighter. "He claims Rockford beat him up and Quinn watched, and he's saying it's Rock's fault that Max got his arm busted and that the boy isn't safe with her."

Logan's and Mason's mouths dropped open at the same time, but her father's lips pulled into a tight line as his jaw set.

"You didn't hear this from me," Len continued, "but I think he's trying to get Social Services involved to see if they'll come in and take Max. I know he's mad and all, but I don't think that's right. I know you're a good mom, Quinn."

"All right, I think we've heard enough. You go on now, Len." Ham's voice was hard, his words a command, not a request.

Lennie ducked his head and hurried out of the house, scurrying across the room like a scared rat.

A hard grip of fear tightened like a fist around her heart. *Social Services?*

She shook her head, her eyes widening, and turned to Ham. "They can't do that, can they, Dad? They can't take Max from me."

Hamilton pushed back from the table and stood up, his body tensed as if ready for a fight. "They can't if he isn't here. I've been thinking about taking the boy camping anyway. This is as good a time as any. If you can get some of his things packed, we can leave in thirty minutes." He didn't wait for an answer but marched toward his room, muttering, "I knew we shouldn't have let that son of a bitch into the house."

Quinn sat, stunned, trying to digest the information she'd just heard. Why was Monty doing this? What was his end game?

And how the heck did he get a preliminary hearing set up so quickly? She knew his brother was a cop, but didn't realize he had that much pull.

Apparently, it took only one string to make something happen, as long as it was the right string. And Franklin was a smaller town than Creedence, so maybe their docket had an opening.

She wasn't sure if having her dad whisk Max off in the night was the smartest decision, but it was the only one she could think of that would keep her son completely safe. She trusted her dad and knew he would die before he let anything happen to Max.

And his behavior this afternoon showed that Monty was a true wild card. She'd seen violence and temper in his eyes and knew he was like a snake trapped in a corner and ready to strike out.

Taking Max out of the county might not be the smartest idea, but she'd be damned if she was going to let that low-life rattlesnake get his fangs into her boy.

"This is ridiculous," Logan said, eyeing Quinn across the table. "But it sounds like there's more to the story about what happened yesterday. Why don't you tell us what's really going on?"

She picked at the seam of the place mat, her gaze trained on the quilted rose pattern, instead of at her brother, as she told him and Mason what had happened.

"That bastard," Logan said between clenched teeth.

"I can't believe Rock didn't break his legs," Mason said.

"He might have if I hadn't pulled him away. Monty had called his brother, and he or someone from the police department was headed toward their house when we got out of there. I'm assuming it was his brother and that he must not have filed an actual police report, because no one showed up here last night. Did they come out to your place?" she asked Mason.

He shook his head. "No. We didn't see anyone last night. I barely saw Rock. He stayed in his room most of the night. I knew he was in a foul mood, and now this explains it."

This didn't explain all of it.

His mood might have something to do with the fact that they'd broken up again. This time for good.

Should she warn Rock? Let him know what was happening?

Maybe he got a summons as well. But his name

hadn't appeared on any of her paperwork. And calling him would just drag them right back into each other's lives again, and she couldn't take that right now.

"What can we do to help, Quinn?" Mason asked. "You want us to come over here tonight? Stand guard in case Hill or his brothers try something?"

She felt the blood drain from her face. She hadn't considered the possibility that they would come to the ranch and try to harm her or her family. The court summons seemed like harm enough. "No. I think Monty is too much of a coward to show up here. He knows both Logan and my dad are armed and wouldn't hesitate to fire at a trespasser, especially one who was threatening their family. Hell, I'm ready to take a shot at the guy myself."

"All right. Well, we're only a few minutes away. Call us if you need us." Mason stood up. "Thanks again for the meal. I'm going to head home. Be prepared for my mom to call you as soon as she hears about this. Or she might just show up."

Quinn smiled, comforted by the idea that Vivi would rush to her side.

Logan stacked the remaining plates in a pile. "I'll get these washed up. Quinn, you better go get Max ready. Dad will be ready to leave soon."

She nodded, wishing that she could pack a bag and disappear with them.

~~~

Rock stomped into the house and threw his gloves on the counter. He'd spent the last hour in the barn, hauling hay and stacking bales. He'd thought the physical work would give him an outlet for his stress, and his body was exhausted, but his mind still reeled with thoughts of Quinn.

And no amount of busywork would heal the wounds in his heart.

The front door slammed, and Mason strode in, a concerned look on his face.

Rock could tell just by the way he walked that something was going on. "What's wrong?"

"I was just over at the Rivers's place, and apparently, that scumbag Hill has filed some kind of petition with the courts to try to get custody of Max."

"What? That's insane. On what grounds?"

"He claims that you sent him to the emergency room yesterday."

"Are you kidding me? I barely touched the guy. I've taken worse hits and played a full period on the ice."

"Quinn told us what happened, and from the sounds of it, the guy is lucky you didn't beat him into a bloody pulp."

"It wasn't for lack of desire. I wanted to and would have done much worse if Quinn hadn't pulled me out of there. But that was between me and Hill. How can he use that against Quinn?"

Mason shrugged. "He's saying something about her putting Max in dangerous situations and arguing that it's your fault the kid's arm got broken at the ice rink."

A heavy weight settled in his chest. It had been his fault. And now look what had happened. He'd caused Quinn and her boy even more pain and harm.

He grabbed his keys from the counter. "I've got to go over there. I need to tell her I'm sorry." But she didn't want to see him. She'd made that perfectly clear the day before.

Rage and frustration boiled in his blood, and he hurled his keys across the kitchen. They hit a glass mixing bowl and knocked it to the floor, shattering it into several pieces.

"FUCK!" Rock yelled, then scrubbed his hands across his face. "I can't go over there. She doesn't want to see me anymore. She doesn't want anything to do with me."

He'd never felt so helpless.

He had power and money and was strong as an ox, yet when the woman he loved needed him, there wasn't a damn thing he could do.

Except… An idea struck him, and he reached for his phone. "She may not let me help her, but I know who can."

Mason had grabbed the broom and was sweeping the broken shards of glass into a dustpan. "Yeah, but who's gonna help you when Mom finds out you broke her favorite mixing bowl?"

Rock ignored him as he scrolled through his contacts. Finding the one he wanted, he tapped the screen and held the phone to his ear.

―⁓―

The next afternoon, Quinn stood nervously outside the courtroom doors. She peered down the hall, watching for her lawyer to appear. She'd considered saving the expense and representing herself. Her bank account couldn't take the hit, and besides, she had the law on her side on this one. It was up to Monty to prove that she'd done something wrong.

But it was Max. And she couldn't take a chance that anything would happen to him. He was worth every cent she had to protect him.

She'd called Bob Dempsey the night before and asked him to meet her at the courthouse today. He was an old friend of her father's, and both the Rivers's and the James's ranches used him as their legal counsel when they were in need of such a thing.

And she was in serious need.

Her dad had taken Max the night before, and she'd spent a restless night worrying about today. Thankfully, she still had Logan.

He'd said he had a couple more things to do at the ranch, then he'd meet her at the courthouse, and she peered anxiously down the hall, watching for both her brother and the elderly cowboy who would serve as her lawyer.

Bile rose in her throat as Monty stepped through the doors instead and swaggered toward her. The left side of his face was swollen, and a purple bruise circled his eye. Three dark stitches under a transparent butterfly bandage held a small cut together on his cheekbone.

The corner of his lip was swollen, yet he still managed to offer her an arrogant grin. "Hey, Quinn." He looked around her shoulder. "Where's Rockford?"

Rock? Why was he worried about where Rock was? If anything, the guy should be nervous that if Rock were here, he'd blacken his other eye.

She was considering doing it herself. "He's not here."

He leaned down, close enough that she could smell the scent of coffee and cigarettes on his breath. "I hope he's at the bank, getting my money."

Money? What money?

He tilted his head. "Didn't he tell you about my little offer to him the other day? I thought you two were closer than that."

She pushed back her shoulders, not wanting him to see that he was getting to her, and putting on a braver front than she felt. "Yeah, he did. Of course he did," she bluffed. "But he's not paying you any money."

"He better reconsider that idea. You tell him this is just the beginning. I don't care if he pays it or your dad coughs it up again, but either they get me my money, or this is just the first of many battles you and I will fight—in court, and otherwise."

Fear spiraled down her back like a trickle of ice water on her spine, and she couldn't speak.

Monty's words spun inside her already dizzy head. *Or your dad coughs it up again.*

Again?

Had her dad paid Monty off before? Is that why he'd left town? Is that why he'd never contacted Max?

Monty's eyes gleamed, like he knew he'd hit a nerve with his threat, and he twisted the knife one more turn. "The internet is full of petitions and forms, and it only costs me fifteen bucks to file them with the county. I can tie you up in court proceedings for years, and that's gonna cost you more than if you just pay up now. Because, honey, I've got nothing to lose. And you've got *everything* to lose."

"Quinn Rivers?" A tall man wearing an expensive suit and carrying a leather briefcase walked up behind Monty.

"See ya inside," Monty said, giving her a lurid wink

before turning toward the courtroom doors. "Remember what I said."

Quinn turned to the man, feeling like she'd just had the wind knocked out of her. "Yes, I'm Quinn Rivers."

The man held out his hand. A gold designer watch shined on his wrist. "I'm Michael Brennan, from Hughes, Brennan, and Baker Law. I'll be representing you today."

She shook her head. "But I already have a lawyer."

"I understand. And I've already spoken with Mr. Dempsey, and we agreed that I'll be taking over your case."

She leaned her head into her hand, rubbing her fingers into her aching forehead. "I don't understand. And no offense, but I can't afford another lawyer."

"It's okay. You don't have to worry about that. Rock sent me. I'm with the firm that represents his team. We take care of the players and their families." He smiled encouragingly at her. "And I owe Rock a favor. So honestly, there's no charge. I'm happy to help you."

Logan hurried up to Quinn and put an arm around her shoulders. "You okay? Who's this?" He eyed the other man suspiciously.

"Michael Brennan. Apparently, he's my lawyer. Rock sent him."

Logan's eyes widened, and a grin spread across his face. "Nice. Good to meet you. I'm Logan Rivers, Quinn's brother."

Michael smiled and shook his hand, then pulled open the door and held it for her. "Call me Mike. And we should go in. We don't want to be late."

Her heart pounded as she walked down the aisle and toward the table at the front of the courtroom. Logan squeezed her shoulders, then slipped into the seats behind her as Michael pulled out her chair and she sank into it.

Feeling stunned and still winded, she couldn't quite grasp the happenings of the last few minutes. She was still reeling from Monty's declaration that her dad had paid him off, and now Rock had arranged for a top-notch lawyer to represent her.

The bailiff stood and called out to the courtroom, "All rise for the Honorable Judge William Moray."

They all stood as Judge Moray entered from a side door and approached the bench. He was a tall man, probably in his early sixties, with a full head of silver-white hair. His eyes were sharp and narrowed as he surveyed the courtroom, then sat down behind the bench.

His face remained passive, but Quinn wondered what he was thinking about Monty's obvious injuries. She almost wished she'd gone sleeveless—she had a few bruises of her own to show.

The judge silently studied her and her lawyer, then turned his gaze to Monty. "Do you have legal representation that you're waiting on, Mr. Hill?"

"Huh?" Monty said.

"A lawyer. Do you have a lawyer?"

"No. I don't need one. I've got the law on my side."

She winced, thankful that she had gone ahead with securing an attorney. Even though she'd been thinking the same thing earlier, she didn't realize how idiotic it sounded until it came out of Monty's mouth.

The judge raised an eyebrow at Monty but didn't say anything more. He turned his attention to Quinn's side of the room.

Michael gave a respectful nod to the judge. "Michael Brennan, Your Honor, attorney for Ms. Rivers."

The judge nodded back, then cleared his throat. "Let's get started then."

Chapter 24

Less than an hour later, Quinn left the courthouse alone and hurried down the sidewalk to her car. She pulled the door shut behind her, leaned back against the seat, and let out a shaky breath.

The hearing was over, and she couldn't believe how well it had gone.

Having Michael Brennan there had been a godsend. He was smart and succinct, answering the judge's questions and making Monty look like a fool.

She'd allowed herself a tiny fist pump at the best part of the hearing when Michael had slipped in the fact that Monty had never paid a dime in child support nor claimed Max as his child until the week prior.

Rock must have filled Michael in on their history, because he seemed to know all the right things to say about what kind of mother she was and about the safety and security of the home that she, her dad, and her brother provided for Max.

He'd been amazing, and from the way Monty had skulked out of the courtroom after being ordered to pay back child support, she figured that she wouldn't be hearing from him again anytime soon.

She crossed her fingers and started the car. With everything going on the past few weeks, she still hadn't taken it into the shop, but Logan had put in a new battery, and it had seemed to be running fine again.

Rolling down the window to let out the summer heat, she headed toward the Triple J Ranch. She had Rock to thank for all of this. And she needed to do it in person.

She called her dad on the way out of town and gave him the good news. He said he'd bring Max home that night. She didn't bring up the subject of him paying off Monty. They'd have plenty of time to talk about that later, and she didn't feel like picking a fight with him now.

Pulling into the driveway of the James's ranch, she noticed that Rock's truck was next to the barn. Her pulse quickened at the thought of seeing him again.

Stop it, she told herself. This was just about a simple thank-you. Nothing more.

Nothing had changed since the last time she'd seen him.

He was still leaving, still going back to Denver, back to the team. And she was still being left behind.

That hadn't changed.

But he had come through for her. He'd been there when she really needed him.

And she did owe him her thanks.

Could she have thanked him over the phone? Probably. But she didn't want to dissect her reasons for showing up at the ranch in person too closely. She felt too good, too happy about the results of the hearing.

And he was the one she wanted to share that happiness with.

Vivi's car was parked in front of the porch steps, and she came out of the house, carrying a Crock-Pot, her hands covered in colorful oven mitts. "Quinn, darlin', I heard the good news. I just got off the phone with Hamilton, and he told me that the judge dismissed that idiot's claims."

Dang, word did travel fast.

Vivi nestled the Crock-Pot in the box of dish towels that sat on the front seat of her car, then stood to give Quinn a hug. "I'm so glad that it all worked out."

"Thank you."

"Listen, honey, I have to get this chili down to the church, but if you need me, I can wait, make some coffee, and sit a spell with you."

"No, really. Thank you, but I'm okay. You go on. I really came to see Rock. To thank him for sending the lawyer. He made all the difference."

Vivi nodded as she circled the front of her car. "I'm glad. But Rock's not here. He went to Denver first thing this morning. He said he had some errands to run and a meeting with his coach. He should be back before too long. He called a couple of hours ago from the bank and said he was almost finished, then he was headed back up the mountain."

"The bank?" A bad feeling rumbled through her stomach. Surely he wasn't considering Monty's threats. "What was he doing at the bank?"

Vivi shrugged "I don't know. I didn't ask. That boy can take care of his own finances. It's got nothing to do with me." She opened the car door, then gestured toward the house. "You're welcome to wait for him. I just made a fresh batch of chocolate chip cookies. Help yourself. I know how you used to love those."

"Thanks. I think I will wait for a bit." Quinn waved, then walked up the porch steps and into the house.

Wandering through the living room and into the kitchen, the smell of chocolate chip cookies in the air, she was flooded with memories of being in this house as a kid, sitting at this table and having cookies and milk with Rock.

That was before.

Before the remodel—before the house and the boy who lived in it had changed.

The renovations were amazing though. At least of the house.

She plucked a cookie from the cooling rack and nibbled on it as she wondered if the boy hadn't changed as well—hadn't gone through his own renovations and improvements.

He really had come through for her today.

Not just in sending her Michael Brennan, but by giving him all of the ammunition he needed to support her against Monty's claims. Rock must have spoken highly of her to Michael for him to have all of that information.

She wandered around the kitchen, wishing he would hurry up and get home already. Pulling out her phone, she tapped the screen to call his number.

She heard the ring in her ear at the same time that a ringtone sounded from a phone sitting on the counter in the kitchen.

She recognized the phone as Rock's, and a lump formed in her throat at the ringtone that played when she called his phone. It had been their song in high school.

Crossing the kitchen, she looked down at his phone and smiled at the simple *Q* that came up as her contact information. She hung up, watching the screen as it changed to his wallpaper of the team's logo.

A text message box was at the top of the phone, and she let out a small gasp as she read the message that was labeled from Coach Sullivan. She could read only the first words of the text, but they were enough.

I refuse to accept your resignation. Call me as soon…

Resignation?

Had Rock really quit the team?

Was that the meeting he had with his coach that morning? She'd assumed it involved setting the timetable for when he would be healthy enough to return to practice.

She sagged against the counter, her mind and her heart trying to comprehend why Rock would quit the team, why he would give up the thing he loved so much.

There was only one reason he would quit and give that all up.

Well, two, really.

Her and Max.

She stood staring at the text message, the other half of the cookie forgotten in her hand, as her heart battled it out with her head.

The choices seemed like many, but really, there was only one.

And that was to stop thinking, stop analyzing every decision, and just act.

Shoving the rest of the cookie in her mouth, she left Rock's house, hurrying down the front steps and to her car.

One of her favorite songs was playing on the radio as she pulled out of the driveway—a song that spoke of warm summer nights and riding in the truck next to the one you love. She turned up the stereo, singing along as the dust flew behind her on the country road leading away from the ranch.

She was on her way to find Rock. She didn't know how, but she knew she couldn't sit and wait for him one more second. She had to move, to act, to run—whatever it took to find him and fling herself into his arms.

They'd waited so long, so many years to finally be together. She knew in her heart that if she just drove toward him, she would find him. They would find each other.

Busting out the last line of the song, she sang with joy in a pure, clear voice, grinning from one ear to the other, her chest bursting with happiness.

But her grin faded as the song played its last notes and the engine of her car sputtered and died.

"What? No," she cried, slamming her palm against the piece of crap car's steering wheel.

This couldn't be happening.

Just moments ago, she'd felt like the universe was working for them, guiding them to each other, and now she wondered if this was the true sign. The sign that said as much as she and Rock thought they should be together, that it wasn't meant to be.

Climbing out of the car, she slammed the door shut and gave it a swift kick. "You piece of crap," she yelled, her euphoria gone, blown away like the dust on the side of the road.

Forget it.

She was going home.

This was too much. Too hard. Screw the whole damn thing.

Leaving the car on the side of the road, she pulled off her heels and strode down the shoulder, walking away from Rock's ranch and toward her own.

—∿∿—

Rock slowed the convertible, shielding his eyes from the sun as he drove down the dirt road toward the ranch.

He shook his head.

No way.

It couldn't be.

He pulled up next to the gorgeous blond who was marching down the road, her high heels hanging from her fingertips as she kicked up dust with every barefooted step.

"Hey there, darlin'. Need a ride?"

She turned her head, her eyes going wide, then blinking back the tears that suddenly appeared there. "Rock?"

"Hey now. None of that. What's wrong?"

"Nothing's wrong. I mean, everything's wrong. I mean…oh hell, I don't know what I mean."

Rock leaned across the seat and pushed open the door. "Get in."

The seat held a white plastic bag from a fancy kitchen store in Denver, and she picked it up to sink into the luxurious seat.

Holding the bag in her lap, she took the bottle of water Rock offered her and tipped it to her mouth, drinking thirstily, then handing it back. She peeked into the bag. "What is this? Why did you have to drive all the way to Denver to get a mixing bowl?"

"It's for my mom. It's a long story." He draped his hand around the back of her seat. "Tell me what's going on with you?"

There was another item in the bag, and she pulled it out and held the zippered money bag embossed with his bank's name on it out to him. "First, tell me about this. Is it what I think it is?"

Dang it.

"Wellll, why don't you tell me what you think it is."

"I think, I'm afraid, it's money that you're planning to use to pay Monty off so he'll leave us alone." She unzipped the bag and gasped down at the strapped fifty dollar bills. "Holy crap. How much is this?"

"It's not *that* much. It's only twenty thousand."

"Only?"

"Yeah. He asked for fifty."

"Fifty?" Her eyes went wide, and her mouth dropped open. "He asked you for fifty thousand dollars?" she stammered.

He nodded. "Yeah, and I considered paying it."

"You did not. That's crazy."

"That's nothing. A drop in the bucket to what your and Max's happiness is worth. I would pay ten times that much to know that asswipe was out of your lives."

She shook her head as if trying to comprehend what he was saying. "Monty told me he asked you for money and my dad had paid him off before, but I had no idea it was that much. Is that how much my dad paid him the first time?"

He winced. "No, and I'm sorry you found out about that. I know Ham was just trying to protect you and Max. Your dad originally gave him ten thousand, so I figured if I offered him twice that, he'd take it and run. But this time, I'm going to get a guarantee that he's gone for good."

"No. I appreciate the thought and that you went to all this trouble, but no. I can't let you do this."

"Quinn, the money means nothing to me. You're what matters, you and Max. I would pay anything, do anything for you."

"But—" she started, but he held up his finger and set it tenderly on her lips.

"Don't say anything. Not yet. I've spent the last few days thinking about this, thinking about nothing but this—about you, and Max, and my life, and how empty it feels without you in it. The life I lead in Denver is full of excitement and parties and late nights, but I feel like I've spent several years chasing after something that was always just out of my grasp. But now, the last few weeks that I've been here, with you and with Max, I feel like I've found what it is I've been missing, what it is I've been chasing all this time. And it's you. It's family. I know I've made mistakes in the past, but I'm trying to show you that I've changed. That nothing is more important to me than you and Max. Not the money. Not even hockey. In fact, I had a meeting with my coach this morning, and I quit the team."

"Rock, you can't. You love hockey. It's part of who you are."

"But I'm nothing without you. My life is nothing without you in it. That's what I'm trying to tell you. I love you, and I want you, you and Max, in my life. More than anything else." He reached into his pocket and pulled out one of the other purchases he'd made that morning. Handing her the small, flat box, he said, "Open it."

Her hands were clasped in her lap, her fingers twisted together as she stared at the box. "What is it?"

He grinned. "Just open it."

She took the box gingerly from his hand and gasped as she lifted the lid. A silver chain lay nestled on the black velvet inside. Hanging from the chain was a diamond-encrusted pendant in the shape of a key. "It's beautiful."

"I told you that I had better taste now." He pointed to the necklace. "That key is just a substitute for the real one."

Her brow furrowed. "The real one?"

"Yeah, the real one that goes to the house I'm going to build you. We can pick a spot, anywhere on our land, and I'll have your dream house built on it. That way we'll be close to both our families."

She stared at the key, her lip trembling, then drew her gaze back to him. "No. You can't. I can't. I can't let you give up hockey, give up your career for me. It's what you love."

"You're what I love. And it doesn't matter. I would give up anything for you."

"But why? I never asked you to give up hockey for me."

He shook his head, confused at her statement. "But it's the reason I left. It's the thing that came between us."

"No, it wasn't. The thing that came between us was your big head and how full of yourself you were over becoming a professional athlete. You acted like you were better than me and that you'd outgrown me. It wasn't about the sport itself. I never asked you to choose between me and hockey. You don't have to quit the team to be with me, with us. All I want, all I've ever wanted, is for you to let me be part of that life *with* you. You don't have to give up what you love to be with me, with us. Just let us share it with you. Let us be with you. You don't have to move up here. We can move down to Denver to be with you."

"You would do that? You would leave Creedence? You would leave your dad? Your brother?"

"Of course I would. I've just been waiting for you to ask me to." She shook her head, letting out a small laugh. "It's not like it's that far away. And we can come back to visit. Besides, we've spent the last eight years living with my dad and my brother. Believe me, I'm fine moving out."

He chuckled with her, then opened the box and pulled the necklace out. "Okay, consider this the key to my house in Denver, and we'll put the dream house on the back burner until I retire. Then we can move back up here." He slid the chain around her neck and fastened the clasp.

She looked down at the necklace and gingerly touched the key-shaped pendant. "I love it."

"I'm glad. But it's not quite complete. It's missing the heart." He reached back into his pocket and pulled free the second box he'd purchased that day. "The necklace also represents the key to my heart. You've always had it, and you always will. But what's in this box represents our lives. Yours, mine, and Max's."

Her eyes were wide as she stared from the box to his face and back to the box again.

"Wait," he said, opening his door and climbing from the car. He circled around the back end and opened her door, then knelt in the dust on the road where he first saw her a few weeks ago, dressed like a pirate and riding a bicycle, and still as beautiful as she had always been.

She'd made his heart start beating again that day, and now it pounded hard against his chest as he looked into her gorgeous brown eyes.

He held up the small box and opened it to reveal a heart-shaped diamond ring. "Quinn, my life is nothing without you. I have never loved anyone the way I love you, and I don't want to spend another day of my life without you in it. I already gave you my heart a long time ago, but now I want to make it official, for the whole world to see. Quinn Rivers, will you marry me?"

Bringing her hand to her mouth, she gazed at the ring, and her eyes filled with tears. The diamond sparkled in the Colorado sun.

Lifting her head, she nodded, a smile breaking across her face. "Yes. Yes. A thousand times yes." She leaned forward, throwing her arms around his neck as she pressed her lips to his.

She tasted like chocolate, and strawberry lip gloss, and the love of his life.

She pulled back, gazing into his eyes, uncertainty shining in hers. "You know I come as a package deal."

"Of course. And I'm going to do everything in my power to be the best dad I can be, to make Max feel like he's my own son. Monty's not interested in being his dad. He didn't find religion or come back to make amends. He heard about you and me being together again, and he thought he could run a con, score some cash off me. And I'm still planning to offer him the money, but with the condition that he lets me officially adopt Max."

Her breath caught as she gasped in surprise, then her smile returned. "You've thought of everything, haven't you?"

He offered her an impish grin. "You know what I like to say, go big or go home."

She threw back her head, letting out a burst of laughter, then she kissed him again, a tender kiss filled with love and joy.

Her eyes sparkled with happiness as she drew back and grinned. "I'm here with you, the man I've loved since I was fourteen years old, the man I plan to marry and love until the day I die. So for me, I'm already home."

The End…

…and just the beginning…

*Read on for a look at the next book
in Nicole Helm's Navy SEAL Cowboys series*

Cowboy SEAL Redemption

JACK ARMSTRONG STOOD OUTSIDE THE STABLES OF REVIVAL Ranch almost wishing he were back in a war zone. He knew how to go about completing a mission.

He didn't know anything about talking to a therapist.

He didn't *have* to talk to her, of course. Gabe had reminded him of that at least ten times today. No one was pressuring him to take this step.

But here he was, and he couldn't even pinpoint a reason. Maybe it had something to do with the way his nightmares had started to include people from his civilian life—Mom and Dad, Becca and her goat. Those definitely ate at him more than nightmares that were distorted memories of a day over a year ago, and the friend he'd actually lost.

Maybe it was watching Alex, his former SEAL brother, put weight back on, come back into himself after making regular appointments with Monica. Alex had gotten together with Becca, the co-owner of their ranch and partner in their foundation, and infused a lightness into their little world that hadn't been there for a very long time.

Or maybe he was just in a rut. Summer equaled plenty of work around the ranch in general; plus, they were putting the finishing touches on the bunkhouse that Alex, Gabe, and he would move into. At the end of the day, he was bone-deep weary and his injuries ached and ached.

But he couldn't sleep, and when he did, the nightmares often plagued him. He was tired. Exhausted. And if this was going to help...

Hell.

"If you're waiting for a welcome dance, I'm afraid I don't know the steps."

Jack tried to smile at Monica, Revival's on-site therapist. She'd appeared at the stable door, that kind smile on her face. Jack liked her enough as a person, and he really enjoyed her ten-year-old son, who helped around the ranch sometimes. But he'd been irritated this spring when Becca had announced she wanted an on-site therapist for their foundation. He wasn't sure he'd gotten over that irritation, but he'd learned to deal with Monica the person.

Neither of them were here as regular people right now though.

"What am I supposed to do, just...walk in?"

Monica made a grand gesture. "Simple as that. Walk in. Grab a brush. I told Becca and Alex we'd handle the horse grooming this afternoon."

Even though Alex had told Jack a little about how his sessions went, Jack still had this prevalent idea in his head of a couch in a corner and a shrink with a notebook. But Monica went straight to the horses they'd all used out on the ranch earlier in the day and got to work with grooming.

Jack could only follow suit. He grabbed the bucket

of tools for his horse and started the tasks he'd learned only this spring. He may have grown up on a farm, but they'd never had horses.

Jack eyed Monica suspiciously, but she didn't talk. She didn't study him. She was doing nothing he expected a therapist to do. Her focus was all on grooming Becca's horse, Pal.

"So, aren't you going to ask me questions?"

"What kind of questions?"

Jack frowned. "I don't know. About whatever we're supposed to talk about."

"Well, what would you like to talk about?"

"I don't know," he replied, wholly baffled. "Whatever I'm supposed to talk about."

"There aren't any supposed-tos, Jack."

"Then how are you going to fix me?"

She raised her eyebrows at him over the back of the horse. "I can't fix your PTSD."

"Then why am I here?" he demanded, exasperation winning out over his confusion.

Monica took a few seconds of silence, as though she was considering the answer, but shouldn't she have known? Wasn't it her job to know?

"My job isn't to be your life coach. It's to listen to whatever you want to say or have to say. It's to offer coping mechanisms if you're having a particular issue, and it's to maybe try to guide you a bit to your own epiphanies. But they have to be yours—your choices, your feelings. I can't map them out for you."

"That's crap."

She laughed good-naturedly. "Perhaps. But it's working for Alex. So why don't you tell me what changed your mind about this?" She waved a hand to encompass the stables. "You didn't want me here."

Jack scowled and focused on his horse. He hadn't wanted Monica, or any therapist, here. Hadn't thought it necessary. Sometimes, he still didn't.

Then he remembered the bone-deep fear of watching Alex fall apart. Alex, their leader, a guy Jack had hero-worshipped in the beginning of his SEAL career, who'd devised this plan for them after the attack that had gotten them all removed from military life.

Even though the past few months had shown Alex getting better, Jack was still haunted by how gaunt and lost Alex had been.

Jack didn't feel that bad off, but he knew he wasn't right. He knew at some point he needed to find a purpose because, with each passing day, he felt like he had less and less of one.

"Alex is better," Jack said, staring hard at the horse's flank.

"He is. And you'd like to be?"

Jack ran the brush over his horse, focusing on the animal's hair. "Yes." He'd like to be, though he wasn't sure he was ready for the work it would take to become better. Didn't that take a certain amount of acceptance? He didn't think he had acceptance in him. Not the driving force kind that Alex had found anyway.

"The first step is realizing it's not a fix or a switch I can flip. Getting better is a process, and it's not going to be comfortable or happen overnight. It's hard, grueling work."

"I was a Navy SEAL."

"You were, and now you're not."

After a few weeks of sessions, no matter that they'd touched on a great many things—his military service, his childhood, his hopes for Revival—the words "you were, and now you're not" repeated over and over in his head like a loop.

He felt worse after having talked to Monica a few times now, and that pissed him off, because he was supposed to be better.

He stalked across the yard from stables to house after another session, grumpy as hell and not in any mood to talk to Alex or Gabe, but they were both on the porch as if waiting for him.

"How's it going?" Alex asked, leaning against the railing, failing at casual.

Jack merely grunted and shrugged. He hated that they both waited after every session and asked if he was okay, if things were okay. He wanted to pretend he'd never been so stupid as to think therapy could fix him.

But he still went to every session, and he still went to where Alex and Gabe were waiting after each one.

"It's not easy. Nothing important ever is. Think of it like BUD/S training," Alex offered with the kind of straightforward pragmatism Jack couldn't help but appreciate, said in a sympathetic tone Jack wanted to burn to the ground.

Jack grimaced. "I hated BUD/S training."

"Exactly."

Jack didn't know why that soothed some of the jagged edges, but it did. Not all of them certainly, but at least some. "Pioneer Spirit?"

"Uh, well, Becca's mom is coming over for dinner."

"Say no more. We're out of here," Gabe said, jumping to his feet from his seat on a porch chair, at least in part for comic effect.

"And I wanted to let you guys know, whenever you're ready, you can move into the bunkhouse."

Gabe raised an eyebrow at Alex. "We? As in not you."

"I'm staying put," Alex said in that tone that brooked no argument.

Not that Jack or Gabe would argue, and Jack supposed it wasn't a surprise. Alex and Becca had been hot and heavy for a while, even more so since Alex had gotten some help. It made sense.

It still felt…weird.

"We'll meet you at Pioneer Spirit later though. Becca and I." Alex shoved his hands in his pockets, rocking back on his heels. "So don't get drunk before we get there, huh? It wouldn't kill either of you to lighten up on that score."

Gabe gave him a mock salute, and Jack tried to smile. He and Gabe had been spending a lot of time at the bar in town lately, but…well, Alex didn't get to boss them around anymore. Especially if he was staying in the main house, while Jack and Gabe moved out to the bunkhouse.

"I better help Becca with dinner," Alex said absently. "See you guys later." He disappeared inside.

"He seem weird to you?" Gabe asked, frowning at the door.

Jack shrugged. "Not particularly. You ready?"

Gabe slung his arm over Jack's shoulders. "I am always, always ready to drink my troubles away."

"And I will always, always drink to that."

———

Rose Rogers surveyed her kingdom: a dimly lit bar sparsely populated by old ranchers and young drunks with Hank Williams Jr. rasping from the jukebox that played mainly country classics.

For three years, Pioneer Spirit had been all hers, and it had yet to get old. For a little girl who'd grown up like she had, owning something, running something, was quite the coup, no matter that it was a run-down townie bar in the middle of nowhere Montana.

She didn't dare take any of it for granted, because it was miles better than anything that had come before.

Which was why she needed to figure something out to protect this. Her father being out of jail put too many question marks in the air. He'd always been a cruel man, but would he be a vindictive one? Would he have the opportunity?

She scowled. She wouldn't give him the opportunity to hurt what or who she loved again. So she needed to find a way to neutralize the potential threat and not wince every time her bar door swung open.

But wince she did, every single time. This time, as every other time before, it wasn't her father. Instead, Jack So-and-So and Gabe Such-and-Such marched in. The two men had become something like fixtures in her bar this summer, and she'd gleaned a thing or two about both from serving them and maybe, on one or two occasions, being a little charmed by them.

Hard not to be charmed, because she didn't know men like them. Their little trio, because Alex Maguire often joined their group as well, had never once sexually harassed her or any of her waitresses, and they'd never gotten in a fight or damaged property.

Not once. They seemed to live up to the fictional idea of honorable military men, and on top of all that, they were building some charitable foundation at the Maguire ranch.

Rose kept waiting for one of them to turn out to be a turd, but they were unfailingly polite, excellent tippers, and sometimes even made her laugh or become interested in their stories—very much against her will.

Gabe was a flirt, but it wasn't that kind of persistent attention she usually nipped in the bud. It was friendlier, somehow. Maybe because he was never handsy, never pushy. Just flirtatious comments whenever she came around. He was also a very equal-opportunity flirt. Any woman who'd ever been in her bar had been charmed by Gabe Cortez, including a few elderly ladies who'd been left blushing.

God help the woman who fell for that mess. Either mess, really. Because both Jack and Gabe clearly had a whole lot of mess underneath their polite, friendly facades. Gabe masked it with smiles and flirtation, and Jack masked it with…well, a stoicism Rose admired.

Until he got drunk. Then she'd catch little glimpses of a guy with a sense of humor. Honestly, if she hadn't spent the past few years watching her sister's husband prove to be an upstanding guy, she'd think they were both serial killers, but she'd finally accepted that not all men were her father.

Even if most were rotten.

Still, Rose couldn't say she minded these two decorating her bar stools. Handsome to a T, the lot of them.

Jack and Gabe were like two sides of the same Navy SEAL coin. One tall, dark, and too handsome for his own good, the other Mr. All-American fair-haired fighter for justice. With a limp.

She wasn't sure if it was the limp or the stoicism that got to her the most, but Jack was a bit of a problem. In that, if he didn't show up on his normal nights, she wondered why. In that she often caught herself watching him when he was in the bar.

One time, he'd gotten really drunk and told her an elaborate story about cow tipping. She'd believed it, hook, line, and sinker, and she never believed liars. But he'd laughed hysterically when he'd realized he'd fooled her.

She'd been pissed for weeks, but ever since, she'd known there was just something different about Jack whatever his last name was.

Someone like her had no business finding him intriguing. She was rotten to the core, snarky and mean at whim, and he was the kind of guy who said *please* and *thank you* and had sacrificed life and limb for his country.

Maybe that's why she was fascinated. Besides, it was a nice little fantasy. The big, strong military man who would protect her from any harm.

Silly, foolish, and utterly untrue, but irresistible nonetheless considering, a few years ago, she wouldn't have even been able to fantasize about such a thing.

"You want those two?" Tonya asked, nodding toward Jack and Gabe as she poured cheap whiskey for a group of ranch hands.

She wanted one of them anyway. "You take them." Rose put two bottles of beer onto a tray and nudged it toward her waitress.

Tonya slid the whiskeys to the man waiting to take them to his friends. "I'm just going to put their tips in the tip jar, so if you're doing that out of charity—"

"Charity doesn't exist here," Rose replied, flashing a menacing smile. Tonya's husband had been hurt in a ranching accident, and they were struggling to make ends meet. She was a good bartender, would make a good manager if Rose could ever back off a little without feeling panicked. Rose would make sure Tonya took all the tips at the end of the night regardless.

Tonya grumbled, but she hefted the tray to take to Gabe and Jack. Rose watched her go. Gabe and Jack smiled politely at Tonya, and she laughed at something Gabe said. Rose couldn't hear it from where she stood, but it was likely a marriage proposal. Gabe threw those out like candy.

Her gaze fell to Jack, and for a second, she allowed herself the happy pleasure of just staring at his face. A classic handsome, really—what might have been wholesomeness if not for the beard and the haunted blue eyes.

Blue eyes that were now staring straight at her. She flashed him a grin, and he lifted his bottle in a little salute.

Sometimes she really considering corrupting Jack the Navy SEAL—at least a little bit.

The sound of the door opening, just a faint squeak under the din of the bar, eradicated that consideration in an instant. She flinched, her gaze immediately moving from Jack to the door.

But it wasn't her father standing there. And what would she do if it turned out to be? She rubbed the knife she carried in a little hidden holster on her belt. She kept a revolver behind the bar in case of emergencies. She could protect herself against her father.

And still fear had sprouted like a weed since hearing he'd been released. That old, shaky fear, those old, defeatist thoughts.

She took a deep breath. She'd gotten this far. Nothing would get in her way again. She'd protect everything she held dear no matter the cost, and she wouldn't allow herself the luxury of falling for any fantasies.

Girls like her didn't get the happy ending, but she'd make sure she was safeguarding her sisters one way or another.

She glanced back at Jack, who was still staring at her, a puzzled frown on his face.

"Not for you," she muttered to herself, and got back to work.

Acknowledgments

As always, my love and thanks go out to my husband, Todd, for your steadfast love and support in my writing career and in our life together! We make the best team!

I have to thank my family as well. My sons, Tyler and Nick, for always supporting me and listening to a zillion plotting ideas. I love you both with more than my heart could ever imagine.

My parents and siblings (all of them) are my biggest cheerleaders, and I'm so grateful for the love and encouragement they all have offered. Thanks, Mom, for being my favorite beta reader and plotting sounding board. And thanks, Dad, for always dropping everything to chat and to offer me great tips and advice on running a ranch and talking me through farming and animal knowledge and that whole cattle-branding scene.

I can't thank my editor, Deb Werksman, enough for believing in me and this project, for your amazing editing talents, and for always making me feel like a rock star. Thanks to Dawn Adams for this incredible cover that makes me fall harder in love with Rock every time I see it. I love being part of the Sourcebooks Sisterhood, and I offer buckets of thanks to the whole Sourcebooks Casablanca team for all your efforts and hard work in making this book happen.

Huge shout-out thanks to my agent, Nicole Resciniti at the Seymour Agency, for your advice, your guidance, your calm answers to my panicked questions, and your editing assistance. You are the best, and I'm so thankful you are part of my tribe.

I must humbly, and with serious fangirling, thank Jodi Thomas, one of my favorite authors, who so graciously offered to read my book and give me a cover quote. Jodi's words and stories have inspired me and given me the strength to persevere when I've felt weary or disheartened. Thanks so much, Jodi. Your kind words mean the world to me.

Big thanks to my writing sisters, Beth Rhodes and Cindy Skaggs, who helped make this work possible through their constant support and lots and lots of writing sprints—whether I wanted to do them or not. Your accountability and support are invaluable!

Special thanks to Kristin Miller for your plotting help. Your friendship and encouragement mean so much to me.

Special acknowledgment goes out to the women who walk this writing journey with me every day. The ones who make me laugh, who encourage and support, who offer great advice and sometimes just listen. Thank you, Michelle Major, Lana Williams, Anne Eliot, Ginger Scott, and Selena Laurence. XO

Big thanks goes out to my street team, Jennie's Page Turners, and for all my readers, the people who have been with me from the start—my loyal readers, my dedicated fans, the ones who have read my stories, who have laughed and cried with me, who have fallen in love with my heroes and have clamored for more! Whether you have been with me since the first book or just discovered me with this one, know that I write these stories for you, and I can't thank you enough for reading them. Sending love, laughter, and big Colorado hugs to you all!

About the Author

Jennie Marts is the *USA Today* bestselling author of award-winning books filled with love, laughter, and always a happily ever after. Readers call her books "laugh out loud" funny and the "perfect mix of romance, humor, and steam." Fic Central claimed one of her books was "the most fun I've had reading in years."

She is living her own happily ever after in the mountains of Colorado with her husband, two dogs, and a parakeet that loves to tweet to the oldies. She's addicted to Diet Coke, adores Cheetos, and believes you can't have too many books, shoes, or friends.

Her books include the contemporary western romance Hearts of Montana series, the romantic comedy/cozy mysteries of The Page Turners series, the hunky hockey-playing men in the Bannister family in the Bannister Brothers Books, and the small-town romantic comedies in the Lovestruck series of Cotton Creek Romances.

Jennie loves to hear from readers. Follow her on Facebook at Jennie Marts Books or on Twitter @JennieMarts. Visit her at jenniemarts.com and sign up for her newsletter to keep up with the latest news and releases.

How do you like your cowboys?

Rugged? • Sassy? • Heartfelt? • Red-hot?

At Sourcebooks Casablanca, we've got 'em all!

"Funny, complicated, a
cowboy isn't perfect but

—JODI THOMAS, *New

THIS COWBOY PLAYS TO WIN

Rockford James was raised as a tried-and-true cowboy in a town crazy about ice hockey. Rock is as hot on the ice as he is on a horse, and the NHL snapped him up. Now, injuries have temporarily benched him. Body and pride wounded, he returns to his hometown ranch to find that a lot has changed. The one thing that hasn't His feelings for Quinn, his high school sweetheart and girl next door.

Quinn Rivers had no choice but to get over Rock after he left. T̶o̶_____roken, she had a rebound one _____ in single motherhood Now _____'s back—and clamoring for a second chance—Quinn will do anything to avoid getting caught up in this oh-so-tempting cowboy…

"An absolute delight."
—*Harlequin Junkie* Top Pick
for *Romancing the Ranger* ★★★★★

EBOOK EDITION ALSO AVAILABLE
SOURCEBOOKSCASABLANCA.COM
SOURCEBOOKS CASABLANCA

Romance $7.99 U.S.
ISBN-13: 978-1-4926-5569-5

50799

9 781492 655695